Oceans Apart

Maritimo Island Book 2

Lisa Stanbridge

Crystal Brook Publishing

This is a work of fiction. Names, characters and incidents portrayed are the product of the author's imagination. Any similarities to a name, character or history of any actual person, living or dead, is entirely coincidental.

Also By Lisa Stanbridge

Maritimo Island series:

Ocean's Embrace – Book 1
Oceans Apart – Book 2

Longing for Home series:

Lonely in Paris – Book 1

Troubled in Paradise – Book 2

Finding Our Home – Book 3

Standalone books:

Abandoned Hearts

Navigate to the link below to read more about her books.

https://lisastanbridge.wixsite.com/lisastanbridgeauthor/books

For anyone who has ever felt like they weren't enough.

You are. You always were.

Chapter 1

Nikki Eckhart never should have watched the *Titanic* documentary the day before her ten-day cruise. Okay, so it'd been over one hundred years since the disaster, but *still*. What if this ship was the next *Titanic*? She'd only been half joking last night when she asked her brother-in-law, Monty, if there were any icebergs in the Pacific.

The enormous cruise liner sat majestically on the water as Nikki stepped out of the terminal. She stumbled to a stop. Passengers brushed past her with muttered curses, nearly knocking her over. Too busy gawping at the ship, she barely registered them. Holy hell! The twelve levels matched the height of some of the tall buildings in the background!

I'll be on that thing for ten days?

A chill sliced through her veins. Bile rose in her throat, and she drew in a shaky breath, willing her lunch to stay down.

This was ridiculous. She was a twenty-six-year-old woman. This shouldn't be so hard. The long queue of people waiting to board proved others did this often.

She closed her eyes and breathed in the salty air through her nose and released it slowly through her mouth.

She cast her mind back to the hours spent researching activities to take part in. Food tasting was at the top of the list, of course, not to mention the foreign island stops to places she'd never visited before. There'd be more food to taste there. Oh, and she couldn't forget the aqua blue water, ideal for swimming, or the white sand for tanning her pale skin.

Releasing another slow breath, she opened her eyes and removed her sunglasses, sitting them on top of her head. She inched forward as people continued to push past, her gaze glued to the ship. To think something that huge could hold its weight on the water!

A gust of wind, surprisingly cool despite the stifling heat in Sydney that day, caught her long hair and blew it in her face. She brushed it out of her eyes, cursing her decision not to wear it up. The salty tang of the sea lingered in the air and Nikki smiled. It'd been too long since she'd been near the ocean.

In her home city of Adelaide, she was only twenty minutes from the ocean. Not far in the grand scheme of things, but appearing in public in a swimsuit? She shuddered.

Hmm. This could put a dampener on her swimming and tanning plans.

She pushed the thoughts aside, relieved to find the nausea and nerves had eased. Yes, she could do this. She'd been so excited for this ever since Monty surprised the family a month earlier. A gift for her parents' thirtieth wedding anniversary, a family getaway to celebrate.

Monty wasn't here, though. He was the life of the party... or the family. He'd insisted this holiday was strictly for the Eckhart family. "A chance to reconnect," he'd said, but Nikki didn't believe him.

You see, living with her parents had its perks. One of them being she had ears everywhere, and those ears had overheard private conversations between Mum and Dad. The point was, she knew things, and Monty's absence wasn't just out of the kindness of his heart.

"Why are you just standing here?" a voice snapped.

Nikki yelped from fright and spun around. Her sister, Katie, stood next to her. *She* was the reason Monty wasn't here.

"You're right in the way," Katie added, hands on hips.

Nikki's spine stiffened. "I'm waiting for Mum and Dad."

Katie harrumphed and folded her slender arms over her tiny chest. "They're coming. Now, will you stop blocking everyone and join the queue?"

Rather than moving, Nikki glanced back at the terminal doors as their parents stepped out. She waved her arm in the air until Mum saw her and waved back.

"Wait a sec," Nikki said. "Let them catch up so we can board together."

Katie only tutted and strode past, pulling her small, expensive suitcase behind her.

Nikki shook her head, surprised yet again by how different she and Katie were. Not just in personality, but in looks. The only resemblances they shared were their almond-shaped eyes. Otherwise, Katie took more after Mum—slim and short, with dark brown hair cut into a bob, and light brown eyes. Nikki took after Dad—tall and stocky, with long honey-brown hair, and grey eyes.

Nikki adjusted the backpack strap on her shoulder, and turned back to the ship again, butterflies returning. She hoped once she boarded and settled into her room, the nerves would disappear for good.

When her parents caught up, the three of them moved with the crowd toward the gangway. Katie stood to the side, arms folded, tapping her manicured fingernails on her forearm.

The ship was so close now. Passengers talked in excited tones as they rushed to board. A surge of excitement replaced Nikki's butterflies. Perhaps this was exactly what she needed.

"Alright, let's go," Dad said when they joined Katie. He grinned, his face alight with excitement. His grey-streaked, brown hair ruffled in the sea breeze.

Dad took Mum's hand, and they joined the line, laughing and chatting like teenagers in love. It was so strange to see them so carefree. At home, they were only her parents. The ones who'd disciplined her and raised her to be the woman she was now. She'd never taken the time to realise they were individuals, too. Two people *in love*, even after thirty years. She only hoped one day she'd experience the same sort of forever love.

Katie huffed. "I can't believe Montgomery made us board with all these people."

"It's Monty," Nikki snapped. Monty hated his full name, yet Katie insisted on using it.

Katie shot daggers at Nikki, then added, "Why didn't he just pay for first-class? It's not like he can't afford it."

Nikki bit her tongue. Katie loved to remind people that Monty was rich, but she hated that no one else cared. Monty was Monty, a good, fun-loving man. No one saw his money... apart from Katie.

As the line inched forward, the breeze died down and the afternoon January summer sun grew hotter. Nikki put her sunglasses back on and moved her backpack to the other shoulder. In front of her, Dad slung his arm across Mum's shoulders and kissed her cheek.

"Ugh, why do they have to act like that?" Katie muttered. "It's so embarrassing."

"Don't be such a prude." Nikki kept her voice low. "I think it's sweet they're still in love."

Katie threw her an icy glare. "You would think that, wouldn't you? You've always lived in a fairy tale. Marriages are *not* like that. Mum and Dad are putting on an act because Montgomery paid for the holiday. I bet all they do at home is argue."

"I said it's Monty," Nikki shot back, "and stop being such a pessimist. I live with them, remember? Don't you think I, of all people, would know if they argued or not?"

Katie huffed as they inched forward some more. "They wouldn't be stupid enough to argue in front of you, would they?"

"You're just bitter because your marriage is failing. You're too much of a wuss to salvage it because it's too hard, so you'd rather live in denial and bring everyone else down with you."

Nikki snapped her mouth shut, but she had no regrets. She had spent too long never speaking her mind. Katie had been a bitch for too long... six years too long to be exact. Her parents refused to get involved, so someone had to.

"You don't know what you're talking about." Katie's tone was flat. "So shut your ugly mouth and leave me alone."

Nikki gritted her teeth. Tears stung the backs of her eyes. Katie's insults still stung even though she'd heard them daily for years. She wouldn't normally retaliate but today was different. She was done with being trodden-on-Nikki.

Her hands balled into fists as she lashed out, "How dare you—"

Dad turned to them with warning in his eyes as he glanced from Katie to Nikki. "Girls, please. This is our holiday. Your mother and I don't want you two bickering the whole time. We have ten days to enjoy a cruise at the expense of your wonderful husband, Katie. Let's make the most of it."

Nikki lowered her gaze. Katie looked away and folded her arms.

After a moment, Nikki lifted her gaze again and mouthed, "Sorry," to Dad.

"Are you okay?" he mouthed back.

She threw him a brave smile and nodded.

Yeah, she could handle it, but she wasn't fine. The confidence to lash out and speak her mind had vanished. Katie's words seeped into her skin, adding to her already tattered self-esteem.

Dad turned and took Mum's hand.

She and Katie were close once. Nikki didn't understand how marrying Monty could change Katie so much. Was there more to it?

More than anything, Nikki wanted to fix their broken relationship. Be close once again. She missed the old Katie. And hell, she missed her old self, too. She'd lost sight of who *she* was. Katie's insults had made such an impression on her mind. Now she saw herself the way Katie did—fat, ugly, and useless.

It had to change.

Tears stung her eyes, but she blinked them away. She could do this. This was an opportunity of a lifetime. A chance to find herself and prove she wasn't a walkover anymore.

The line continued to inch forward, the crowd chattering and laughing as the holiday spirit settled over everyone. Before too long, they made their way up the metal gangway. Up close, the ship appeared even more overwhelming. It held up to three thousand passengers alone, with plenty of room for activities, restaurants, and bars. Not to mention crew. *Wow!*

She took one slow step after the other. People came up behind her, their voices bouncing off the ship's exterior. The higher she got, the faster her heart pounded.

When the doorway appeared, her parents and Katie went in first. When she reached it, she stopped for a split second and peered inside. Other passengers were directed to their rooms by crew, while other smiling crew waited at the door to view their passes.

This is it.

Nikki stepped over the threshold, displayed her pass, then followed her family.

In her periphery, a tall, broad, figure approached, but he appeared further away. Until she took one more step inside and she connected with a hard chest. Closer than she thought!

She lost her footing, a shriek escaping her lips.

Gasps rang out around her.

Her backpack slipped off her shoulder and she stumbled, but a pair of muscular arms halted her.

Heart racing, breath caught in her throat, she stared into golden-brown eyes. The world and everyone in it turned hazy. She'd always been a sucker for eyes, and these ones, God they were beautiful.

His curious gaze remained fixed on her and she wondered if the holiday could offer a chance at love, too.

Chapter 2

Gavin Fletcher stared into beautiful grey eyes. He hadn't been watching where he was going. The woman appeared out of nowhere and there was no chance of stopping their collision. His instinctive reaction was to stop her from falling, but he hadn't expected to find a beautiful woman in his arms.

After steadying her, he stepped away but couldn't tear his eyes away from her pretty round face, her porcelain skin tinged with pink from the sun. A breeze wafted in from the door, catching on her long hair. The sweet scent of coconut tantalised his senses.

He finally found his voice. "I'm so sorry. Are you okay?"

She smiled and tucked her hair behind her ear. "I'm fine." Her voice was sweet and husky. "My dignity has taken a holiday, though." She giggled and cleared her throat. "I'm sorry. I wasn't concentrating on where I was going."

She glanced at the floor and gasped, her cheeks turning a brighter shade of pink. Gavin followed her gaze and understood her embarrassment. The zip on her backpack had burst, spewing out various pieces of clothing, underwear and personal hygiene items for all to see.

When she crouched to pick them up, he followed suit. He picked up the closest thing to him but didn't notice what it was until he handed it to her. He chuckled quietly when she snatched the box of tampons and shoved them in the now broken backpack. Her already pink cheeks turned a violent shade of red.

"Thanks." She scooped up the last of her items and stuffed them into the bag. They both stood. She held the bag against her chest and held out her free hand. "I'm Nikki. Sorry again." She quirked a crooked smile and his insides turned to mush.

"Gavin." He took her hand and shook it. One touch of her soft skin and his heart raced.

"Nikki!"

She grimaced the same moment he let go of her hand and stepped back. A dark-haired woman approached, appearing annoyed.

"What's taking you so long? Hurry, will you?"

"I'm coming," Nikki muttered. She turned back to him and smiled. "It was nice to meet you, Gavin."

He watched her walk away with the other woman, who talked in rushed, annoyed tones. Once they were out of sight, he turned and headed for the stairs.

Nikki was a stranger to him, but he couldn't stop thinking about her. She wasn't his usual type. She was softer... curvier, but there was something undeniably sexy about her. He'd love to see her again, but what was the likelihood he'd find her in this crowd?

When he reached the outdoor deck, an image of her pretty face and sparkling grey eyes entered his mind.

"Seriously, pull it together," he muttered to himself as he sat on a stool at the bar.

"What did I do?" a female voice asked, sounding affronted.

He blinked, his twin sister, Sophie, coming into view behind the bar. "Not you."

"Are you talking to yourself again?" Her golden-brown eyes, the same as his, narrowed.

"Foster homes will do that to you." The words slipped out before he could stop them.

Sophie's eyes widened, the all-too-familiar pain clear in them. Awkward silence fell over them and he shuffled on the stool. They didn't speak about the past. Ever.

He fiddled with the bar mat. "What are you doing here? Aren't you a steward?"

She picked up a glass and dried it. "I'm doing a favour for someone. I'll be heading to my assigned deck next."

Gavin slid off the stool and joined her behind the bar. She shot him a disapproving look. "You're not crew anymore. You shouldn't be behind here."

He shrugged and picked up a second towel. "There are no customers. I won't tell if you don't." He winked.

Sophie tried to frown, but a thankful smile won in the end. Gavin had worked enough bars to know that drying glasses seemed endless.

He'd spent the last two years working on cruise liners. His last job ended a few weeks earlier, so now he could enjoy being a passenger. He'd paid extra for a first-class room so he could board early and offer Sophie some moral support.

She'd had a rough time over the last twelve months, and this was her first job in years after being a stay-at-home mum. Now a single mum after a failed marriage, with two kids to support, she had to take what she could get. Her two sons were staying with their father.

"Will Richard be okay with the boys?" Gavin referred to her ex, who was a little wet behind the ears.

He'd never understood what Sophie had seen in him. Yeah, he'd provided for the family, but he'd never made Sophie happy. Didn't seem to know *how* to. Just worked, ate, and slept.

A wave of guilt washed over him as he wondered for the umpteenth time if the demise of their relationship was his fault. When Sophie had admitted to him that she was lonely and unloved, he hadn't held back in telling her she deserved better. Someone who knew how to love her and make her happy. The next day, it was over. Had he been too honest?

"He'd better be." Sophie answered his question, a shadow passing over her face. "I hope to hell they won't be feral when I get home. Richard never puts them to bed on time. He feeds them beans on toast for dinner, and he lets them run wild." She grimaced. "Why did I let you talk me into this, Gav?"

He held up his hands. "Hey, I only suggested it. You're the one who ran with it."

"I know, I know." She picked up another glass. "It's my first time away without them, that's all. I'm probably worrying over nothing. His parents live close, and they promised to check on them."

Gavin chuckled. "And you wonder why I don't want kids." Though as the words left his mouth, an unexplainable feeling passed over him. Something akin to... longing?

Sophie interrupted before he could contemplate it. "I love my kids, but sometimes I think you have the right idea." Sophie gave a wistful smile. "Despite the way things turned out, I wouldn't trade my boys for the world."

"Look, Soph, just in case I haven't told you yet, I'm sorry about what happened between you and Richard."

Her shoulders went rigid and her eyes shimmered. "It's alright." Her voice wobbled. "I don't blame you, just so you know. You only told me what I needed to hear. I wasn't happy and neither was Richard, even if he denied it at first. It would've happened one day."

Gavin nodded but dropped the subject. His guilt eased, and they entered a comfortable silence while they worked. When passengers appeared, Gavin moved to the other side of the bar, perching himself on a stool once more.

He stared out over the deck. Some people found a seat among the copious amounts of deckchairs while others wasted no time jumping in the pool. The bright summer sun glistened on sprays of water from a young boy who cannonballed into the water. As he admired people laughing and getting into holiday mode, he contemplated his own life.

He'd been a nomad for so long, he knew nothing else. The life suited him. No one to answer to, no stifling debt, his choice of foreign women. What wasn't there to love about it?

"So," Sophie sat on a stool next to him, "Las Vegas, hey?"

"Huh?" So consumed by his thoughts, he didn't notice she'd finished her shift.

"You were deep in thought. I figured you were thinking about the big trip."

He grinned. It couldn't come soon enough. He spent the last two years saving for Las Vegas. It had been his goal for years but had put it off, wanting to save enough money to fully experience it.

"I can't wait. Everything's booked and paid for. The moment the cruise is over, I'm off."

Sophie's smile slipped, but she said nothing. She slid off the stool, and pulled her long hair back into a ponytail, deftly tying a hair tie around it. "I should get to my next shift. Come check up on me from time to time, okay?"

He couldn't respond before she sped away. Gavin frowned. What was up with her? He shook his head and shrugged it off.

After ordering a beer from the bartender, Gavin turned back to people watch while he sipped it. A family of four were setting themselves up near the pool. The two kids, a girl and a boy, were giggling and trying to whip each other with their towels. The mother scolded them, telling them to be careful, then turned to rummage in her bag. With her back turned, the father grabbed his own towel and ran after the kids. This ended up in a three-person chase around the deck, the mother watching on, shaking her head in dismay.

Gavin turned back to the bar and took a long swig of beer. The image played in his mind like a movie reel. What would it be like to have a family like that? The same longing from moments earlier returned with force and settled in his gut.

The unanswered question only intensified it, so he shook it off and guzzled the last dregs of his beer. He placed the empty glass on the bar and gestured to the bartender for a refill. He'd been in one place for too long, that was all.

In between his cruise jobs, he'd lived with Sophie and her sons. It had been nice being with them, and he loved his nephews, but it only confirmed that a life of travel was for him. He couldn't think of anything worse than settling down, holding down one job while stuck in a life doing the same mundane thing day in, day out.

As soon as he was on his way to Las Vegas, the feeling would pass.

Chapter 3

When Nikki entered her room and glanced around, she saw someone had pulled open the curtains over the balcony doors, which gave her an unobstructed view of the ocean. The cool breeze wafted in, tinged with a hint of salt and sand.

The door clicked shut as she stepped further inside, blocking out the din of other passengers talking and laughing. The room wasn't as VIP luxury as Katie had hoped, but Monty *had* got them their own rooms. For that, Nikki was grateful. It would've been hell sharing a room with her sister.

With an ensuite, a queen-size bed, two-seater sofa, television, bar fridge, and coffee making facilities, she had no complaints. Home away from home, with plenty of storage for her clothes and a desk where she could set up her laptop. Though she'd probably spend most of her time on the balcony.

She set her broken backpack on the end of the bed then flopped down next to it into the softness of the mattress. A sigh of pleasure escaped as she closed her tired eyes. It'd been a real expedition so far, and she wanted to enjoy a few quiet moments before unpacking her overnight bag. The rest of her luggage would arrive later.

The minutes passed and her tension eased. When she opened her eyes and sat up, she noticed a vase of yellow tulips on the bench by the door. She strode over to them and found a note leaning against the vase, a box of chocolates next to it.

She picked up the card and read the message inside.

I know how difficult this is for you, Nik, but I appreciate it. Please try to enjoy your holiday. Don't let Katie bully you. Be you and have fun. Eat what you want, enjoy these chocolates guilt-free and don't be afraid of what others say. You are an exceptional woman and the best sister any brother could ask for.

See you in ten days, and thanks again.

Monty

Nikki grinned and picked up the chocolates—her favourites, too. After stealing one, she placed the rest in the top drawer of the bedside cupboard with the card. She'd save the rest for another time.

She walked over to the balcony doors, staring out into the harbour where the smaller boats bobbed up and down in the shimmering water. Monty was not only her brother-in-law, but her best friend. There'd never been any romantic feelings between them. He was the brother she'd never had. He knew her better than anyone. Around her parents, Nikki pretended like Katie's insults didn't affect her, but Monty saw straight through the façade. He knew she struggled with her self-image and was always at the ready with an encouraging word.

Turning back to the bed, she dragged her bag closer. After emptying the contents, she sorted everything into piles. Her mind drifted back to her run-in with Gavin, her cheeks growing warm.

He was everything she *didn't* look for in a man. She liked boyish, clean-shaven, well-defined men with longer hair.

Gavin was far from boyish. Ruggedly handsome described him better. Short, dark brown hair, square jaw covered in three-day stubble, mild definition, and those golden-brown eyes... *damn*. She shivered and wrapped her arms around herself.

With a shake of her head, she returned to the task at hand. When she reached for the box of tampons, her face heated. *How embarrassing.* She wasn't due for her period, but she *was* an overthinker and catered for every scenario. She cringed and added them to the pile for the bathroom.

Once she'd sorted through everything, she started putting it all away.

It was so nice of Gavin to come to her aid. So many men lacked chivalry... or at least the men she'd dated in the past had. He proved it wasn't difficult to lend a helping hand.

After she'd put everything away, she stepped out onto the balcony enjoy the salty breeze on her skin. Her nerves were long gone, and now all she had to do was enjoy the holiday and embrace the challenge of finding herself.

I'm so done with Katie treading all over me and dictating who I am. Today it stops.

She stepped back inside with a decisive nod. On that note, she'd start day one of the cruise with a bang and face her biggest challenge by going for a swim.

Removing the black, one-piece swimsuit from the cupboard, she stared at it and released a shaky breath. Last night she'd battled with herself internally. At first, she refused to go swimming. Katie would only come up with yet another insult. The last thing she needed was strangers doing the same thing. In the end, she pushed her negative thoughts away and added it to her luggage.

It was damn hard, though. She'd become self-conscious after many years of being insulted. Self-deprecating comments spewed out from her mouth before she could think. It had to stop. Besides, just because Katie insulted her didn't mean other people would.

Boosted after the pep talk, she embraced the challenge and changed into the swimsuit. With the rest of her luggage not due for a while, she had time to kill. It was hot enough. Plus, it was the only way she'd ever learn to be comfortable in her own skin.

Before covering the swimsuit with a dress, she took in her reflection in the mirror with an open mind. She pushed Katie's harsh words aside and stared at the woman in front of her. Pretty, almond-shaped grey eyes on a round face and long, honey-brown hair falling in waves below her shoulders. She turned sideways, seeing a far from perfect figure. In the swimsuit, all her flaws were visible. The extra tummy she hated, the bigger thighs, and arms with their own wings.

When she faced the front again, Katie's insults flooded back. Now all Nikki could see was a whale—a tall woman without a gap between her thighs, wider hips and large breasts. Katie once told her that being a D cup was too big and she needed a breast reduction. It'd haunted her ever since.

Her chest ached, emotion built up. Tears spilled from her eyes, one after the other until she collapsed to the floor, sobbing into her knees. What was the point? Katie was right. She was always going to be right.

Whatever happened to not letting Katie tread all over you anymore?

At that moment, nothing could console her from the darkness shrouding her. She was sick of being belittled and made to feel worthless and ugly.

She glanced up and wiped her tears away. It was time to stop crying and stop being so affected by her sister. But, God, it was hard. When tears threatened to fall again, she sniffled and held them back. This was the first day of her holiday, and she wasn't about to let her sister ruin it.

Standing, she ignored her reflection and grabbed a towel from the bathroom. A knock sounded on the door when she came back. She threw the towel on the bed and answered it.

"Hi, my name is Sophie. I'm—"

"*Sophie*? Is that you?" Nikki's jaw dropped as she stared at the tall, slim woman standing in front of her, looking just as surprised.

"Oh my God, *Nikki*?" Sophie's pretty golden-brown eyes gleamed.

They grinned at each other, then laughed and embraced, jumping up and down. They'd been friends in high school. Sophie was three years older. She started grade eleven when Nikki started high school, but they were unlikely friends. For two years, they were inseparable, only losing contact after Sophie's graduation.

Nikki pulled back, happy tears blurring her vision. "I can't believe it's you! What happened? I never heard from you after you graduated."

Sophie frowned. "I'm so sorry, Nik. Life spiralled out of control. I turned eighteen just after graduation, moved out of the foster home, and the next thing I know, I'm here." She spread her arms out and let them fall to her side again.

Nikki opened her mouth to respond when Sophie regretfully said, "As much as I'd love to catch up, I'm on the clock."

It was then Nikki noticed the work uniform. "You work here?"

"Yep, servicing the rooms. Thought I'd pop by to see if anyone needs anything." She tugged on her ponytail as she leant in and whispered, "This is my first cruise job and even though I've been trained, I feel *so* out of my depth. Don't tell anyone."

She stepped back, shaking her head. Sophie may've grown up, but she hadn't changed a bit. Easily flustered, outgoing, fast-talking.

"If it's any consolation," Nikki said, "this is my first cruise and I've been a nervous wreck the whole morning. Monty said there were no icebergs in the Pacific, but I'm not sure I believe him."

Sophie's eyes lit up. "Who's Monty? Is he your boyfriend? Husband?"

"No!" The thought of Monty being either made her laugh. She loved him like a brother, that was all. "My sister's—"

As if on cue, Katie appeared next to Sophie. *Speak of the devil.*

"What's your room like?" Katie pushed her way in.

"I didn't invite you." Nikki turned to face her sister.

"I'm your sister. I don't need an invitation," Katie said over her shoulder.

Nikki gritted her teeth and watched as her sister took in every inch of the room with a critical eye. Less than thirty seconds passed, but when she turned back, annoyance passing over her features.

"Why did Mum and Dad get such a large suite and we didn't? Have you seen it?" She harrumphed.

"Yes, I saw it on the way." Nikki tutted. It was so typical of Katie to be jealous. "Why does it matter?"

Katie's eyes bulged. "It matters because—"

Nikki regretted her question instantly. "Actually don't bother answering that. Why can't you just appreciate what Monty has done for us? Can't you see how generous—"

"Generous?" Katie scoffed. "If he was, he'd at least get *me* a suite like Mum and Dad's." Her gaze zeroed in on something over Nikki's shoulder and she shrieked, "*Flowers?*"

Katie pushed past and Nikki turned with a sigh as Katie stomped over to the tulips. Nikki rubbed her temples while Katie ranted. "Are these from Monty too? How dare he? He's *my* husband."

"Oh, for goodness' sake, just stop!" The words tumbled out. Katie's eyes widened and her mouth snapped shut. Nikki took advantage of her silence, and continued, "Why does it matter who Monty sent flowers to? He sent some to Mum and Dad, and I assume he sent some to you, too. And why does it matter what size our rooms are? Show some bloody appreciation, Katie. This trip is a gift for Mum and Dad's anniversary."

"For your information," Katie recovered, "Montgomery bought this as a *family* holiday. We should be treated the same."

"Oh my God!" Nikki clutched her hair in frustration. "Why can't you get it through your thick skull, Katie? It's for Mum and Dad's *anniversary*." She spoke slowly, emphasising the words. "*They* get the special treatment this time. Stop being such a selfish brat and appreciate your husband for once." Katie's jaw dropped and, despite her anger, Nikki had the urge to smile in triumph but held it back. Instead, she pointed to the door. "Leave."

Katie pulled her shoulders back and stuck up her nose, spotting Sophie for the first time. She hadn't moved and stood to the side of the doorway with her head bowed and hands clasped in front of her.

"Who are you?" Katie demanded.

Sophie smiled politely. "I'm your cabin steward. I was just popping by your rooms. I'll come past soon to make sure you've got everything you need."

Katie forced a smile. "Oh, yes, please do. I have some requests."

Sophie nodded but said nothing.

Katie stepped out the door but turned back to Nikki and hit her with the final blow, "By the way, you look horrible in those swimmers.

The ones with the skirted bottom are much more flattering for your shape." With a triumphant smile, she stormed away.

Nikki had forgotten she didn't have anything over her swimsuit. Suddenly feeling exposed, she wrapped her arms around herself. She'd stood up for herself for the first time ever, but Katie had overshadowed it by stabbing her where it hurt most. Harsh words always won. It was why Nikki stopped trying to fight her sister.

Tears stung her eyes, but she held them back.

"Holy cow," Sophie said. "I knew you had a sister, but you never said she was a bitch."

Sophie's words broke the wall and tears cascaded down Nikki's cheeks, her face flaming in embarrassment. If she wasn't running into hot guys, she was bawling her eyes out in front of friends she hadn't seen for years.

What a way to make an impression.

Chapter 4

N ikki wiped away tears only to make way for more. "I'm so sorry."

She turned away from Sophie, covering her face with her hands. She willed the tears to stop, but they were endless.

It wasn't the end of the world, the insults were nothing new, yet they still hurt like hell.

"Is she always like that?" Sophie stepped further into the room.

Nikki didn't answer. Instead, she walked over to the bedside cupboard where a box of tissues sat. She grabbed a couple and wiped her face dry, her tears abating.

"It's okay." Nikki threw the used tissues into a bin beside the cupboard. "She's nothing but a prickly thorn."

"No, it's *not* okay." Sophie strode over and stood in front of Nikki. "You're avoiding my question, which funnily enough, actually gives me the answer I need, and I don't like it. Why do you put up with it?"

Frustrated and wanting to forget the incident ever happened, she shook her head. "Just forget it, okay? You should go see Katie. She's not known for her patience."

Sophie didn't move. Her eyes bore holes through Nikki, genuine concern oozing out of them. There was something familiar about them, but Nikki put it down to knowing Sophie in the past.

"I won't forget it," Sophie persisted. "You were never this... this..." She waved her hand up and down.

"Fat?" Nikki offered sarcastically.

Sophie gasped in horror. "What? No! What the hell? I was going to say fragile. My God, she's destroyed you!"

"I said forget it, Sophie." Nikki gritted her teeth. "You should go. You have a job to do, remember? I'm nothing more than a forgotten acquaintance."

If the hurt on her friend's face was anything to go by, Nikki had hit a raw nerve. Her emotions were all over the place and she'd lashed out. She'd gone from never being able to speak her mind, to saying too much. There was no excuse for her harsh words.

"That's not fair, Nikki," Sophie said. "I didn't have a normal life like you."

Nikki opened her mouth to apologise but Sophie wasn't done.

"The moment I left school I had to grow up. Fast. My foster parents gave up fostering when my foster mum got sick with cancer. The day I turned eighteen was the same day we had to leave. Those under eighteen were shipped off to other homes, and I had to find a job, a place to live, and somehow survive when I knew very little about life. I'm sorry we lost contact, but you know what? It's difficult being eighteen and weighed down with responsibilities. Suddenly all your focus is on working for the next payday so you can stay alive."

Nikki winced. She'd known her friend lived in a foster home but never considered what happened after school.

When Sophie turned to leave, Nikki called out, "Sophie, wait."

Sophie stopped before she reached the door and turned back.

"I didn't think and I'm sorry," Nikkie shrugged helplessly.

Sophie's shoulders sagged. "It's okay. You weren't to know. I didn't mean to freak out. It wasn't *so* bad. It could have been much worse."

Katie's voice floated down the hallway. "Where's the steward?"

Nikki winced. "Sorry about her. For what it's worth, she wasn't always like that."

"That's hard to believe." Sophie shot daggers at the open door. "*You* don't have to be sorry. And, for the record, I think your sister is wrong."

"About what?"

"About you. You rock the bathing suit. You're *hot*. I was always jealous of you."

Nikki wrapped her arms around herself. "You're lying! I'm a blimp and you need to get your eyes checked."

Sophie stepped further into the room and approached Nikki. "I'm not lying, Nik. I remember a time when you were much more confident."

Nikki smiled sadly. *If only I could be that person again. I had dreams once, too.* She shook the thoughts from her head. Those days were long gone.

"I mean it," Sophie persisted. "You have *no* idea how many boys wanted to get in your panties at school. I was the string bean with no boobs. You had natural curves and a sweet and innocent personality to boot. The boys went gaga for that."

Nikki's face flamed and she averted her gaze.

"You are *not* fat and you are *not* ugly," Sophie added.

"Steward!" Katie's voice was louder this time.

Nikki glanced up. "You better go. I don't want you to get into trouble."

"I'll make sure I pop by when I'm doing the rounds."

Nikki nodded. It would be nice to pick up where they left off all those years ago.

Sophie grinned. "*And* I'm determined to find that confident woman I know is still in there somewhere. It's time to put your sister in her place."

With a wave, Sophie rushed out the room, closing the door after her.

Nikki stared at the door. What to do? Katie's words still stung, but Sophie's compliments counteracted them. *Perhaps I will go for that swim after all? Prove I'm not letting my sister get to me.*

With a firm nod, she donned a dress over her swimsuit, slipped on a pair of sandals, then picked up her towel and keycard and left.

She stopped by her parents' room first.

"I'm off for a swim. Do you guys want to join me?" Nikki asked when Mum answered.

It had become a habit to include them whenever she went out. She loved her parents dearly and enjoyed spending time with them, but in hindsight, she'd been lonely. Oh, how she missed going out with friends her own age.

Mum shook her head. "Thanks, Nikki, but we'll pass. We're going for a walk soon."

"Well... okay."

The problem with this new realisation was that she still didn't have those friends she desired and didn't know anyone on the cruise. She'd have to meet new people, and *that* was terrifying.

She turned to walk away when Mum said, "Nikki, this is your holiday, too. Your father and I will be fine. Besides, you don't want to spend all your time with us old fogies, do you?"

Nikki glanced back and laughed weakly. Who knew finding oneself was so difficult? At home it was easy. She did her chores, babysat Monty and Katie's twin daughters occasionally, and created websites for her small business. This cruise required her to *do* things. It was all so overwhelming.

"Don't worry about us," Mum encouraged. "Have some fun, do something crazy. Not many parents would tell you to do that."

Nikki cast a glance up and down the hallway where the crew flittered about and more passengers claimed their rooms. She was almost jealous of them because they were busy. She appeared to be the only one who had no clue. It felt like one of those choose-your-own-adventure books, only she wasn't sure what page to turn to.

"Nikki—"

She spun around. Mum leaned against the doorframe, a small smile on her face. "Don't let your sister upset you like she always does." She walked up to Nikki and they embraced.

"You need this," Mum said in her ear. "Don't let your sister dictate who you are."

She pulled away and Nikki smiled. Her heart swelled with love for her mother, filling her with confidence.

With a brighter smile, she pulled back. "Alright but we *are* doing something special on your anniversary. I'm sure you and Dad have your own plans, but I insist on having a family dinner. No arguments."

Nikki wasn't keen on having dinner with Katie, but for better or worse she *was* family. Nikki only hoped Katie behaved herself.

Mum held her hands up. "No arguments from me. Let me know when and where and we'll be there. Now go. Have fun and don't worry about us. I'm sure we'll pass like ships in the night."

Nikki groaned and turned away. "I'll pretend I didn't hear that."

The further away she got, the worse her insecurities became. She pushed on, doing her best to ignore them. At the elevators, she stopped and pressed the button and waited. The doors opened seconds later but it was full. Changing her mind, she walked away and took the stairs instead. *Maybe I'll burn some calories*, she thought. *Katie would love that.*

She gritted her teeth as she pushed the negative thought aside.

Each deck she bypassed seemed busier as more and more people arrived. Passengers laughed, talked and shouted over each other.

On the outdoor deck, the pool glistened in the afternoon sun. There was also a spa and lots of deckchairs dotted around. Now she had a choice. Swim or drink?

The drink nearly won, needing the confidence boost, but then she figured the swim made more sense. Get it over with. Butterflies fluttered in her stomach, and she swallowed the lump in her throat.

She stopped at a deckchair near the steel ladder in the pool, placing her towel down and hiding her keycard underneath it. A glance around settled her nerves. It wasn't packed yet. A few people sunbathed, some swam, a handful of others sat at the bar with their backs to her.

Before she could talk herself out of it, she pulled her dress over her head and kicked off her shoes. She walked around to the shallow end and waded into the water. The coolness caught her breath, so when she was waist deep, she dived straight under. When she emerged seconds later, she was grinning.

She swam a couple of laps, then stopped and leaned against the wall, just enjoying the coolness of the water. Heart raced, smile going nowhere, she wondered why she'd waited so long to do this. No one had laughed. No one ogled, pointed or called her ugly. She'd overcome this hurdle. Perhaps next time would be easier.

The sun burned her skin, and she winced, chiding herself for not wearing any sunscreen. She'd stupidly left it in her room. Her pale skin never tanned but burned easily. There was shade at the bar, and she'd earnt that drink, so she swam over to the ladder. A newfound confidence hung over her as she pulled herself onto the first step.

With one foot on the bottom step and the other on the second, movement caught her eye. A man slid off a barstool and walked towards her. As she pulled a foot up so both were on the second step, her breath caught when the man looked directly at her. Close enough to see those familiar eyes. One chance meeting and already they were already etched in her mind.

Gavin.

All too aware of her swimsuit that hid nothing, her legs turned to jelly. She fought the temptation to fall back into the water and conceal herself, because what was the point? He'd already seen her. He grinned and stopped a few feet away, waiting for her.

On unsteady legs she took the last two steps, but her toes caught on the edge of the pool. She tripped with a yelp and for the second time that day, the ground came up to meet her, and—

Strong arms caught her!

Heart racing, she glanced up into those beautiful eyes and for the first time, she really took him in. Low brow, hooded eyes beneath neat eyebrows and a chiselled, masculine face. With his help, she stumbled to her feet, hopping when her bruised toes throbbed.

"Th-thank you." Embarrassment flamed her cheeks. "You've got good reflexes."

He chuckled, still holding onto her. "Good thing too. Are you okay?"

Her skin prickled, his touch sent sparks to all her nerve endings. She managed a nod and stepped back, drinking him in. Tall, broad, toned with enough muscle to be sexy but not overdone. Exactly how she liked it. There were some tattoos on his right arm but she couldn't see what they were.

She shivered when Gavin took her in from head to toe, his eyes flashing. There was no mockery or disgust in his gaze, just pure, unadulterated appreciation. Like he saw past what *she* saw. Her mouth turned dry, his attention doing nothing to slow her racing heart.

"Looks like I'll have to stay close," he said with a wink. "You may not survive this cruise otherwise. Do you have time for a drink? My shout."

She managed a weak smile, admiring his smooth pickup, but a sense of unease clawed through her. So used to insults from Katie, she didn't know how to deal with this sort of attention. Her feelings fought with each other. The ones that believed Katie's insults overshadowed the ones that enjoyed and craved his attention.

Nikki took an instinctive step to the deckchair and picked up her dress, donning it. "I don't think that's such a good idea. You've seen how much of a klutz I am. I might unintentionally hurt you."

"That's a risk I'm willing to take." His eyes glinted.

Nikki stopped short for a second, butterflies fluttering in her stomach.

The desire to take him up on his offer was strong but she knew better. "Trust me, it's not worth it. I'll only embarrass you." She slipped her feet into her sandals.

The truth of the words sat heavily on her shoulders as she stared at her feet. The toes she'd hit were red but not bleeding and the throbbing had become a dull ache.

Her short-lived confidence disappeared. "See you around, Gavin," she added with a sigh, picking up her towel and keycard.

When she turned away, he called, "I'm going to be at the sail away party at four-thirty. I'll be at the bar if you're interested in that drink together."

Nikki stopped for a second, contemplating, then started walking again. *No. If I go, that's only asking for trouble.*

Chapter 5

Gavin stared after Nikki, a smile tugging at his lips. She played hard to get but something possessed him to keep pursuing. He was intrigued.

He hadn't expected her curves to be such a distraction. All he wanted to do was hold her again.

Once she was out of sight, he made his way to the deck where the sail away party would take place. If he arrived early enough, he could secure a place to sit.

Thoughts of Nikki consumed him, and he hoped she'd show up. He wanted to ask her to dinner, which was *not* like him. Dates complicated things too much. One-night stands were much easier. No strings. No feelings.

This time, he had an overwhelming desire to figure Nikki out. She was a puzzle begging to be solved. He sensed she wasn't a one-night stand type of woman and it appealed to him. He didn't do relationships, and with his upcoming trip, he wouldn't start one now, but there was nothing wrong with a harmless fling. All he had to do was convince her.

⚘⚘⚘⚘⚘ ⚘⚘⚘⚘⚘

Later that afternoon, Gavin sat at the bar while the sail away party ramped up. He glanced around at the masses of people, hoping to spot Nikki. The crowd was huge, though. It would be impossible to see her.

He turned back and sipped on his bourbon and coke. He was the only one sitting. Everyone else grabbed their drinks before moving away to mingle and dance. As more people filled the party area, they pressed up against him. Music from the live band blasted from the speakers and there was an all-round merry atmosphere. People laughed, danced and waved off their relatives and friends. The ship's horn sounded and a loud cheer rose.

Next to him, a tall, long-legged woman stopped beside him, between his stool and an empty one. "Martini, please," she yelled across at the bartender.

Gavin downed the last of his drink and requested a refill at the same time.

The woman stood close, her long, blonde hair that hung to her waist in natural waves, tickled his arm. She was dressed in a short, see-through summer dress, a skimpy black bikini visible beneath it, leaving nothing to the imagination.

She fluttered her eyelashes and sent him a flirty smile, turning so her cleavage was on display. He averted his gaze. Once upon a time, she was the type he'd pursue, but this time he wasn't tempted. Nikki's beautiful face was etched in his mind. He glanced around once more, but it was pointless. Just a sea of faces.

The bartender returned and placed their drinks down. The woman took her martini and sauntered off with her nose in the air.

Gavin's shoulders slumped as he sipped his drink. Despite the jolly atmosphere, he didn't *feel* the vibe anymore. Didn't experience the same excitement everyone else did. It was probably because this was his last cruise for a long while. Too excited about his big trip to enjoy it. He'd be boarding a plane bound for Las Vegas the day after the cruise. Eleven days and counting. The usual thrum of excitement washed over him, and he hoped the next few days would pass quickly.

"Hi," a voice yelled over the music.

Gavin's heart leapt as he stared into a pair of familiar grey eyes. *Well, maybe the days shouldn't pass too quickly.* He gestured to the empty stool next to him. When Nikki sat, she appeared on edge... guarded.

He leant in so he could talk to her better, getting another intoxicating whiff of her coconut scent. It sent his pulse into an erratic frenzy.

"What made you change your mind?" His lips almost touched her ear. He smirked when she shivered.

She smiled shyly. "Guess I realised I'm on holiday and need to live a little."

"Can I get you a drink?"

She shook her head and held up her cruise card. "I can get it."

Unable to resist touching her, he took her hand. Her skin was so soft and warm. "I insist. What would you like?"

She regarded him warily.

"I'm not trying to get you drunk," he said. "Do you drink wine?" She pulled a face, and he laughed. "Okay, no wine. Cider? Beer? Spirit?"

She moved her hand back and put her card away. "A cider would be nice, thank you."

He missed her touch but didn't initiate it again, not wanting to scare her away. Gavin summoned the barman again and requested a cider.

He turned to Nikki, who took in the crowd with doe-like eyes. The noise irritated him, too.

When her drink arrived, he suggested they go somewhere quieter. Nikki hesitated but then cast her gaze around once more. The crowd had doubled in size. She nodded.

They stood and he gently took her by the elbow, guiding her through the masses of people. Eventually, they made it outside to the outer deck where there were a few people milling around but not too many.

They wandered past deckchairs, away from the noise, while the ship sailed away from the dock. Gavin spotted a couple of free deckchairs a safe distance away where the music could still be heard but wasn't so loud. Nikki sat on the side of one and Gavin sat on the other, facing her. She rested the cider on her jean-clad leg.

"So, not a wine drinker?" he asked, recalling her reaction to the suggestion.

She wrinkled her nose adorably. "I'm not a big drinker and wine gets me tipsy too fast. Plus, I find it generally unpleasant."

"Duly noted." He held his glass up in a toast. "Well, here's to the holiday of a lifetime."

She clinked her glass to his, and they sipped, his gaze holding hers.

Nikki cleared her throat and averted her eyes. "I'm sorry for being so standoffish earlier." When she looked up, there was a vulnerability in her eyes.

"You don't need to apologise."

"Yes, I do. I was rude to you."

"Well, then, perhaps we could start over. Have dinner with me?" He held his breath in anticipation.

He watched her intently as she appeared to struggle with an answer. She wore her emotions on her face, but he wasn't good at reading them. Had he been he too full-on? They *had* only met that day. It'd been a long time since he'd asked a woman out on a date. His stomach dropped, expecting a rejection.

"I'd like that."

He breathed a sigh of relief. "How about tomorrow night?"

She nodded and smiled, averting her gaze to the ocean. The smile remained fixed on her face, but she still appeared conflicted. He almost asked what she was thinking but held his tongue. Instead, he followed her gaze.

The ship sliced through the water, creating ripples which made the other nearby boats bob up and down. His breath caught when he turned back to Nikki. The sun on her face gave it a yellow hue. Her grey eyes shone brightly, appearing almost blue.

She sipped her cider, her tongue darting out to lick the moisture off her pink lips. Gavin groaned, and Nikki turned to him in surprise. Never had he wanted to kiss a woman so much.

And that was why, without so much as a second thought, he leaned in. He was never so bold unless he knew the woman was on the same page, but with Nikki, he lost all common sense. He drew closer. Her eyes widened, a gasp escaping her lips when he brought his hand up to caress her smooth, porcelain skin. Her warm breath fanned his face.

He closed the distance. The moment their lips touched, lightning struck. An overpowering force spread through him right down to his toes. He'd kissed many women and never had he experienced anything so intense. Her lips were as soft as he'd imagined. She tasted of apple, and the sea air mixed with the sweet, creamy hint of coconut from her hair made his head spin. He wanted to deepen the kiss, wholly taste her, but he sensed her reluctance.

He pulled back, the gravity of the situation weighing on him. *This is so not like me.*

Nikki bit her lip and it took all his willpower not to kiss her again.

"That... that shouldn't have happened," Nikki said, her brow creasing in confusion as her fingers touched her lips.

Gavin understood her confusion. There was no way *he'd* forget such a kiss.

"I'm sorry." Gavin didn't mean it. It may have been out of character, but he had no regrets.

"It's okay." She folded her hands in her lap. "You don't have to be sorry. It's just..." She shrugged. "I'm complicated." She shook her head and pursed her lips.

He wanted to ask questions, but she erected an invisible wall around herself. He let the subject drop, but his mind replayed the kiss. *I'm doomed. All I'm going to want to do now is kiss her, and I can't. Damn it.*

Awkwardness filled the semi-silence. Gavin glanced out over the water again. The sun had disappeared behind a cloud, rays of light shining out from behind it. In the background, the music changed to the popular sea shanty *Drunken Sailor*. The crowd cheered, drowning out the music for a few seconds. Beside him, Nikki laughed softly. The sound enveloped and caressed him like a summer breeze.

"Do they always play shanties?"

Gavin glanced across at her. "It depends. Most times it's a request from a passenger for a bit of fun. Sometimes the band will play it for a reaction."

Nikki raised her eyebrows in question. "This isn't your first cruise?"

"I've lost count how many I've been on. I worked on them before now. I finished my last job a few weeks ago and decided to have one last hurrah before I jet off to America."

"You're a traveller?"

He nodded enthusiastically. This led into easy conversation, all awkwardness dispersing. Yet questions formed in the back of his mind. Somehow, in a matter of a few hours, something inside him had changed. One woman whom he'd never met before, one kiss that clouded his mind, and suddenly he was feeling things he'd never experienced before.

Chapter 6

What were you thinking letting him kiss you? And dinner? Jeez, what's wrong with you? Nikki power-walked through the ship, ignoring the sights and people. She needed to get to her room where she could hide.

She hadn't intended to meet him for a drink, but she was sick of never doing anything and a harmless drink would be fine, right? Apparently not!

The memory sent a trail of goose bumps along her skin. She rubbed at her arms as she reached her deck. Her lips still tingled. She'd barely managed to kiss him back, so shocked by it, along with the alarm bells going off in her head. Yet, there was no way she'd ever forget how his lips felt.

Slowly walking along the blue and gold carpeted hallway, she distracted herself by viewing the pictures on the wall. Most were photos of beautiful island locations and the local Polynesian people. Some were of the sun setting and others were of previous passengers with the crew.

No amount of admiring them would rid Gavin from her mind though.

She couldn't remember a time she'd enjoyed being in a man's company so much. Gavin was so easy to talk to. Attentive and unjudging, he appeared to appreciate everything she said. It was disconcerting because she'd never truly enjoyed the company of previous boyfriends. It was a rude shock.

At her room, she stopped at the door and dug into her jeans pocket for the key card. That was when something occurred to her.

Her time with Gavin had only reinforced how being cooped up for so long had done her no favours. She'd forgotten how to have fun and everything had become irrationally terrifying. That was the real reason she'd initially said no to meeting. A broken heart she could handle. But living and having fun? That was scary as hell.

She cringed as she removed the keycard. Even the thought of having dinner with Gavin scared her. For so long, Katie criticised everything she ate. What if Gavin was the same? It was a fear she'd had in her previous relationships too, so she'd always order a salad. Why couldn't she enjoy a steak or pasta guilt-free? If she could ignore Katie's words, perhaps she'd be able to.

She shook her head as she swiped the card and pushed open the door.

"Where have *you* been?"

With one foot over the threshold, Nikki raised her eyes heavenward. After offering a silent prayer for strength, she turned around to face her sister. "Exploring. Is that a problem?"

Katie smiled smugly and leant against her doorframe. "It's that guy, isn't it? The one who stopped your fall when we arrived."

Nikki frowned. Why did Katie remember that specific moment? To anyone else it was long forgotten. Her parents hadn't mentioned it either. Katie's tone implied she was... jealous? It was so absurd Nikki ignored it.

Refusing to rise to the bait, Nikki didn't falter. "I have no idea what you're talking about. I was checking out what activities there were to do onboard. It's not like I have to tell you where I am every second of the day."

She turned back to her room when Katie retaliated with, "He would never be interested in you, anyway. You're too fat."

The words made her bristle. Rather than biting back, she walked into her room, slamming the door after her. Her delivered luggage sat next to the sofa, but she ignored it for now. There were so many things she wanted to say, words that wouldn't die on her tongue this time, but she kept silent. She wanted to think. Something about the ridiculous notion of Katie being jealous.

It didn't stop the sting, though. Didn't stop the realisation that perhaps her sister was right. What if he'd only kissed her out of politeness? Or worse... pity?

The negative thoughts were so overwhelming, anything she tried to quiet them would be useless. In the end, she did the next best thing. Settled down to design a website. She promised herself she wouldn't work much while she was away, but she needed to keep busy.

Only for a couple of hours.

***

When a knock sounded at her door, Nikki stood and stretched her arms over her head.

The knock sounded again so she strode over and opened the door. Sophie stood there, arms folded, fingers tapping her right forearm.

"Oh, hi." Nikki still hadn't recovered from the shock of seeing her again after so long. "I didn't think I'd called anyone."

What was supposed to be a couple of hours turned into a couple of days. No one bothered her. Once she started designing, she couldn't stop. Not only did it keep her thoughts occupied, but she was having a blast with her newest assignment—a website for an online baby clothes store. Even the chocolates from Monty hadn't been spared, a perfect snack when she was working.

Honestly, locking herself in her room hadn't been intentional. On the first day, she'd planned to check out one of the comedy shows but changed her mind when she remembered her date with Gavin. By that point she'd decided she wouldn't go but had no way of contacting him. As much as she tried to ignore Katie's words, they taunted her mercilessly. He really could do so much better than her.

Guilt ate away at her, mixed with disappointment over wasting two days when she could've been enjoying onboard activities.

"You didn't," Sophie said, gesturing to her casual outfit of skinny jeans and a white, fitted t-shirt.

Nikki scowled at her slim figure. *Not a curve in sight. Damn her.*

"I'm here to take you out," Sophie added.

Nikki's grip tightened on the door. "Are you allowed to be here? I don't want you to risk your job on my account."

Sophie's eyes flashed. "I don't care about my bloody job and besides, I'm not scheduled to start until later, so right now I'm a free woman for the next few hours. We haven't seen each other for years, so sue me for wanting to spend time with you."

Her words warmed Nikki's heart. She almost caved but the prospect of running into Gavin was too great. She began to close the door. "I appreciate it, but I don't want to go out. Besides, I've got work to—"

"Work?" Sophie pushed her way into the room. Nikki stumbled backwards, losing her grip on the door.

It took her a few seconds to recompose herself. By that point Sophie had made short work of closing the lid of her laptop and packing it in the bag.

"Hey!" Nikki took two strides and made a grab for the bag but Sophie held it behind her back. "What are you doing? You can't just barge into my room and take my stuff."

"I'm not 'taking' anything. You're so dramatic." Sophie rolled her eyes. "I don't know what the hell has happened to you but if I remember correctly, you never let work interfere with fun. What about the times we skipped school? Or left homework to the last minute just so we could see a late movie?"

Nikki missed those times. Life was so much easier. "Things change," she muttered.

"What? A personality transplant? I know it's your sister, despite what you say."

Always passionate, anger radiated off Sophie.

Nikki didn't answer.

Sophie huffed. "Fine, ignore me, but I know it's true. The last time I was here, I heard what your sister said. Understandably, you were upset, but locking yourself in your room for two days? I *did* see your 'do not disturb' sign, but if I'd known you were working, I would've barged in earlier."

Nikki's cheeks warmed and she looked at the floor. The sign had been a godsend. Her suite was so comfortable, making it harder to leave. She was content sitting on the balcony, or if it was cold, at the desk indoors.

"Come on." Sophie snapped Nikki out of her thoughts. "There's a classic movie starting in half an hour. I really want to go, and I want you to come with me." She shook her head in disbelief. "I still can't believe you've been working. What part of 'holiday' don't you understand? Why did you bother coming?"

"It was a gift for Mum and Dad's—" she gasped. "Oh my God!"

Glancing at the watch on her wrist, she breathed a sigh of relief when she noticed it was only ten in the morning. She still had time.

"What's wrong?" Sophie asked.

"It's Mum and Dad's anniversary today. I'm sorry but I can't come with you. I need to shop for gifts."

She *had* remembered to make a dinner booking, thank goodness.

Sophie's eyes lit up. "I'll come with you!"

"Sure." It would be nice to spend time with her long-lost friend too.

After pulling out a pair of jeans and a t-shirt, she threw throwing them on the bed. "I've got to shower," she said to Sophie. "You can hang around if you want. I'll only be a few minutes."

Sophie nodded and removed the laptop and bag from behind her, placing it on the sofa. Nikki eyed it longingly.

"No more work, Nikki," Sophie said.

"But I have a deadline! I need to get it finished by tomorrow or else I won't get paid."

"What exactly do you do?"

"I design websites. I really do need to finish it."

Sophie sighed. "Fine, but later. Not right now. After you've reached your deadline, you're going to enjoy your holiday, okay?"

Nikki pulled a face. "You're not my mother."

Sophie grinned. "No, but I'm your friend and I only have your best interests at heart."

Nikki gave an exaggerated sigh. "*Fine.*"

Ten minutes later, she was showered and wrapped in a towel, her hair hanging around her shoulders. She found Sophie sitting patiently on the sofa, but the jeans and t-shirt Nikki had put on the bed had been replaced with a light blue and white knee-length dress. She glanced suspiciously at Sophie, who paid her no attention.

She picked up the dress and went to hang it back up when Sophie reacted. "Don't put it away!"

Nikki turned to her. "Why? I don't like this dress. I don't know why I packed it."

"Don't like it? It'll look great on you. Besides, it's such a beautiful day out there, you'll look like you're really on holiday."

Nikki frowned and shook her head. "No thanks. It shows too much of my legs."

Sophie sighed in exasperation. "Seriously, girl, you need to stop being so self-conscious and start showing off your assets."

Nikki's laugh was bitter. "What assets? Fat legs, fat arse, fat tummy, fat—"

"Will you *stop*?" Sophie's eyes were dark, her fists clenched at her side. "Why do you do this? Why do you constantly put yourself down? I know you've never been the most confident person in the world but you were *never* this bad."

Stumped for words, all Nikki could do was shrug. "When you hear it all the time you begin to believe it."

Sophie sighed and grabbed Nikki's hand, leading her to the full-length mirror. Nikki squeezed her eyes shut.

"You need to *stop* believing it, Nikki." Sophie's voice grew soft. "I know your sister has drummed it into you, but you need to ignore her. It's time to embrace who you are... a beautiful woman."

"Please stop." Nikki's voice wavered. "I know what I am."

"No, you know what you *think* you are. What your sister has made you believe you are. Now, I want you to open your eyes and look at yourself."

"But I'm only in my towel."

"Even better. Now, open them."

Nikki shook her head and squeezed her eyes tighter.

"Do it," Sophie said, her tone firm.

Nikki shook her head again, standing strong in her resolve. She was *not* going to look at herself. She knew what she would see.

"Nikki." Sophie's voice turned low. "Do. It."

Nikki didn't budge.

Sophie sighed in exasperation. "Why are you so stubborn? I thought it was only the teenager in you. Obviously not."

Nikki shrugged, a small smile tugging at her lips.

"If you *don't* open your eyes, I'm going to rip the towel away."

Gasping, Nikki's eyes flung open, and she held on to the towel for dear life, glaring at her friend for tricking her.

Sophie laughed, slapping her hand against her leg. "Your face!" She chuckled and shook her head. "It got you to open your eyes, didn't it?"

Nikki scowled, but this time she did as she was told. She looked at her reflection with Sophie next to her.

"Better." Sophie smiled.

"This isn't helping." Nikki compared herself to her friend. "Look at us! We're like the elephant and the mouse."

Sophie snorted a laugh. "Oh, stop. Don't compare yourself to me or anyone else. You need to stop seeing the version of yourself Katie planted in your head. Because the version I see? She's gorgeous. I'm not going to laugh at or judge you, Nikki."

With a sigh, Nikki took a good look at her reflection. All she could see was a frump. A woman with long, honey-brown hair that needed a trim because she had split ends. Who was twenty kilos over her recommended weight to height ratio. Who had a tummy, thunder thighs and—heaven forbid—fat rolls. It disgusted her.

Tears stung her eyes. *This* was how her sister saw her and it hurt like hell. Nikki had tried all the fad diets, and even though she hated exercise she'd tried that too, but *nothing* worked. She was always hungry, miserable and still the same weight. She'd rather be fat than starve to death.

"I can't." Nikki stared at her reflection. "All I see is what Katie does."

Sophie shook her head. "Your sister must stop this. She has no idea what she's doing to you." She sighed. "I'm sorry, Nikki, but I have no choice. This is the *only* way I can get you to see what I see. Once and for all."

In one swift motion, while Nikki was defenceless, Sophie ripped the towel away.

Chapter 7

"Oh my God!" Nikki crossed one arm over her breasts while her free hand covered her private parts. Tears of humiliation dripped onto her chest. "What are you trying to prove?" She'd *never* in a million years felt so exposed.

Sophie stepped back and threw the towel away from them on the floor.

"Why?" She glared at Sophie through tear-filled eyes. "Why are you doing this to me? As if I don't feel bad enough."

Sophie stepped forward again. "I'm sorry, really I am. I'm not trying to humiliate you. I want you to appreciate your assets. If you can accept yourself like *this*, you're more likely to accept who you are when you go out."

"I can't believe you did this to me."

Her face was on fire. She wanted to hide, turn back time and tell Monty she didn't want to go on the cruise. It had done nothing but ruin her life.

What about Gavin?

She mentally shook her head. There was a reason she'd avoided him. Guilt still ate away at her but she pushed it aside. She'd done him a favour.

"Don't be embarrassed," Sophie consoled. "I'm not going to feel you up. You know I don't swing for women."

This elicited a small smile from Nikki. "Me either but I'm so embarrassed."

Sophie waved a dismissive hand. "Don't be. I spent a few months travelling with my brother. We were—"

"I keep forgetting you have a brother," Nikki interrupted. "I didn't meet him, did I?"

Sophie shook her head. "No. He dropped out of school when he was fifteen and started working. He wasn't around much."

Everything from all those years ago was a blur.

"Anyway, as I was saying." Sophie frowned at Nikki for interrupting. "My brother and I backpacked around Europe, staying in hostels. The showers were communal, so I couldn't be shy around other women. We all have the same parts, so what's embarrassing about it? Just so you know, I'm not turned on by you."

Nikki burst out laughing and, to her surprise, both of her hands fell to her side. Nikki let herself relax. After all, she was in the company of a good friend. Despite years of no contact, it was like they'd never been apart.

She turned to the mirror with a sigh, closed her eyes for a second, then opened them again and stared at herself... naked. It was the hardest thing she'd ever done. Could never bear to. All she saw was fat... fat everywhere. She looked like—

"No," Sophie said sternly. "I know what's going on inside that head of yours. Embrace who you are, Nikki. You are a voluptuous woman. You have curves, you have breasts bigger than fried eggs, you have *so* many things men love. Who gives a crap if you carry a few extra kilos? It's what's inside here," she tapped Nikki's temple, "that counts. But all that aside, you're *still* a beautiful woman. Now," she stood behind Nikki, both staring at her reflection, "I want you to look at yourself objectively. Okay?"

She was so out of her comfort zone, but so desperate to feel good about herself she went along with it. There was no one else she would dare do it with. She and Sophie had always been comfortable around each other. Confident in their friendship and never shy, happy to change in front of each other when they needed to. It was a painful reminder of how Katie had damaged her so much. It was time to find that confidence she'd lost.

With a single nod, Nikki undertook the painful process of allowing herself to see who she was... as a *woman*. Her skin milky white with very few blemishes, her figure naturally curvy. Her face round and pretty with large, hazel eyes protected by long eyelashes. But beyond that, deep within, she was Nikki Eckhart... a sensitive and selfless woman who cared for others.

Those things, she realised, helped her understand that some excess fat didn't matter.

It wasn't a miracle cure, but she could begin to accept the woman inside and with that, the woman on the outside wasn't so ugly. Her confidence issues wouldn't disappear overnight, but it was a start. She'd be forever grateful to Sophie for helping her.

"Thank you," she whispered. Then glancing over her shoulder, she added, "Can I get changed now? This is super awkward."

An hour later, Nikki and Sophie were shopping for an anniversary gift. Nikki wore the dress she initially refused to wear. After her awkward confrontation, Nikki had to admit she felt and looked pretty in it. It was summery and perfect for the cruise.

"Thirty years you say?" Sophie asked.

Nikki hummed a yes. She glanced around at the array of shops lining each side of the deck. It was a mall on the water. They'd visited a few, but Nikki hadn't found anything appropriate for an anniversary gift.

"Okay, traditional gift is pearl."

Nikki glanced across at Sophie who read from her phone.

"Modern is diamond." Sophie wrinkled her nose and glanced up. "They both sound expensive. Do you have any other ideas?"

Nikki shrugged as a jeweller caught her eye and she pointed it out to Sophie. "Let's check it out."

They weaved through other passengers and stopped at a display window. "Pearl could be nice for Mum," Nikki mused. "I think diamonds would be more suitable for Dad. He's not big on jewellery but he has a—" Her eyes widened. "Hold on a sec."

She walked into the store and stopped at the silver watch that'd caught her eye. The style was manly, the face encrusted with tiny diamonds. Perfect for Dad.

"These people and their money," Sophie muttered from beside her, eying the watch in the glass case. The price was already exorbitant but had been inflated onboard.

Nikki's cheeks warmed. "I'm far from rich but I've managed to build a decent savings. That's one advantage of living with your parents."

"Wait a minute." Sophie grabbed her arm and Nikki turned around. "You still live with your *parents*?"

"Yes, why?"

"But... but you're like, what? Twenty-six now?"

Nikki nodded. "What's the problem?"

Sophie's jaw dropped. "No problem, but I don't know many people who still live with their parents at your age. I don't think I would... well, if they were alive."

The atmosphere changed. "Do you miss them?"

Sophie's smile slipped as she shrugged. "I barely remember them. I miss having parents. I wish I had a mother." Her eyes brimmed with tears, a stray one dripped down her cheek, but she managed a bright smile. "I can't believe we bumped into each other like this." She wiped the tear away. "You were always like family to me."

Nikki beamed. "Ditto." And she meant it. Sophie had been like a second sister, and Nikki regretted losing contact. If they hadn't, it was possible Nikki wouldn't be in the state she was in now. Sophie would've been a wall of strength, like she'd always been.

Nikki turned back to the watch as a shop assistant materialised, ceasing further conversation. She considered a few other options but, in the end, settled on the watch for Dad and a lovely pearl necklace for Mum.

With gifts sorted and wrapped, she and Sophie sat down for a coffee and a light lunch before Sophie had to leave for her next shift. Nikki found a little booth in the corner away from the crowd of holiday makers grabbing coffee while searching for the next activity to take part in. In their little quiet corner, they sat, ate, and chatted like old times.

"You said you had to adjust to living alone," Nikki said, recalling their conversation a few days ago. "Where was your brother? He didn't help out?"

Sophie finished her coffee and placed the cup back on the saucer. "He was desperate to travel and I wasn't about to stop him. We'd been cooped up in foster homes for too long. It was time to live our lives. I didn't mind. Once I'd adjusted, I enjoyed my life. I got married two years later. I met Richard when I was backpacking around Europe with my brother. I even cut my trip short to go home with Richard."

Nikki gasped. "I didn't know you were married! If you tell me you have kids, I'll cry. You look amazing." Nikki sipped her cappuccino, glancing at Sophie over her cup. Her friend's eyes had lost their shine, and she lowered her face but Nikki saw her bottom lip wobble.

"Oh no, I'm sorry. Did I put my foot in it?"

Sophie looked up again wearing a brave, watery smile. She held up her left hand, sans wedding ring. "We divorced six months ago, and yes we have two boys."

A lead weight settled in Nikki's stomach. "Oh God, how horrible!"

Sophie shrugged like it was nothing, but Nikki could tell it was a big *something*. "It was for the best." Sophie's words came out on a whisper. She cleared her throat. "We were both so young and not ready for what married life entailed. I'm surprised we lasted as long as we did, but we both tried to make it work for our sons. Until we couldn't."

Nikki reached across for her friend's hand, giving it a squeeze. "I'm so sorry."

"It's okay." She pulled her shoulders back. "It was amicable and we're on good terms. I have sole custody, but we have an agreement to share the care of the kids. It's the only reason I'm here now. I know I'm working, but it sort of feels like a holiday too. It's nice to get away after everything."

Nikki nodded but had no idea what to say. So much could change in ten years.

"Where do you live now?" Nikki changed the subject.

Sophie shoulders drooped. "Still in Adelaide."

"No way!"

Her eyes lit up. "Yes! You too?"

Nikki nodded and grinned. How had they never run into each other? Adelaide wasn't that big, but then she realised they led very different lives. Nikki didn't leave the house often and Sophie had kids to run around after.

"That's so awesome!" Sophie exclaimed, back to her old self. "You can be my babysitter!" When Nikki gave her a deadpan look, Sophie laughed. "I'm kidding. We'll have Wednesday coffee, go out for dinner and a movie on Friday nights, breakfast on Monday's, and—" She held a hand to her forehead. "I'm exhausted just thinking about it. I'm not a teenager anymore."

Nikki chuckled and finished her cappuccino. "What time is your next shift?"

Sophie tapped her phone to check the time. "Crap, twenty minutes. I totally lost track of time. Sorry to rush but I need to change first." She stood and came around to embrace Nikki. "I'm glad we got to do this. I'll see you around."

With a wave, she dashed out of the café and was swallowed up by the crowd within seconds. Nikki picked up her purchases and made her way back to her room.

Chapter 8

Back at her room, Nikki locked her purchases safely away, then stepped out onto the balcony. The deep blue ocean sparkled in the afternoon sun, and Nikki was surprised how carefree and confident she felt in that moment. How long would it last? It was a question she couldn't answer but did she want to? She was a terrible overthinker so she would embrace the feeling instead.

So, doing exactly that, she headed back inside and changed into her swimsuit. Time to do something that terrified and thrilled her all at once. She'd done it once, she could do it again. When she spied her reflection in the mirror, the instinct to cringe was overwhelming but she caught herself. Instead, she forced herself to stop, look, appreciate.

She didn't think she'd ever agree she looked good in a swimsuit, but she conceded that she didn't look bad. That was a start, right?

After lathering herself with sunscreen, she donned a dress and sandals, stuffed everything she'd need in a tote bag, then left her room. When she reached the outdoor deck, memories of Gavin saving her fall for a second time flashed through her mind. The guilt of standing him up assailed her, so this time, she ventured to the opposite side of the deck where another, smaller pool was. She placed her bag down on a spare deckchair.

Butterflies whipped up a storm when she glanced at the pool. The time had come. The warm summer sun beat down on her but a cool ocean breeze took the edge off.

Once composed, she stripped down to her swimsuit and placed her clothes on the chair next to her bag. She wandered to the pool and glanced around. When no one laughed or called her names she relaxed and sat on the edge, sliding into the water.

She swam for a bit, enjoying the freedom. After a few laps, she stepped out, dried off and lathered herself in more sunscreen, then laid on the deckchair to sunbathe. Waterslides above her cast shadows over the deck, adults and children alike shrieked as they slid down into another pool behind Nikki.

Closing her eyes, the sun warmed her skin. With any luck, she would turn brown. Moments passed. She heard people talking, some shrieking down the slide and others laughing. It was deliciously relaxing. No hustle and bustle of city life. No stress, tension or rudeness.

She sighed in contentment. For the first time since arriving, she was glad she'd come. Nothing, not even Katie's harsh words, could ruin her mood.

"Hello Nikki."

Then again...

She didn't need to open her eyes to know who it was. That voice. That overwhelming guilt. That pull.

"Gavin." She sat up. "Hi." Her stomach churned at the thought of confessing *why* she'd stood him up. "How are you?" It was a lame question in a desperate attempt to draw out the inevitable conversation.

He sat on an empty chair next to her, shoulders rigid. She swung her legs around. The sun shone on his tanned skin, giving it a bronzed look. His brow was creased, and he was frowning.

He ignored her question and instead he calmly said, "You didn't show up. Everything okay?"

She winced. He'd put on a front to conceal his annoyance, which only made her feel worse. She shrugged, having no idea what to say. In the end, she muttered, "I figured you'd have a better time without me."

His frown deepened. "Isn't it up to me to choose who I have a good time with?"

She admired him for keeping his cool. Yet another thing to like about him.

Nikki clasped her hands between her knees. "Of course, I didn't mean it like that. It's just..." She didn't know how to say it without confessing her deepest insecurities, which would probably scare him off for good. "I'm really sorry."

"That's all? No explanation?"

She dropped her chin. This was why she'd avoided him. She had no good reason. It was awkward being the woman who had so many insecurities. Men didn't understand them.

Yet it appeared as though Gavin was different. In three short encounters, he'd shown interest in *her*. They shared chemistry. The memory of his touches still made her heart race. It was like nothing she'd ever experienced before. Brand new territory. She was desperate to explore and enjoy these new feelings but doing so would put her heart at risk as it would only end up being a fling. She could handle the heartbreak but why would she set herself up for it?

Gavin cleared his throat, reminding her that she hadn't answered. Snapping out of her thoughts, she shrugged and averted her gaze. A gust of wind whipped across the deck, blowing her hair in her face. She tucked it behind her ears again and glanced back at Gavin who waited for an answer with eyebrows raised.

She sighed. "I freaked out. That's all I can say and I'm sorry."

His shoulders slackened and gave a short nod. "I haven't seen you since. Have you been avoiding me?"

"I felt guilty." She smiled in apology. "So, yeah, I have. It's great being able to work anywhere you go with internet access. You can lock yourself away and forget the world."

Gavin looked half appalled, half amused. "You've been *working*?"

"You're the second person to say that to me today. Why is it so shocking?"

He stared at her like she'd grown two heads. "Perhaps because you're on *holiday*." He paused and glanced up at the sky, stroking his chin in thought. "Well, it's official." He slapped his hands on his thighs. "Tomorrow I'm taking you into Suva. We're going exploring."

"What... where...?" She shook her head. *Speak normally, girl.*

Gavin laughed, any awkwardness between them dissipating. "It's our first stopover. Suva, Fiji. Markets, white beaches, street food that'll blow your mind. You'll love it."

"Why do you want to take me? I could go on a tour."

He held his hands out, palms up. "Why not? I want to spend the day with you, and besides, I've been there tons of times and would love to be your personal tour guide."

"Oh... well..." She was about to say yes when something occurred to her. "Why are you bothering after I stood you up?"

He shrugged and got to his feet. "Let's call it a second chance. If you stand me up a second time, I may not talk to you again."

They smiled at each other, but Nikki read between the lines. Gavin was serious. *This is your chance. Stand him up again and you don't have to worry about him anymore. If you go with him, you could enjoy a holiday fling.*

It wasn't an easy decision. She was supposed to be finding herself, not having flings.

"We dock at eight," Gavin said. "I'll meet you at the bottom of the gangway. If you're not there by nine, I'll assume you're not coming."

He winked, then turned and walked away.

It should've been simple, but nothing ever was when it came to her heart. She wanted to spend time with him, enjoy a holiday romance, but it would play with all the wrong emotions. What if she fell in love?

Well, don't. Simple.

With a sigh, she stood and wrapped a towel around herself. She'd decide later. Picking up her things, she made her way back indoors.

⁕⁕⁕⁕⁕ ⁕⁕⁕⁕⁕

After leaving the pool, Nikki did some shopping. She bought a backpack to replace her broken one, then, on a whim, also bought a new dress for dinner. She'd packed formalwear with her, but she wanted a new outfit to match the woman she was becoming. To her surprise, it didn't take long to find the perfect one and she was back at her room by five-thirty p.m.

With only twenty-five minutes to get ready, she dumped her purchases on the bed and rushed to the bathroom to shower. She washed the chlorine out of her hair in record time but had no time to style it, so blow-dried it enough to stop it dripping then let it hang around her shoulders.

It reached ten to six and she still wasn't ready. If she wanted to be on time, she'd have to leave in five minutes, but that wasn't going to happen. They'd just have to wait. Mum and Dad wouldn't mind, but Katie would probably complain.

Screw her. She's not worth your worry.

Easier said than done, but Nikki would make a concerted effort to not let her sister bring her down. It was time to prove to herself and her sister that she could look pretty and feel good regardless of her size.

Removing her new dress out of the protective bag, butterflies did loops in her stomach. No amount of confidence would remove the fear of Katie's harsh words. They would come, no doubt about it, but Nikki would put on a brave face.

Don't let her belittle you. Don't let her make you feel worthless. Hold your head high and be confident.

It was funny how some people never changed. Sophie had always been encouraging, seeing what others didn't, and already her voice was taking over the negative one in Nikki's subconscious.

Ten minutes later she was ready. She took a deep breath, stepped in front of the mirror and stared... and continued to stare at the *beautiful* woman looking back at her.

Wow.

She viewed herself from all angles, a slow smile forming on her lips. She was worried the dress might've only looked good in the store thanks to the bright lights, but she was wrong.

The strapless mint green dress clung to her torso, then fell in an A-line from the waist to the floor, capturing her natural curves. It was made of satin with a sheer overlay. The bodice was covered in silver sequins to the waist and then continued down, thinning out until there were none at all along the bottom.

Nude heels topped the dress off nicely, along with a silver teardrop necklace and matching earrings.

With a grin from ear to ear, she grabbed the bag with the gifts and walked to the door. *Eat cake, Katie. If you dare say I'm fat and ugly I'm going to laugh in your face, because right now I know I'm not.*

Chapter 9

Gavin rushed to the restaurant. He should've been there at six and it was already five minutes past. He took the stairs two at a time until he reached the deck where the restaurant was located. When he spotted it, he sped up, weaving in and out of the crowd.

A group of people clustered together stopped in front of him. His eyes widened. Moving too fast, he swerved out of the way, narrowly missing them, but ran into someone else. A feminine shriek filled his ears, and he reached out to steady her.

Still breathless, he smirked. "*Again*?" he teased, holding onto Nikki's arm.

Her cheeks flushed as she smoothed down her dress. He took her in for the first time, his breath catching. *She's stunning.*

"Why were you running?" Her eyes glinted. "I thought we were told not to?"

Gavin grinned and drew in a steadying breath. "I'm late. I can do what I want."

She chuckled and clasped her hands in front of her. Her natural beauty drew him in. He'd noticed it the first day they met, but tonight, it rolled off her in waves.

"Out of, like, three thousand people, why do we *always* run into each other?" Nikki asked, cocking her head to the side.

Gavin leaned in and whispered, "Fate," before walking away.

He shivered, sensing her eyes on his back. How far was she willing to take it? Flirting was one thing, but since their kiss a couple of days ago, he figured it wouldn't go any further. Could he break through her walls and convince her to enjoy a harmless fling? He so needed to taste those soft lips again.

"Gavin, you're here, thank God! You're such a lifesaver." Gavin nodded at the man in charge. "You're serving tables one to ten. Number eight is an anniversary dinner. Don't forget the complimentary wine."

Gavin got to work. He made his way to the bar first to grab the wine. He placed it in a wine cooler and took it to table eight. The three people sitting there appeared familiar, but he dismissed it. All passengers became recognisable after a while.

"Happy anniversary." He focused his attention on the husband and wife. He placed the cooler in the middle. "I hope you enjoy the wine on us."

They exchanged surprised glances. "Oh, how lovely," the wife said. "Thank you."

"Are you ready to order?"

The wife glanced over his shoulder and shook her head. "Not yet, thank you. We're waiting for our other daughter."

He nodded, told them he'd return soon, then continued to wait on his other assigned tables. After taking drinks orders, he rushed back to the bar to fulfil them. He glanced at the door where groups of people waited to be seated as Nikki strode through.

His heart skipped and he couldn't tear his eyes away.

She walked through the restaurant slowly, her eyes darting around as though searching for someone. His fingers itched at the reminder of holding her only moments earlier. If only he could hold her all night long.

He drew in a sharp breath. Questions floated around his mind… *serious* lifechanging questions. He'd been looking forward to his big trip, but Nikki came along and it no longer held the appeal it once did. *She* took the appeal away. No woman had ever done that before.

A strange unease crept over him. He couldn't explain it, but he couldn't shake it off. The only certainty were his feelings for Nikki, but he had to reel them in. Fast. Otherwise, he'd end up hurting himself, or worse still… Nikki.

He still couldn't bear the thought of never travelling again. Of settling in one place with the same person. *What if it's because you've never found the right one? What if Nikki's it?* His breath caught and cold fear clutched at his heart.

He used brute force to push the unsettling thoughts and feelings to the deepest recesses of his mind. *Not going there.*

Nikki remained in his periphery as he turned to the bar. Her hair swayed with her movements. She walked with caution, tucking her hair behind her ear or tugging self-consciously on the bodice of her dress. She was so unassuming, unaware of the way other people admired her.

When the bartender filled up his tray with drinks, Gavin picked it up and turned. Nikki stood next to him, still glancing around.

When her eyes met his, she smiled. "I can't get away from you," she joked.

He moved the tray to the other hand and gave her a lopsided smile. "Perhaps it *is* fate."

She looked at the floor, her fingers fiddling with the fabric on her dress. "I'm looking for my family." She glanced back up at him. "I'm not sure if you'd know... it's an anniversary dinner."

Ah, that first day. That explains why I recognise them.

"They're over there." He pointed in the direction. "Table eight."

She glanced over to where he pointed. "Oh, thanks!" She stepped forward then turned back, brow furrowed. "Wait a sec. Are you *working*? You're on holiday, yet you told *me* off for the same thing?"

He smiled sheepishly. "I know most of the staff here. Someone called in sick and they were desperate, so they asked if I'd volunteer to fill in."

"Volunteer? So you won't get paid?"

"I can't. I haven't signed the paperwork. Besides, I don't mind helping. The staff are always so busy."

She shook her head but grinned. "You're such a hypocrite."

He held up his free hand in defeat. "Guilty."

"I better join my family. See you later, Gavin." She left him with a fleeting smile.

He stared after her, admiring the seductive movement of her hips. *Good God, this woman will be the death of me.*

He returned to work delivering the tray of drinks to table nine, passing Nikki's table the same time she approached. Her parents commented on how beautiful she looked, but then the other woman, presumably her sister, spoke. "What *are* you wearing? You look hideous!" Nikki stopped abruptly, her face turning white.

He almost dropped the tray as a shaft of anger speared through him. If he hadn't forced himself to keep moving, he would've spoken his mind. It wasn't his place.

Did her sister always speak like that to her? If so, it explained a lot about Nikki.

He stopped at table nine and placed the drinks down. He was close enough to hear the blasted woman speak again. "What on earth possessed you to buy such a horrid-looking thing? You look like a—"

"Katie!" The father's tone could cut ice. "Will you *stop*? Your sister looks lovely."

Gavin moved away, unable to hear any more of the conversation. He managed a quick glance over his shoulder. Nikki sat with her shoulders slumped, a crestfallen look on her face.

How could anyone be so cruel, and why on earth did Nikki take it?

N ikki avoided her sister's gaze, feeling like a blimp. A few harsh words and her confidence was in tatters yet again. The whole way to the restaurant she told herself she wouldn't let her sister win. She *knew* she was pretty, but Katie's words cut through her confidence like a sharp knife.

The worst part? Gavin had heard it. She knew this because she saw his shoulders tense. She didn't want his pity. All she wanted was for the ground to swallow her up.

She kept her gaze on her lap, hands folded, listening to the surrounding chitchat while holding back tears. The tension between her and Katie was thick.

Nikki only looked up when her mother spoke. "Wine, Nikki?"

Nikki opened her mouth to say yes, but Katie beat her to it. "No, wine is full of calories. I'll just have water and so will Nikki."

Enough was enough. Fed up and hating Katie for causing a scene at their parents' anniversary dinner, Nikki didn't hold back. "You don't make my decisions for me, *Kathryn*." Using Katie's full name would rile her up, as proven by her stiffening spine. "I will have a glass of wine because I want some and because it's Mum and Dad's anniversary. Stop dictating what I should or shouldn't do."

Katie's face reddened and her nostrils flared. She stood and slapped her napkin down on the table.

"Fine!" She huffed. "If you want to put on more weight and look like an inflated elephant, be my guest. But *I* don't want to be seen with a freak like you."

She stormed away, Nikki staring after her with her mouth hanging open. For a moment, she couldn't move. Then Katie's words hit like daggers. Tears threatened to fall, but she held them back. It was time to grow a backbone and stop letting Katie's words affect her. Besides, she didn't want to ruin her parents' anniversary more than it already had been.

"I'm so sorry." She glanced at her parents, who appeared shellshocked. "I didn't want to ruin your special dinner."

Mum reached across and squeezed her hand. "You didn't, Nikki." She pursed her lips and turned to her husband. "We have to do something about this. It's getting out of control."

Dad offered Nikki a sad smile. "What can we do? Katie's an adult. We can't send her to her room anymore."

"Guys, please don't do anything on my account. This is a battle between Katie and me. Hopefully one that will cease if I can ever get through to her. But I will *definitely* take that glass of wine, thanks."

The topic was dropped so they could enjoy the meal together. Mum poured the wine, and Nikki took a grateful sip. Placing her glass down, she perused the menu, salivating over the ribeye steak with red wine jus. A little voice tried to tell her Katie would disapprove but she pushed it aside.

It was a celebration and she wouldn't apologise for enjoying it.

Chapter 10

Nikki hated that dinner was more enjoyable without Katie. She gave her parents their gifts, which they loved, and they enjoyed a nice meal together. Gavin waiting on them helped, too. He'd give her little smiles or winks, and when he waited on other tables, she'd often catch him glancing at her.

For once in her life, she didn't think he was pitying the fat girl. Even after what Katie had done, he still flattered her. That had to mean something.

Towards the end of the evening, he passed by the table to ask if they wanted desserts or another drink. Nikki couldn't take her eyes off him. He wrote something on his notepad, then glanced up. Their gazes met and a slow smile spread across his face. When he repeated himself, asking if she wanted anything, she turned her attention to the dessert menu and ordered the chocolate lava cake.

"Great choice," Gavin said. "It's rich, chocolatey and tastes like heaven."

A pang of doubt had her saying, "Perhaps I shouldn't?"

Dinner was exquisite and no doubt high in calories, would enjoying a rich dessert be pushing it too far?

"No, you really should." Gavin appeared behind her. He reached down and took her menu. He stood so close his body warmth enveloped her. His woodsy scent made her mouth water. She looked up and caught his gaze. "You deserve it," he added sincerely.

"It does sound good," Mum added.

"Would you like to change your order?" Gavin asked.

Nikki glanced across at her parents who were huddled over the menu with indecisive looks on their faces.

"Go on," Nikki coaxed. "If I have to, so do you."

Mum smiled. "Oh, go on then. What about you?" she directed to Dad.

He shrugged. "It's not every year we celebrate thirty years of marriage, so why not?"

Gavin chuckled. "You won't regret it."

With one more glance at Nikki, he sped off to the kitchen. Nikki released a shaky breath and clasped her hands in her lap. She stared down at them so she didn't have to look at her parents. They weren't stupid. They would've seen Gavin's attention towards her. She just wasn't ready to answer their questions.

She spent the next few moments admiring the expansive room—the burgundy balustrades, slick brown floor and crystal chandelier. A live band played soft music, some couples dancing to it. Her parents were now talking amongst themselves, laughing like a young couple in love.

When Gavin reappeared, Nikki's eyes were drawn to him again. He chatted with her parents, laughing, joking and being attentive. When he came around to her with her dessert, his eyes never left her. She drowned in their golden depths.

He placed the dessert in front of her. "Come for a walk with me later. Meet me in the atrium at ten-thirty."

Her heart leapt, and she nodded. Once Gavin had left, Nikki glanced at her plate. The lava cake sat in the middle, icing sugar sprinkled on top. It was garnished with a handsome dollop of cream and a delicious-looking chocolate sauce.

She glanced up, saw her parents feeding each other, and smiled. Katie would've been disgusted but Nikki admired the love they shared. She picked up the little dessert fork and pierced the cake, chocolate oozing out of it.

She dipped the cake in the cream and placed it in her mouth. Her eyes fluttered closed as she savoured the sweet yet slightly bitter chocolaty richness on her tongue. It really *was* heaven. When she opened her eyes again, she caught Gavin staring at her from the other side of the room. The look in his eyes made her insides turn to mush. Her face flushed from his attention, and she looked away, stabbing another piece of cake.

She was halfway between embarrassed at being caught eating and thrilled she had that effect on him.

Half an hour later, she and her parents were done with dinner. They stood first and Dad said, "We're going back to our room." He sent Mum a knowing look.

Nikki's stomach lurched. Yes, she wanted to experience the love her parents had, but she didn't want to think about them having sex. Ever.

"No worries." Nikki shuffled in her seat.

"Enjoy your walk with Gavin," Mum teased.

Nikki's cheeks flamed. "How—"

She came around and kissed Nikki's cheek. "It's obvious. Just be careful, okay?"

Nikki managed a nod. Dad waved as they left and she remained at the table, considering Mum's words. Was a fling with Gavin careless? If he ended up being someone special, how would she be able to let him go?

They were questions for another time. Right now, all she wanted was to spend a bit of time with him and get to know him. There was no harm in that.

It was eight p.m. when she left the restaurant, and she spent the next two and a half hours wandering the ship. She made a mental note of the places she'd like to visit, determined to make the most of the cruise and not waste any more time.

At ten-thirty p.m. she entered the atrium, still in the same outfit from dinner. She didn't want to change because Gavin had appreciated it.

With her head held high, she wandered to the bar in the centre of the room and sat on a stool. People milled around the beautifully decorated room, some smiling at her when they walked past, while others stayed in their own groups. Everyone appeared happy and relaxed.

When the bartender asked if she wanted a drink, she shook her head. Her watch read quarter to eleven. She ran her sweaty palms along her dress, trying not to think the worst. When it ticked over to eleven, she sensed a presence behind her. She turned to find Gavin a few feet away, staring at her with an expressionless face.

She slid off the stool, smiling in relief. "I was beginning to wonder if you were paying me back for standing you up." She chuckled nervously.

Gavin blinked as though breaking out of a trance. "Would I do that?"

"Maybe? I wouldn't blame you if you did."

He grew serious and stepped forward, placing a hand on her arm. His touch made her skin sizzle. "I'm not that sort of person, Nikki. When I say I'll be somewhere, I'll be there."

She cringed and looked away.

"Damn it, I'm sorry." Gavin's apology sounded genuine. "I didn't mean to imply anything."

"It's fine." She glanced back at him and forced a smile. He wasn't being nasty, but it hit a nerve. "I am sorry, though. Really, I am."

He took her hand in his. "It's all forgotten. I'm sorry I'm late, though. I got held up at the restaurant. Do you still want to go for that walk?"

She looked into his eyes and breathed a little easier. *He doesn't hate me.* She nodded and together they walked out onto the outer deck. The breeze was cool off the water, but the sky was clear and full of twinkling stars.

"It's so beautiful out here." Nikki stopped to let a couple pass. She glanced across at Gavin, who shrugged.

"I've been on so many ships, it doesn't really do it for me anymore."

"How can you ever get sick of such a beautiful sight?"

"It depends what it is." His voice was husky. "I could never get sick of looking at you."

Nikki whipped her head around to look at him, her eyes wide. His gaze was so intense, confirming the truth in his words. She'd dated a few men, but none of them had ever told her she was beautiful.

Rendered speechless, all Nikki could do was stare. He smiled and stepped closer, one hand still holding hers while the other reached out to stroke her cheek. She shivered and leaned into his touch.

"You have no idea how beautiful you are, do you?" His eyes searched her face. The hand stroking her cheek moved back into her hair to caress the back of her neck.

She tried to speak but failed, only managing a weak shake of her head. His sensual caress sent bolts of chemistry to every part of her body.

Gavin frowned, eyes full of disbelief. "You. Are. Stunning." He leaned forward, their lips only inches apart. "No one should ever tell you otherwise."

He crushed his lips against hers. The air was sucked out of her lungs, an explosion of heat and crackling chemistry drowning out everything around her. All she was aware of was Gavin's soft, sensual lips caressing hers... again. This time she reciprocated, wanting to experience this properly. Cool air whipped around them but she didn't feel cold because Gavin's arms tightened around her, warming her like the summer sun.

She needed air, *now*, but she was too caught up in the moment to care. When her head spun, Gavin broke away as though reading her mind. She gulped in a lungful of salty air, her eyes fixed on him.

"Why does your sister talk to you like that?" He rested his forehead against hers.

She swallowed hard. "I-I don't know." She could barely form words, her head cloudy. "Things changed so suddenly a few years ago. I don't know why it started."

"You shouldn't have to put up with it." Gavin's eyes flashed in annoyance.

She moved away and turned to stare out over the ocean. The light of the full moon glimmered on the choppy water lapping against the hull.

"I can't stop it," she said after a pause. In her periphery, Gavin stood next to her. "She doesn't listen to me, our parents, or her husband."

"She's married?"

Nikki turned to him and leaned on the railing. "Surprising, huh?"

"I hope she doesn't have kids."

When Nikki only nodded, Gavin's eyes widened. "She *does*?" He ran a hand over his head and released a breath. "Those poor bastards."

Nikki unfolded her arms and glanced behind her. Spotting a deckchair, she sat down and crossed her legs at the ankle, making sure her dress didn't drag on the deck.

"They're great kids." Nikki smiled wistfully, missing her nieces so much. "Take after their father more than Katie, thank God."

Gavin sat on her deck chair and took her hand. "How old are they?"

"Six... they're twins."

"I'm presuming, based on who I saw at the table tonight, your nieces and brother-in-law aren't on this holiday?"

Nikki tucked her hair behind her ear. "No, they're not. Monty told me it was about family, a chance to reconnect and celebrate a milestone, but I overheard Mum and Dad saying Monty wanted space to 'assess their marriage'. Katie has no idea."

Gavin was so easy to talk to, and it was nice to open up to someone about it. Overhearing things she wasn't supposed to became a burden after a while. Why Monty never told her himself, she didn't know. He probably had his reasons. Perhaps one day she'd ask for the full story.

"It's a tangled web." Gavin's gaze captured hers once more.

"Tell me about it. I'm trying to figure my sister out, but I can't. She hasn't always been like this, but something changed her."

He smiled, his eyes lighting up. "Don't worry about her. It's time you worried about yourself. I heard what she said tonight and it's not on. You need to know how beautiful you are."

Nikki's cheeks turned warm, and she glanced away.

"Hey." Gavin's finger tilted her chin to look at him. "Please don't hide. Trust me, I don't tell a woman she's beautiful unless I mean it."

Nikki laughed off her awkwardness. "I'm glad to hear it. So, what's your story, Gavin? You know about my screwed-up family, but I know very little about you. Well, apart from your love of travelling."

She'd forgotten that titbit of information. She'd been so caught up in the overwhelming chemistry, she didn't want to think about the gaping difference between them. He was a traveller, a man who'd probably never settle down. The opposite to her.

Her head screamed at her to walk away. If she didn't, she'd get hurt, no doubt about it. It wasn't that easy though. She was drawn to him like a honeybee to a flower. Her heart told her to throw caution to the wind, forget why she came here, and just enjoy *him*.

"There's not much to say," Gavin answered. His voice had gained a hard edge to it. "I have a sister and two nephews." He shrugged and became tight lipped.

No mention of parents. Interesting.

She didn't persist, sensing it was a sensitive topic. Instead, she changed tack. "So, if you travel so much, what do you do for work?"

Gavin's shoulders relaxed. "Hospitality, mainly. Bars, waitstaff, that sort of thing. It's easy to pick up random jobs wherever I go."

"You don't ever tire of travelling?" She played with the sequins on her dress.

He hesitated a second longer than necessary. "Never. It's who I am. It must be in my blood." He spoke as though he was trying to convince himself.

She wasn't convinced.

"You've never considered getting a permanent job?" She asked this hesitantly, not wanting to appear judgemental. It was also an experiment to see if she could get another hesitation out of him. Travellers often grew weary. Was that where Gavin was at in his life?

There was no hesitation this time though. "Be stuck in a dead-end job for the rest of my life? No thanks. I'm so used to freedom. Picking up any work I can, travelling, roughing it... to settle down in one job and one place..." He shrugged. "It sounds boring."

And this just confirms my suspicions. He'll never settle.

Sadness weighed down her heart. This was her chance to run.

She didn't.

"It doesn't have to be." She looked up at him, thankful that he didn't appear annoyed at her questions. "I design websites and make good money. I can take it anywhere."

"Even on cruises." His eyes danced with amusement.

She laughed and tucked her hair behind her ears. "It's a good escape when you don't want to see people."

"Was it your sister who made you not meet with me?" His gaze connected with hers.

"She didn't *make* me per se. She said you'd never be interested in someone like me and I figured she was right."

"Do you always believe what she says?"

Nikki winced at his harsh tone. It wasn't aimed at her though. It was aimed at Katie.

"She's usually right." She folded her hands in her lap.

"Well, she's not this time, because I *am* interested in you."

Her heart pounded against her ribcage.

He lifted her hand and kissed it. "I mean it. You're unlike any woman I've ever known."

"Yeah, I'm fat." The words spewed out before she could stop, but she regretted them. She'd been trying to stop the self-deprecating talk, but she slipped up sometimes.

Gavin's expression turned fierce, and he sat back, eyes dark. "Do you always do this to yourself? Put yourself down?"

Nikki shrugged and looked away, twiddling her fingers.

"Do you think I care about that sort of thing?" he persisted.

Nikki looked up. Now that she'd opened the floodgates to her insecurities, she embraced it. "I don't know. So many men do." She looked away again.

"I'm not most men, Nikki." He sounded annoyed. "I find you very attractive and I wouldn't change a single thing about you."

"Not even a few kilos?" Nikki's bottom lip quivered.

"No definitely not." Gavin's voice was calm again. "You're perfect the way you are and your sister needs to stop saying such horrible things."

Nikki risked looking at him again, her pulse thrumming. A lone tear escaped and slid down her cheek. Gavin leant in and kissed it away. With his face still close to hers, he said, "I hope this means you'll be joining me tomorrow?"

Frozen, she could only nod.

"Good," he said, lifting a hand to run his knuckles across her cheek. She leaned into his touch, her eyes fluttering closed.

"If I'm not careful, I could easily fall for you," Gavin murmured.

Nikki's heart leapt and her eyes flung open. For a split second she witnessed a vulnerability in his gaze, but he dropped his hand and glanced away, appearing annoyed.

He mumbled something she couldn't quite hear, but she could've sworn he said, 'I can't have that.' She hoped like hell she was wrong because she was already freefalling.

Chapter 11

It neared midnight when Gavin walked Nikki to her room. He'd enjoyed her company, her laugh, the way she looked at him, how she blushed after that kiss. He'd meant what he'd said earlier. If he wasn't careful, he *could* easily fall for her. It was time to apply the brakes before they careened out of control. Nikki was so fragile. If he went too far, then slowed down, he'd destroy her.

He didn't understand women very well, but he understood playing with their feelings was wrong and downright mean. If he led Nikki on then dumped her, he'd be worse than her sister. *Damn.*

This led to another issue. He *wanted* to spend the rest of the cruise with her. Have a harmless fling. Unfortunately, she wouldn't see it the same way. She'd want more than he could give.

Yes, it was time to press on the brakes *now.*

By the time they reached her room he was ready with a spiel. Instead of looking at him though, she fiddled with the sequins on her dress. Something she did a lot during the night.

He so wanted to kiss her again, another thing he shouldn't have done, but, *damn*, he couldn't help himself. She'd kissed him back and it was everything he'd imagined and more. She was near to perfection, and for someone who wasn't his usual type, this surprised him.

Do it. Now.

"Look, Nikki—"

She jerked her head up so fast, eyes wide, the words died on his tongue. He knew that expectant look. She *knew* what was coming. Her self-esteem was so low, she wouldn't think she was good enough for him.

Goddammit. How could he do this to her? She needed to know she was plenty good enough, but to continue was a bad idea. A *very* bad idea.

He opened his mouth to speak when he heard Sophie screech, "Nikki! Oh my God, you look *hot!*"

Wait. *Sophie* knew *Nikki?*

Gavin's brow furrowed as he glanced down the hallway to where Sophie headed towards them. He looked from her to Nikki. They were smiling like they knew each other well. But how?

"Gav, what are *you*—?" Sophie glanced between him and Nikki. "Ooh," she drew the word out, "you two..." She gestured between them. "But how—?"

"Wait, you know each other?" Nikki asked.

Sophie laughed. "He's only my twin brother. How do *you* two know each other?"

"*This* is your brother?" Nikki pointed at him. "You never said he was a twin!"

"It wasn't relevant." Sophie shrugged.

"How do *you* know Nikki?" Gavin was getting confused.

"Okay," Nikki laughed and held up her hands, "Sophie, I know Gavin because I accidentally ran into him when we arrived. Gavin, I know Sophie because we attended the same school. She's also my cabin steward, which is how we ran into each other. And now I know you're the brother I never met. I think that clears everything up, right?"

Gavin glanced between his sister and Nikki. They appeared so chummy, like they were the best of friends. Then again, if they'd known each other in school that would explain why. He wished they'd met all those years ago. Perhaps things would've been different. The image of a decade long relationship with Nikki flashed through his mind then faded, leaving an ache he'd never felt before. He shook his head then turned to look at his sister.

"You two seem cosy," Gavin and Sophie said in unison, then laughed.

Nikki's eyes widened and she shook her head in a daze. "That was weird."

"What are we doing?" Gavin and Sophie spoke at the same time again, exchanging confused glances.

"Talking at the same time and saying the same thing." Nikki leaned against the door and shook her head. "It feels like I'm in some twilight zone."

Sophie grinned. "We don't really look alike, so I suppose we have to do something 'twinny'."

Nikki didn't look convinced. "Okay... well, I'm going to bed." She still looked dazed as she turned to Gavin. "Thanks for everything. I'll see you tomorrow?"

He nodded. It was the wrong time to say anything now, so he'd deal with it tomorrow.

Not caring that his sister was there, and having no strength to stop himself, he leant in to kiss Nikki goodnight. When he pulled away, her cheeks were pink and he chuckled, loving how she blushed so easily.

"Goodnight. I'll meet you where we planned."

Nikki nodded. After bidding goodnight to Sophie, she entered her room. Once the door had clicked shut, Sophie grabbed his wrist and dragged him away.

After they'd rounded a corner, Sophie let him go and screeched, "You two are *dating*? Since when?"

"We're not dating." He rubbed his wrist. She had a hell of a grip.

"You so are." Sophie placed her hands on her hips and gave him the same glare she bestowed on her children when they misbehaved. "If you dare hurt her, Gavin, I swear I'll castrate you."

He swallowed and held his hands up in surrender. "I don't intend to." He heaved a sigh. "I mean it, we're definitely not dating. We're going into Suva together tomorrow and we shared a couple of kisses. That's all. I kiss a lot of women."

Sophie frowned. "That's what I'm concerned about. Nikki's very fragile at the moment, thanks to her sister."

Gavin shuddered. "Yes, I had the pleasure of encountering her tonight."

Sophie shook her head in disgust. "I'm serious, Gav, please be careful. She's a nice woman and she doesn't need a guy like you breaking her heart."

Gavin held a hand over his heart, feigning surprise. "Me? A heartbreaker? I would never do such a thing."

Sophie glared at him. The fire in her eyes unsettled him and he knew what she was going to say. He tried to stop her, but he wasn't fast enough.

"Do I need to remind you about Angela?"

Gavin returned the glare. "Don't go there."

"I'm going to, because I can see Nikki getting hurt the same way Angela did. If she's just a fling to you, like the rest of the women you've been with, end it now."

Gavin continued to glare at his sister for a few more seconds but remained silent. In the end, he cursed under his breath and stormed off towards his room. She always managed to push the right buttons that lathered on the guilt.

He stuffed his hands in his pockets, gaze firmly on the carpeted floor as he ignored the late-night passengers making their way to their rooms. He muttered and cursed again, hating that Sophie brought up such a sensitive topic.

Angela was his first and last girlfriend in high school before he dropped out. They were both only fifteen, but she'd fallen for him. Hard. She was beautiful, easy-going, and fun to be around. When it became clear she'd fallen for him, rather than backing off, he fuelled her fantasies by leading her to believe he felt the same way.

In hindsight, he hadn't realised his commitment fears and how deep they ran. He was still just a stupid, immature teenage boy. A coward for being too scared to tell her he didn't feel the same way.

It all came to a halt when she found him kissing another girl behind a classroom and the fallout had been terrible. He didn't even apologise. Not one of his proudest moments and it'd haunted him ever since. It was the trigger for only ever having one-night stands, and the realisation relationships were not for him.

He cringed and shook his head. Was he setting himself up for things to go wrong again? This situation with Nikki was different, but heartbreak was still inevitable.

His heart twinged at the thought of hurting her. It was the last thing he wanted to do. He'd seen her fragile state and Sophie was right. He had to end it and he was about to before Sophie appeared. Now look where he was.

Nikki wasn't another Angela. She was the first woman he'd truly connected with, and not just in a sexual way. Emotionally too.

I really shouldn't have kissed her.

Arriving at his room, he unlocked the door and walked inside. Slamming it behind him, he fell to his bed without changing and groaned into the pillow. They were, without a doubt, the best kisses of his life. He didn't want to regret them but he did because Nikki would expect more than he could give. There was one major difference this time, though. He *did* have feelings for Nikki. It only made the situation worse, because they'd both end up hurt.

What will you do if you fall in love with her? Leave the ship? Forget about Las Vegas? Live happily ever after? Find a permanent job, permanent house, with the same woman?

The familiar cold fear clutched at his heart. That life wasn't for him. How could he change after ten years? He was so out of his depth. What if he was always meant to be a nomad? Perhaps he'd become a hitchhiker... an adventurer. The guy who hiked around the world just because he could.

With another groan, he rolled onto his back, stared up at the ceiling and flung his arms out. *This isn't a good situation to be in. End it. Tomorrow. Before it goes any further.*

He reached over to the lamp and switched it off.

He had a lot to think about.

Chapter 12

Nikki stood leaning against her door for countless minutes after she left Gavin and Sophie. *It's no wonder I recognised the eyes.* How was it possible she'd bumped into both people?

She pushed away and undressed. The night had been an emotional rollercoaster. Even before Sophie had stumbled across them, she was certain Gavin was about to end this thing between them. Had this overwhelming feeling in her gut, which never let her down, but he hadn't. Now she was so confused.

Perhaps ending it was the right thing to do, save any further heartache. But she'd forever have a million unanswered 'what ifs'.

Hanging her dress in the closet, she changed into her pyjamas. Once she'd brushed her teeth, she sat up in bed with her laptop to finish the website she'd started. It was late, but she was so close to completion and wanted it done before succumbing to sleep.

An hour later, when it'd ticked over to one-fifteen a.m., she shut down the laptop and snuggled deep into the covers, pulling the duck feather duvet up to her chin. Her eyes drooped, sleep not far off, when her phone rang, jerking her awake again. She hadn't touched her mobile for days but kept it charged in case Monty called.

She turned the light back on, fumbling in the top drawer for her phone. Pulling it out, she slid her finger across the screen without looking at the caller ID. Monty was the only person who'd call her while she was away, but why so late?

"This had better be good," she snapped. "There's only half an hour difference between us so it's late for you too."

There was silence on the other end, followed, seconds later, by a shaky breath.

"Monty?" She felt guilty for snapping at him. "Are you okay?"

"Katie wants a divorce." In the room's quiet, those words sounded like they were being shouted for the entire ship to hear.

Nikki fell back onto the pillows, releasing a breath and closed her eyes. This was the first time Monty had actively sought her out to talk about his marriage issues.

Nikki sighed, anger towards her sister boiling low in her belly. "Oh, Monty, I'm so sorry." She held a hand to her forehead.

She heard a chair scrape across the floor on the other end of the line. "I needed someone to talk to before I lost my mind." He sounded like a broken man. "I can't sleep. The girls are dead to the world, but I'm terrified to tell them. What if they blame me? What if they want nothing more to do with me? The divorce papers came through a couple of days ago. Katie wants full custody of the girls."

He stopped talking so quickly, the sudden silence hung around her. She ran over Monty's words in her head. What was going on inside her sister's mind?

"They won't blame you, Monty. They'll be upset but you need to let them know you love them and that you'll fight for them. You have as much right to custody as Katie does and I'm certain they won't want to be apart from you. Just make sure you fight, because Katie won't give up without one."

Monty quietly sobbed. It broke Nikki's heart. How could Katie do this to him? Why had she become such a terrible human?

"What am I supposed to do, Nik? Despite all this, I still love her, but I don't want to because it hurts so much. And those kids, hell, I'd do any damn thing for them but she's going to take them away like they're nothing. Doesn't seem to care that I have feelings. How am I supposed to cope with this? All I want is her and the kids. Is that too much to ask?"

Nikki couldn't answer because nothing would make it better.

"I vowed to make this work," Monty added, a catch in his voice. "I want to fight for us but it's clear she doesn't want to."

Nikki rubbed her eyes. "Have you spoken to her since you got the papers?"

"I called a few hours ago but we only argued. It was useless."

"That explains it," Nikki mused.

"What?

"Oh, just something she did tonight." She explained the dinner incident then added, "I can't do much, Monty, but I can try to talk to her."

"Are you really the best person?"

Nikki's laugh held no humour. "Probably not, but I can be nasty with words too."

"Don't be too hard on her. Being nasty will only push her away."

"Or it might make her think. Tough love, and all that."

Monty sighed. "Touché. Well, I trust you. I'm not signing the papers, Nik. Not without a fight. I refuse to do anything until I figure out why she's like this. There must be a reason."

"Well, I'll find out somehow. For now, though, I need to sleep. Will you be okay?"

"I'll survive. I have two little princesses to keep me occupied. They miss you by the way."

"I miss them too. Please give them a big hug from me. Take care of yourself, Monty. We'll figure it out."

"I hope so. Bye, Nik."

They hung up and Nikki placed her phone back in the drawer. She switched the light off and rolled over, closing her eyes. She'd worry about Katie tomorrow. Perhaps pay her a visit before they disembarked.

It was after two by the time Nikki succumbed to sleep. When her alarm sounded at seven, she didn't want to get up. Her head pounded with a headache, and she doubted her decision to pay Katie a visit. Headaches made her irritable, and she'd probably make the situation worse.

She pushed the covers back with a groan and flopped her legs out on top.

Squeezing her eyes shut, she rubbed her temples but the ache persisted. She'd rather stay in bed all day, but she didn't want to stand Gavin up again. Besides, she promised to help Monty.

After a few minutes, she pulled herself out of bed and drew the curtains apart, wincing at the bright sunlight. She opened the doors to the balcony and stepped out. The ocean was dark, the early morning sun still low in the sky. Land was visible now, it wouldn't be much longer until they docked.

Dressed in a flimsy short and top pyjama set, the cool morning sea breeze scattered goose bumps across her skin. It was a nice relief from the stuffy room and her headache eased a little. Over the last couple of days, she'd spent a lot of time out here. The ocean view was bliss and she'd experienced the odd sunset too.

After a few moments, she stepped back inside but left the doors open to air the room. She took some painkillers to help clear her headache and started getting ready.

After a shower and dressing in shorts and a t-shirt, her headache had reduced to a light throb. Picking up a tote bag with her keycard, sunscreen, hat, purse, passport, and travel documents, she turned to leave when a knock sounded on her door.

Sophie smiled brightly on the other side. "Morning! Are you excited about getting off the boat? Most people are by now."

"Ugh, I forgot how chirpy you are in the mornings." She gave her friend a hug. When they pulled away, she added, "I'm not bothered either way. I'd be quite content staying in my room."

Sophie rolled her eyes. "Well, go and enjoy. Suva is beautiful and Gavin knows all the great places."

"How did you know I was going with Gavin?"

"Duh. He told me."

"Oh, of course. It's not like you're related or anything. How is it possible I met him *and* ran into you amid three thousand or so people? The odds aren't very high, you know?"

"True, but it's not impossible." Sophie turned serious. "Be careful of my brother, okay?"

"Why?" Nikki tried to ignore the knot in her stomach, but it was impossible. It weighed like a brick.

"I care about you, Nikki, and I don't want to see you hurt. He's my brother and I love him, but he doesn't do relationships. If you're after a fling, go ahead, have fun, but if you're not, be careful. The last thing you need is a broken heart."

Nikki shuffled from foot to foot and looked away. She didn't want a broken heart, but she didn't want to stop seeing Gavin either. It was time to decide. Have an amazing fling or tell him she couldn't see him before he told her? It'd been a contributor to her sleeplessness the night before and she still didn't have a clear answer.

"I'm not trying to make decisions for you," Sophie added when Nikki didn't speak. "I don't doubt my brother cares for you, but don't expect anything long-term from him, okay?"

Nikki looked up and swallowed over the lump in her throat. "Thanks for the warning, but I'm on holiday and having fun. If this becomes a fling, so be it. A girl's gotta live sometimes, right?"

Sophie smiled but it didn't reach her eyes. "Of course. Now, do you need anything?"

"Nope. I'm about to see Katie, then I'll have breakfast before we dock."

Sophie pulled a face. "Don't torment the tiger. It might attack." She growled and clawed the air with her fingers.

Nikki left her room with a laugh, waving as Sophie headed in the opposite direction. She wanted to ignore what Sophie had said but it was impossible. *Why do my emotions always get involved? For once, I just want a bit of fun without any consequences.*

She ignored her thoughts and walked to Katie's room. Knocking loudly, she stepped back and folded her arms, hoping she looked imposing. It probably wouldn't work but she had to get some confidence from somewhere. It was time to put Katie in her place.

The door opened, and Katie appeared. The moment she saw Nikki, her lips pursed and her face darkened. She stepped outside. "What do *you* want?"

Nikki flexed her hands and lifted her chin. *You can do this. Tell her what's on your mind. Don't let her win again.*

"Well?" Katie smirked and eyed her up and down. Nikki took a sharp intake of breath. "You look hideous. Your legs are so fat. How can you even show them in public?"

This time the words pinged off her like she wore armour because she had an epiphany. Katie didn't insult her because it was true, she did so because she wanted a reaction. The smirk before her comment revealed the truth and it only angered Nikki more. *Well fine, if she wants a reaction, she'll bloody get one.*

Years of constant belittling, demeaning and insults rose to the surface. Nikki stepped forward, breathing in and out through her nose. Katie's smirk disappeared and she stepped back, fear flashing in her eyes.

Glaring at her sister, she erupted, "Shut the fuck up." Katie flinched and Nikki was also momentarily surprised at what came out of her mouth. She never spoke to anyone that way. It had to be said though, so she steamrolled ahead. "What do you have against me? Why do you hate me so much? What the hell have I ever done to you?"

She gritted her teeth and waited for Katie to say something. Anything.

She didn't. All she did was stare with wide eyes.

"Then there's Monty." Nikki couldn't stop the words from spewing forth. This snapped Katie out of her trance. She tried to step back into her room and close the door, but Nikki was too quick. She stuck her sneakered foot beside the doorframe.

"Don't go there," Katie threatened.

"Oh, I'm going there. What's your problem, Katie? When will you ever see Monty for who he is? A wonderful man, a caring husband and a brilliant father. Do you have *any* idea how much he loves you?"

Katie blinked a couple of times as though hearing a foreign language. Rather than responding to the question, she bit back with, "If he's such a wonderful person, why don't *you* have him? It's obvious you fancy him."

Nikki's jaw dropped. "Is that what this is all about? You think I want your husband? Oh my God, you are so, so wrong."

"You don't know what the hell you're talking about. You can have him for all I care. He's just a thorn in my side."

"Why do you hate him?" Nikki's anger bubbled over like a volcano. "Why do you hate me? Are you so determined to make people unhappy, you'll do *anything*? Insult me, divorce Monty... what's next, huh? Put the kids up for adoption?"

A shadow of something Nikki couldn't decipher passed across Katies' face. Her eyes shone with tears, but Nikki was too far gone to care. She was saying what should've been said years ago and she didn't experience an ounce of guilt.

"I don't know what the hell is going on in that head of yours, Katie, but you're a worthless piece of rubbish. You don't want anyone to be happy, not even yourself, so you go out and make everyone's lives miserable. I'm sick of it. As of this moment, nothing you say or do will ever affect me again." Nikki stepped forward and poked Katie's chest as she hissed the words, "You. Are. Nothing."

She spun on her heel and stormed away, ignoring the crowds of people who'd congregated in the hallway to see what the commotion was about. Ignoring her parents with shocked expressions on their faces. Ignoring everything but the overwhelming call to be with the one person who cared, even if it was going nowhere.

Gavin.

Chapter 13

G avin stood at the end of the gangway, watching people file off the ship, their excited chatter lingering on the warm breeze. Some made their way to the booths along the wharf to look at tours on offer or join a pre-booked one. Others continued on foot to explore the city and surrounds.

Gavin never bothered about tours. He preferred to explore at his own pace.

Lying awake in bed the night before, Gavin decided he *would* spend time with Nikki. Guilt free. He'd make it clear this was a fling and wouldn't hang around at the end. When they parted, there'd be no heartbreak. Well, at least none he'd have to feel guilty about.

A group of giggling young women in their early twenties, most likely university graduates, filed down the gangway. They smiled flirtatiously in his direction and accentuated the sway of their hips. He smiled politely but averted his gaze to scan the seemingly endless line of passengers disembarking the ship. He only had eyes for one woman.

Where was she?

When it reached nine a.m. and there were only staff flitting on and off the ship, Gavin shoved down his disappointment and turned away.

He'd taken one step when he heard his name called. His heart leapt into his throat as he spun around. Nikki stood at the top of the gangway, grinning. She waved, then sped down to meet him, holding onto the rail.

With her hair pulled back in a ponytail, she was the picture of beauty in her own way. She was dressed in simple denim shorts, a white tank top, with a bag swinging over her shoulder. For the life of him, he couldn't figure out why her sister labelled her as fat.

Seconds later, she stopped in front of him. "I'm sorry I cut it fine," she said between pants. "I went to have breakfast but there was a queue. By the time I got my food, I was too nervous to eat, and it was already nearly nine so..." She shrugged and smiled. "Guess I'm going hungry today." Her cheeks turned pink. "Though that's not a bad thing, I guess." She averted her gaze.

He frowned and tilted her chin to gaze into her eyes. "Don't do that. I won't let you go hungry, and we'll have a great day together. Okay? There's no need to be nervous."

She blinked at him, giving him a weak smile. He wrapped his arms around her, holding her flush against him. She fit so perfectly in his arms, like she was made to be there. Her curvaceous body had a softness to it, a warmth that drew him to her in a way he'd never experienced before.

Add to it a vibrancy that came off her in waves every time he saw her. Despite her low self-esteem, Nikki was happy, full of life, strong, sometimes confident, and undeniably beautiful, inside and out. She didn't deserve the cruel label her sister had set. Nikki might not be a size ten, but she was her own unique shape. Gavin hoped to experience every inch of her before their time together ended.

He kissed her briefly, then let her go and took her hand instead. "Did you have any plans? Or are you happy to explore?"

Her eyes glinted and she shrugged. "I'm happy to explore."

They walked hand in hand past the line of booths, some of them packing up where tours were full. The warmth of the sun beat down on them, causing a sheen of sweat to form on his brow. It wasn't too hot, but it was heavy. Apart from a few puffy white clouds, it was a clear day with a bright blue sky.

Towards the end of the line of booths, some others remained open and displayed local wares of jewellery, clothing, and souvenirs.

"I was thinking we could walk into the city," Gavin explained. "We can have a look around the markets, catch public transport to some hotspots."

Nikki didn't respond straight away and when Gavin glanced over to check if she'd heard him, he saw her staring straight ahead. He followed her gaze to where a middle-aged Fijian woman stood at the end of the line. She wore a floral style dress with sandals and held up a placard with the words '*Day Trips to Maritimo Island*' written in large, colourful letters.

"Have you ever heard of Maritimo Island?" Nikki asked.

Interest piqued, he shook his head. "Nope." He let go of her hand and rushed forwards.

When he approached the woman, she smiled broadly and lowered the sign. "*Bula*! Are you interested in a day trip to Maritimo Island?"

"You don't have a booth like everyone else," he observed.

The woman had the decency to look sheepish. "Advertising at the wharf is only a new venture and today was about searching for interest. Unfortunately, I arrived late and most passengers had already disembarked when I arrived. Are you interested?"

In normal circumstances he'd say yes in a heartbeat, but today he had Nikki to think about. Someone who was frustratingly sheltered and it was his number one goal to help her step out of her comfort zone. Undo whatever her horrible sister had done. What harm could come of a day trip to one of Fiji's many islands?

"Maybe—" He turned his head when he felt a hand on his shoulder. Nikki stood beside him, worry lines creasing her brow.

"We can't leave the main island, can we?" Nikki asked.

"Sure you can," the woman enthused. "It is only a short forty-five-minute flight on a seaplane. You will be back in time to board your cruise."

"What does the island have to offer?" Gavin asked, sending Nikki a mischievous grin.

"Maritimo Island is one of Fiji's many islands, but a true a hidden gem. It has become a tourist hotspot after it was featured on a travel documentary about two years ago. Imagine crystal clear waters, pristine beaches, lush tropical rainforests. Much smaller than this island, you can spend the day exploring the vibrant coral reefs, perfect for snorkelling or kayaking, or take a hike to the peak of the island."

She spoke as though reading a script, but she said it so confidently he was sold. He loved exploring hidden gems. Now to convince Nikki. A glance at her confirmed she'd need a bit of work. She worried her bottom lip, a war of uncertainties in her eyes.

"If that does not sell it," the woman continued, "you'll be able to enjoy a delicious meal on the beach of fresh seafood and local produce cooked in lovo pits. Whether you're after a day of exciting activities, or just a day to relax and unwind, Maritimo Island offers both."

"What do you think?" Gavin asked, turning to Nikki and taking her hands in his.

"I don't know. It's a bit risky, isn't it? What if there are delays getting back? Or bad weather? Or—"

"When was the last time you were spontaneous?" he asked, capturing her eyes and imploring with her. "When did you last let your hair down and just have *fun*? Not worried about every little thing?"

She lowered her gaze and shrugged.

A long time. "Come on," Gavin coaxed. He leaned closer and whispered, "It'll just be the two of us. We'll get to see a place no one else on the cruise will."

This got her attention, and she lifted her gaze to meet his, a small, reluctant smile tugging at her lips. "Alright, fine, but we must be back on time."

"We will be." Gavin kept hold of one of Nikki's hands and turned back to the woman. "We'd love to go on a day trip."

"Wonderful!" she said, rolling up the placard and placing it under her arm. "Follow me and I will take you to the seaplane. It leaves in twenty minutes, so we must be quick." As they started walking, she said over her shoulder, "My name is Adi. I will join you today so I can make sure everything runs smoothly. It will give me a chance to see my niece, who works at the resort there."

She rattled on as she walked, stopping at a car a moment later and gesturing for them to get in. On the ten-minute journey she never stopped talking and didn't have any concerns telling strangers about her family's sordid past. Secrets, deceit, and how it all worked out a year ago. She proudly talked about her own transformation as a person. How she learnt from her mistakes and now lived her life making up for past wrongs.

Gavin struggled to wrap his head around how someone could be so forgiving of a person who lied and kept their identity hidden for so long. Then again, there were always two sides to every story, and he was only hearing one of them.

What intrigued him most was how in places like Fiji, where family was more important than anything, they were still capable of having issues. It only confirmed why family was overrated. He loved his sister, but she had her own problems. At least when he travelled, he could escape the drama that came with broken families.

The car stopped as Adi announced, "We're here!"

Thankful for the interruption, he followed Nikki out of the car. Adi continued talking, barely taking a breath as they wandered along a path towards a floating pier. When they stepped onto it from the sand, Adi told them to stay put while she continued to the dock where a small seaplane bobbed on the water. A middle-aged Fijian man stood next to the plane. He wore shorts, a colourful, tropical shirt, and a pilot's cap. When Adi approached, they greeted each other with a handshake.

Gavin watched as Nikki walked to the side of the pier overlooking the sparkling soft, white sand, aqua blue ocean, and the Fijian coastline of lush green hills covered in dense tropical vegetation. In the distance, he could make out a red structure of some kind. A cabin perhaps? The contrast of green vegetation against the blue sky with scattered white clouds took his breath away.

Water lapped at the pier, seagulls squawked and flew above them while a soft, warm breeze kissed his skin. Apart from some locals walking or driving past, it was quieter than the wharf. Gavin had been to Suva a few times and explored the city and surrounds, but he didn't remember ever coming here.

He joined Nikki and rested his arm across her shoulders. "It's beautiful, isn't it?" he whispered in her ear, grazing his lips along her earlobe.

She shivered and snuggled closer into his side. "It's incredible."

Noticing goose bumps on Nikki's arm, Gavin leant down and placed a gentle kiss on her shoulder. He chuckled when more appeared. "Are you cold?"

She turned to him, winding her arms around his neck. "No," her eyes searched his, "but your touch gives me goosies."

He laughed out loud, throwing his head back. "Goosies? I haven't heard that word in years!"

She laughed and turned away, but he grabbed her hand, pulling her back. He smothered her lips with his, unable to contain himself and sensually ran his tongue along her bottom lip. When she granted entry, the world disappeared until it was just the two of them with the warm, salty breeze enveloping them. His heart hammered and his body responded. This woman did things to him… lots of things.

He pulled away, panting and gazed into her eyes, swallowing hard. Her pupils were dilated. He barely knew her but deep down he recognised the fear of losing her. Of never seeing her again.

Then *that* feeling returned. The strange, unexplainable one. This time, two words flew into his head, which explained it so simply.

Emptiness. Longing.

Terror pulsed through his veins at this revelation, and he stumbled back. *I can't let this happen.* Nikki's arms fell to her side, her brow creasing in confusion.

"You may board now," Adi said, coming up to them. "We will leave in five minutes."

Gavin cleared his throat and sent Adi a small smile. "We'll be there in a moment."

She nodded once, then returned to board the plane.

"Are you ready for an adventure?" Gavin asked with a forced smile, his voice uncertain to his own ears.

Nikki glanced at anything but him, blinking fast. He closed his eyes for a moment and breathed in deeply. When he opened them again, Nikki stared at him quizzically.

"Well?" he asked softly.

She nodded and he breathed a sigh of relief.

He walked along the pier towards the seaplane, gesturing for her to follow. She followed beside him, her arm hanging temptingly by her side, swinging as she walked. He wanted to take her hand but resisted. He'd only confuse her further if he did.

Guilt sat in his chest. This wasn't going as he'd planned. He really needed to get them both on the same page.

Chapter 14

Nikki fidgeted in her seat as the plane descended. Apart from Adi and the pilot, she and Gavin were the only other passengers on the six-seater seaplane. Butterflies had fluttered in her stomach the entire flight. Even if Gavin had twisted her arm into leaving the main island, it *was* risky. This was so not her.

It used to be.

Nikki drew in a sharp intake of breath as she glanced out the window, thoughts of the past consumed her.

A medium-sized island, much smaller than Fiji, came into view as they descended. White sand and boats bobbing in the aqua blue ocean dotted the coastline. Rainforests, agricultural areas, and buildings were visible. Even so high up she could see people walking around or driving in... were they golf carts?

It looked idyllic. She vowed to enjoy this spontaneity. Embrace the girl she once was. Adi *had* insisted they'd be back in time, so Nikki would sit back and enjoy the adventure. Gavin was right, they were the only two from the cruise visiting today.

She glanced over at Gavin opposite her. He stared out the window and hadn't said a word since they'd boarded. He'd gone weird ever since that mind-blowing kiss on the pier. Hands down the best kiss of her life. It had made her lose all rational sense and she would've pretty much done *anything* he'd asked. Then a shutter came down and he'd gone cold. She almost didn't agree to come, doubting everything.

Did she really want to jet off to some isolated island with a near stranger who changed hot and cold so drastically?

Then that same overwhelming feeling she experienced on the ship returned. To be with Gavin. Figure him out. Explore what could be, even if it didn't go anywhere. She wasn't blind. He was a heartbreaker, a nomad, but she needed this. It was time to live her best life, no matter how scary it was.

The hardest part was working through the negativity and anxieties that came with the new experience. It would take a long time to stop stressing about every little thing. It'd take longer to stop the self-deprecating talk, but she was up for the challenge.

New day, new Nikki.

The plane landed and skidded along the water, coming to a stop next to the dock. As soon as the seatbelt sign switched off, Adi stood and made her way to the front of the plane. Nikki had liked her honesty back at the island. It gave her hope that no matter how dire her situation was with Katie, maybe there was some hope.

"Welcome to Maritimo Island!" Adi said. "Please meet on the pier at three forty-five for a four o'clock take off. I hope you enjoy your day."

Nikki wasn't wearing a watch, so she glanced over at Gavin, but he wasn't wearing one either. She hoped he had his phone, because she'd left hers onboard. Uncertainties tried to crowd her mind, but she pushed them away.

Gavin met her gaze and smiled. Whatever had bothered him earlier had vanished. "Are you ready for this?"

Her stomach let out an almighty growl and she giggled. "Yes, but I wouldn't mind some food along the way."

"The resort has a restaurant if you want something immediately," Adi said. "Otherwise, you can visit the markets or come back to the beach at midday to enjoy local food cooked in lovo pits."

Gavin got to his feet and held out his hand to Nikki. "Let's go."

She took it and he hauled her to her feet. She slung her bag over her shoulder and followed him out of the plane. When they walked down the pier, a Fijian woman came up to them wearing a bright and welcoming smile. She looked to be Nikki's age, perhaps a little older, and *stunning* with glowing skin, tight curls, big brown eyes, hourglass figure. *Ugh.*

"Welcome to Maritimo Island!" she said with an Australian accent, which Nikki hadn't expected. "I'm Tenika and if you need anything you'll find me over at the resort. How long are you here for?"

"Just for the day," Nikki said, tucking her hair behind her ear. "We have a cruise to board later, but Adi convinced us this was the place to see."

"Fantastic, I hope you have a wonderful time! The carts are available for all to use if you want to make the most of your day. They'll get you to each place quicker." Adi joined them and Tenika's face brightened. Nikki figured Tenika was Adi's niece. "Adi, it's so nice to see you!" They embraced then Tenika turned back to Nikki. "I hope you have a wonderful day. If you have any queries, come to reception at the resort." She linked her arm through Adi's and they breezed past, talking in excited tones.

Gavin released Nikki's hand and slung his arm over her shoulders as they continued down the pier. Negative thoughts came back one by one, so fast she couldn't stop them. Nikki sighed, her feet growing heavy. She didn't fit in here. She wasn't built for tropical islands where women wore bikinis and showed off perfect figures like Tenika's.

Nikki would look like a bloody whale if she sunbathed in a bikini. The thought made her shudder and Gavin glanced over at her.

"Are you okay?" he asked as they stepped onto the sand, fine grains filling Nikki's sandals and massaging her feet.

"Fine," Nikki muttered. She didn't want to burden him with her thoughts. "Do you have the time?"

He nodded and removed his phone from his shorts pocket. "It's ten-thirty. Let's find something to eat, then we can explore."

Food suddenly didn't appeal to her. "Um, let's wait until lunch."

"I thought you were hungry?" Gavin stopped and stared into her eyes.

She averted her gaze, afraid he'd see right into her soul.

"I'd rather wait," she lied. "The lunch sounds great so I want to save my appetite." She turned back to him with a practiced smile. "Unless *you* want something now, of course?"

Gavin assessed her for a moment before he shook his head. "I'm fine. If you're sure, then let's grab a cart and have a look around."

She followed him onto the path, shook the sand out of her shoes, then walked a little way until they came across an abandoned cart. They jumped in, Gavin taking the driver's seat, then sped off.

Truth was, she was *famished*. She'd had every intention of eating earlier but the nerves had come on so unexpectedly and she couldn't stomach it. Sophie's warning of heartbreak had played over and over in her head.

Her little pep talk on the plane helped for a few minutes, but now... now the fears that sent her into hiding after she first met Gavin resurfaced. Of eating in front of him, worried he'd judge what she ate and how many calories it contained.

That's what Katie thinks. You're supposed to be done letting her ruin things for you.

She squashed the thoughts down and focused on the view. The island was stunning. Concrete paths ran around and through the island leading to various points. Coconut palms, ferns, shrubs with hibiscus flowers of various colours, and other tropical plants lined the paths and grew in density where there were no buildings.

When the path ended at some cliffs, Gavin turned left and drove towards the centre of the island where the rainforest was built up and the sun blocked by the canopy. The air grew heavy and humid, tinged with an earthy tropical scent. Local islanders waved and greeted them with happy smiles. Nikki's concerns vanished as she smiled and waved back.

"Everyone's so friendly," she exclaimed, turning back to Gavin with a grin as they approached a market area.

She breathed a little easier and settled into the adventure, letting go of the worries that threatened to overwhelm her.

Her stomach let out a loud growl again, easily heard over the cart tyres on the path. Gavin frowned at her.

"We're getting some food into you," he said, slowing down and taking the next turn that led to the markets.

"I'm okay, really." As soon as the words left her mouth, her stomach let out another growl.

Gavin gave her a deadpan look but said nothing. She gave up arguing. It was silly to be so self-conscious about eating in front of him anyway. He appeared to genuinely find her attractive, his looks and kisses alone proved that.

They drove a short way before Gavin stopped and got out of the cart. He came around and held out his hand, a no-nonsense expression on his face. She took it and let him lead her into the open-air markets. A mixture of delicious, savoury aromas drifted on the balmy breeze and tickled her nose. They stepped into the market area with rows of stalls selling food, souvenirs, arts, crafts, jewellery, and clothing. They were outside of the dense rainforest, but the trees and tropical foliage surrounded them. The sun now beat down on them from the clear blue sky. The humidity lifted but the intense warmth of the sun caused a sheen of sweat to form on her back.

They headed straight to the food stalls and ordered fish tacos, a side of cassava chips and a tropical drink. They sat at a picnic table and chair setting at the edge of the rainforest.

Nikki hesitated, warring with her irrational thoughts, before tasting the chips and groaned. "These are amazing," she said as she popped another into her mouth.

She swallowed her mouthful, then picked up the taco, stopping when she noticed Gavin staring at her, his own food untouched. She couldn't figure out what the wide-eyed look meant. Was she right? Was he judging her eating habits?

Her face turned hot and she put the taco down. "Sorry, I got carried away."

"Don't ever be sorry for enjoying food. I like a woman with an appetite." He grabbed one of his chips and ate it with an appreciative nod. "You're right, delicious. Now come on, let's eat quickly. We only have," he pressed the side button on his phone, "four and a half hours left."

After eating, they located the cart and Nikki ran around to the driver's side. "My turn to drive."

Gavin didn't argue and sat next to her. She hadn't driven one before, but it was easy to figure out. With no idea where to go, she just set off in a random direction and followed the path. They continued past the markets and drove past a large agriculture area where they grew crops. Back on the path along the outside of the island, they came across a large warehouse and fish markets, the fishy aroma strong but not unpleasant.

She followed the island to the north, a large white structure came into view through the palms. It must've been the resort Tenika had mentioned. On the beach was a jetty that extended into an L-shape into the water with multiple bungalows coming off it. As they drew closer, Nikki saw the resort through the trees, including a pool with the sun glimmering on the water.

"What a beautiful place," Nikki said, slowing down as she drove past.

"Hey," Gavin said. "Can you stop for a sec?"

She did so and looked at Gavin to see where he was pointing, then followed his gaze to the beach where a line of kayaks rested on the sand. Her stomach plummeted to her toes. *Oh no.* But Gavin's excited grin said a resounding 'yes'. Without words, he jumped out of the cart, came around to her side and grabbed her hand, all but dragging her along to the sand. Getting on the cruise ship was difficult enough.

Her breathing turned uneven. "You... you want to go kayaking?"

"You're not afraid, are you?" he teased, eyes glinting.

Her cheeks grew warm as she looked away, casting her gaze over the kayaks once more. Would she *fit*?

"Of course not," she said, keeping her gaze averted.

"You're such a rubbish liar." Gavin chuckled. "You've just been on the water for three days. A little kayak shouldn't scare you."

Her eyes widened. "That titchy thing would probably sink if a pin pricked it. The ship at least is large enough to hold its own."

He draped his arm over her shoulders. "I'll teach you how to row. It's a piece of cake."

She doubted it.

"What about sharks?" she asked lamely, looking for any excuse to get out of it.

His eyebrows shot up. "Sharks? Um... well, I don't know. If we stay close to the coast, we'll be fine."

Nikki tensed, her heart rate increasing too fast for her liking. She ran her sweaty palms along her shorts.

"What if the boat sinks when I get in?" The question was out before she could stop it and she mentally kicked herself. Then, to make matters worse, her mouth ran away with her words, "I mean, I'm not small—"

The truth came out and she cursed under her breath. *Damn Katie*! Deep down she knew she'd be fine, but it was so difficult to grasp those thoughts.

Gavin's eyes grew dark. "Nikki, stop." He removed his arm and turned so they faced each other. He grabbed the tops of her arms and stared into her eyes. "Stop doing that. Did nothing I say get through to you last night?"

She blinked up at him. Opened her mouth to speak but no words came out. "I'm sorry," she managed in a whisper. "I... I can't always stop it."

He closed his eyes and took a deep breath. When he opened them again and met her gaze, everything faded away. His eyes weren't just looking at her. They were looking *into* her. Piercing through layers of insecurity and doubt. There was no judgement, no frustration, just pure, raw honesty.

The depth of his expression took her breath away and she forgot how to breathe. It was as though he saw her in a way no one else ever had. Not as a reflection of Katie's words, but as the person she was at her core. His expression softened and she could see in his gaze he found her beautiful in more than just her appearance.

Something inside her stirred, something locked away for so long. In that moment, she couldn't *not* believe him. There was no doubt in his eyes, only a fierce, unwavering belief in her worth.

When he leant down to kiss her oh so softly, she could've floated away. But the memory of his coldness back in Suva floated back into her mind. She pulled back and put some distance between them, her heart aching.

"I don't understand you," she said. "One minute you're cold, the next you kiss me like that?"

He grimaced and raised his eyes heavenwards. "Nikki, I'm sorry. I just…"

"You're only into flings? I know, Sophie already told me."

All he did was shrug. What other reaction did she expect? At least he didn't lie about it. Now she had a big decision to make. Fling, or no fling? After her encounter with Katie, she'd all but made up her mind. It would be fine if she told her heart that's all it was. There didn't have to be any heartbreak.

Although, even if there was heartbreak, perhaps it'd be worth it. She'd barely been living these last few years. *Something* had to give, and maybe this was it.

So, she held her head high and said, "I'm not one to have flings, but I *am* on holiday, and I *am* trying to find who I am without my sister's influence, so…" she shrugged. "As long as we're clear where this stands, we might as well enjoy it, right?"

Gavin stared at her for a long moment, his eyes wide. What was going on in that head of his? Before she could doubt anything, he smiled and kissed her again. This time he didn't pull away and neither did she. Just let herself drift and enjoy this lifechanging experience.

When they parted, Nikki was certain she wore a dazed smile. Her eyes fluttered open and her smile widened into a grin. "You kiss really well. I'll miss that a lot when this holiday ends."

He held a finger against her lips and shook his head. "No talk of departure. Let's enjoy our time together. Now, how about that kayak?"

Chapter 15

Five minutes after they arrived, an instructor turned up along with a handful of other people. After a brief lesson, the small group started their row around the island. Gavin hung back in his kayak while Nikki stayed a little way ahead. She'd picked up the skills for rowing fast for someone who'd never done it before. He was impressed and proud she'd stepped out of her comfort zone.

Gavin needed a moment to gather his bearings. He was happy he and Nikki were on the same page, but what was this strange, unsettled feeling in his gut? When she'd talked about the holiday ending, it had struck and wouldn't budge.

Then there was the fact Nikki had chosen to enjoy a fling with him, despite it going against her entire being. Apart from Sophie, no one had ever made such a sacrifice for him before. That he remembered. Memories from his childhood were hazy.

In the grand scheme of things, it was a small gesture, but *damn* it hit hard.

Nikki glanced back and called out, "You coming, slow poke?"

He pushed it aside for now, but it hovered over him like a raincloud. "No one calls me slow poke," he said loud enough for her to hear as he increased his speed.

Nikki's giggle caught on the breeze and caressed him in all the right places. She was such a breath of fresh air and he was at full risk of falling for this woman. A part of him wanted a taste. To see what all the fuss was about. Why being in love was supposed to be the most amazing experience of one's life.

A cold chill ran down his spine despite the humidity.

Don't go there.

Growing up in foster homes, and with few memories of his parents, had left a bad taste in Gavin's mouth. Not to mention Sophie wearing fresh scars from her own failed marriage. He had zero good examples, and Nikki deserved someone who could love her back. *Not someone incapable of love.*

Gavin mentally shook his head to rid the thoughts, focusing instead on the now. He rowed beside Nikki, who took everything in with wide-eyed appreciation and lots of gasps. He loved her genuine awe that came with visiting a new place.

After a little while, the water became clearer. So clear, he could see the bottom of the ocean floor along with the fish, shells, and rocks. Soon it changed to a stunning marine world where coral and giant carpet anemone decorated the ocean floor and colourful fish swam past. This would be a great place to snorkel if they had time.

Cliffs loomed on the coast of Maritimo Island on their left. When they ended, there was wild rainforest with an aquamarine lagoon visible through the trees.

As Gavin drank everything in, his gaze shifted to the right and a much smaller island. From here he could see cliffs and tropical foliage, but that was it. It was within rowing distance but might take a little while to get there. He calculated it in his head and was confident they had time.

His explorer streak took over and he rowed up to flank Nikki. "Fancy a detour?"

She glanced across at him with uncertain eyes. There was something adorable about the kangaroo-caught-in-headlights look, but he was still so sad she had missed out on so much.

"*Another* detour?" she asked.

"No seaplane involved this time. We'll just go over there." He pointed to the island in the distance. The instructor *had* said it was fine to stop along the way, but to return the kayaks when they were done. He didn't say they couldn't take them away from Maritimo Island, so Gavin was willing to take the risk.

Nikki followed his gaze, worrying her bottom lip. He wished he could kiss her right now.

"Alright," Nikki said. "As long as you're sure we'll be back in time."

He grinned and manoeuvred his kayak to change direction. "Come on," he said, inclining his head.

Nikki glanced back at the group disappearing around a bend, then followed him, her face alight with unmissable excitement. The fact she was having fun, and he'd helped her step outside her comfort zone, made this day a success.

For the next forty-five minutes, they rowed in comfortable silence, the only sounds the splashing of the oars slicing through the water and the occasional seagull squawk. They approached the island from the right, Gavin gawped at the wild, untouched place of looming cliffs and swaying palms.

They rowed to the shallow water, the kayaks banking on the sand. Gavin removed the sprayskirt and pulled himself out of his kayak, his shoes sinking into the water and wet sand. He glanced around at the masses of palms spanning left and right, following the curve of the small island.

He turned back and noticed Nikki struggling to get out of the kayak. Not surprising for her first time.

"Need a hand?" he offered as he stopped beside her and held out his hand.

"Thanks." She took his proffered hand and stepped out of the kayak, her own shoes sinking into the sand and water sludge.

"Come on, let's look around."

They dragged their kayaks onto the sand, then Gavin took Nikki's hand and led her into the small island. So small, he could see the other side through the lush, tropical foliage.

They walked a few metres before they entered a large, natural cave. Towering rock faces surrounded them like walls, their surfaces worn smooth in places, others rough and streaked with moss and lichen.

The air inside was cooler and the ground beneath their feet was uneven with exposed rock and sand. The roof had a large hole in the centre where sunlight poured down in a shaft, illuminating the shallow lagoon below.

Around the edges of the water was tropical foliage and large stones, some slick and smooth, others jutted up like sculptures.

"It's like we stepped into a hidden world," Nikki said.

Gavin nodded, speechless, and released her hand. Cautiously, he stepped over the rocks towards the lagoon, exploring the entire cave, running his hands over the walls, comparing the smoothness of some to the roughness of others. He'd visited so many places, but nothing was as perfect as this.

He glanced back at Nikki, who sported a soft smile.

"What's that look for?" he asked.

"You love this, don't you? Finding new places. Exploring."

He nodded.

"It's pretty spectacular," she added.

He removed his shoes, then glanced over and gestured for her to join him. She came over and removed her own shoes, then he took her hand, and they waded into the water that came to their knees.

When she gasped at the coolness, Gavin laughed. "Sissy."

She used her foot to kick water at him, only to slip on a rock beneath her. She shrieked and grabbed on to Gavin to stop her fall. It didn't work. Instead, she brought him down with her and water splashed around them. His backside hurt from landing on the rocks. He blinked in bewilderment, glancing across at Nikki, who was dripping wet. When she met his gaze, they burst out laughing.

"You're a crazy woman," Gavin said when he'd composed himself. "If you don't run into me, you pull me into lagoons. I can't take you anywhere."

"Didn't I warn you the first day we met?"

"Yes, I suppose you did."

Nikki bit her lip and a snort came out. There was no stopping her giggles and she shrugged in response but said nothing for laughing too much.

Gavin loved this carefree side of her. He slung his arm across her shoulders and pulled her into his side. The water rippled around their hips. "It's quite comfortable in here, don't you think?"

Nikki hiccupped. "No, not really. I'm all soggy."

When she attempted to stand, her foot slipped on another rock. This only made her giggle again, which made it impossible to stand. Gavin watched on, enjoying every second, until she looked at him pleadingly. He grinned, stood effortlessly, then held out his hand. She grabbed it and he hauled her to her feet.

He kept his arm around her, guiding her out of the water. They found a space to sit on the sand where they could dry off. He lost track of time as they relaxed in companionable silence. Gavin leaned back on his hands, enjoying the tranquil setting.

Apart from the faint sound of waves lapping the shore and birds chirping, it was blissfully silent. When Nikki also sat back, she glanced across at him the same time he glanced at her. Their eyes met and without a moment's hesitation, he leaned across and captured her lips.

She wrapped her arms around his neck and pushed herself against his chest. The kiss became one of passion and hunger. He bravely ran his hand along her flank, sneaking under her top. When his fingers brushed her silky-smooth skin, she gasped, and he smiled against her lips.

He moved his hand around to her back, pulling her closer. They fell onto the sand, Gavin on top, and he wasted no time in deepening the kiss, his hands roaming. This had to be the single most exhilarating moment of his life. Only when his lungs begged for air did he release her.

As he stared into her eyes, terrifying thoughts entered his mind. Thoughts of heartbreak, of hurting Nikki, of being hurt himself, of wanting a future with this woman, all the things that terrified him. He pulled away and rested his head on her shoulder. After a few seconds, he rolled off to lay beside her, leaning on an elbow so he could look at her. Nikki stared at him with wide eyes.

"I don't know what you're doing to me," Gavin ran a finger along her cheek, "but I'm terrified."

Nikki swallowed and nodded. "Me too."

He shuffled back, putting distance between them and willed his heart to slow down. This was too intense. It wasn't meant to be like this. A fling. That was what they agreed on.

Tension developed between them and Nikki asked, "What's the time? We should head back soon."

Gavin dug into his pocket and his heart stopped.

"Shit," he muttered.

"What's wrong?" Nikki's voice held a hint of alarm.

He jumped to his feet and glanced around the area for his phone with no success. How had it slipped out? Remembering the tumble into the lagoon, he waded back into it and his heart skipped. There it was, sitting on the rocks at the bottom.

"What's wrong?" Nikki asked again, sounding annoyed.

With a heavy heart, Gavin retrieved his phone and turned around holding it in one hand. "My phone slipped out of my pocket."

Nikki got to her feet, not looking too concerned. "It's waterproof, isn't it? Most modern phones are."

He scoffed and waded out of the water as he pressed and held down the side button. Dead.

"Not this one. It's old and cheap. Besides, it's been in there for a while."

Her eyes widened. "Bugger." She touched her lips, worry lines forming on her brow. "Um... how long is a while?"

He put the phone back in his pocket so as not to litter, but it was useless now. For the first time in years, he had no contact with the outside world. No way to check the time. He didn't wear a wristwatch, and he noticed Nikki didn't either.

"I don't know," Gavin said, trying to sound upbeat. "But I'm sure we're fine."

"We should go," Nikki said, panic lacing her voice.

"Hey, I'm sure it's fine."

Nikki wrung her hands together. "It won't be if we stay here much longer. Can we go? Please?"

Gavin nodded while trying to estimate how long they'd been gone for, but it was impossible. They'd spent so long enjoying the silence, then he'd got caught up in Nikki's kisses, and time as he knew it disappeared. They could've been here for hours for all he knew.

"Come on," he said, trying to remain positive. "Let's go."

But he didn't miss the worry lines on her brow or the knot of worry forming in his gut.

Chapter 16

The row to the little island had been a breeze with Nikki high on excitement and the adventure of it all. Her arms had ached from the unusual rowing motion, but it had eased while they relaxed.

On the way back, she gripped the paddle tight, her knuckles white as the blade sliced through the water. The row back was ten times harder. Her arms burned, muscles protesting with every stroke, but she pushed forward. The rhythmic rowing sounds were almost meditative and had kept her calm for a short time.

It wasn't just the physical exertion that wore her down. The more time passed, the more her anxiety grew into a knot in her stomach, threatening to send her into a panic. Having no idea of how much time had passed was not her idea of fun. It was the worst-case scenario she was certain *wouldn't* have happened but had.

What if we miss the flight?

Her heart skipped. This was what happened when she was reckless and spontaneous! Maritimo Island was visible in the distance, but it looked so far away.

The afternoon had slipped away in the haze of their impromptu adventure and too much kissing. But, *damn*, they were great kisses. She'd become a different person, someone she didn't recognise, and it rattled her.

It had been *fun*, though. *So* much fun. Exploring. Kissing. Falling in the lagoon. Just being in the same space as Gavin. She couldn't quite believe they'd both forgotten to keep an eye on the time. How stupid!

A little way ahead, Gavin appeared relaxed and unworried as he paddled with ease. His casual nature was both comforting and maddening. How did he do it? Shut off the worry?

She'd do anything to quiet the anxiety that gripped her stomach. God, was this the sort of person she'd become? Anxious? Unable to take risks? Was this who Sophie saw? What happened to the teenager who'd been like Gavin once upon a time? Ten years ago, this would've been the adventure of a lifetime.

Don't you see? You were *that woman on the island.*

The thought sent a jolt to her core. It was true, she *had* reverted to her teenage self for a short time. The carefree teenager without the rest of the angst that came with it. Deep down, that was who she wanted to be. With a little more maturity, of course.

Her arms screamed for relief but the worry of missing the flight kept her pushing forward. As time passed, the sun inched lower in the sky. Nikki wished she could estimate the time by the position of the sun. Her chest tightened as they rowed, her worry growing with each stroke of the paddle.

If they missed the plane, they wouldn't be back in time before the ship departed. They'd been warned many times it wouldn't wait if they were late. The departure time was set and anyone who didn't make it would be left behind. She swallowed back the lump in her throat.

Gavin glanced back and sent her a reassuring smile. "You good?"

"Yeah, just a little tired," she said with a strained smile.

"Not far now." He threw her one last smile, then rowed harder, sending him further in front.

Nikki gritted her teeth and followed. It wasn't easy though. Her arms were lead weights, each stroke more difficult than the last. Her muscles trembled. Her entire body heavy, sore, the fatigue catching up with her.

She heard Gavin shout something but couldn't make out the words. Instead, she glanced at where he pointed. Maritimo Island was so close, the water became shallower. The resort stood tall and proud behind the palms.

Relief pulsed through her veins. They were going to make it! This gave her a boost to row harder, managing to catch up to Gavin. Her body begged for relief, but she knew they could do this. She'd been worried about noth—

A buzzing sound filled the air and Nikki's stomach dropped to her feet.

Oh no. No, no, no!

The seaplane lifted into the air a moment later and climbed into the sky, way, way, out of reach. Nikki's breath caught and she stopped next to Gavin, the realisation hitting her like a punch to the chest.

Gavin stopped too and glanced at her with wide eyes. His casual expression faltered and for the first time he seemed to truly understand the gravity of the situation.

"Shit," he muttered.

The buzzing faded, and all she could hear was her own pounding heart. The stress, the anxiety, the worry she'd tried to ignore, built up and her eyes brimmed with tears.

"We... we missed it."

Gavin plastered on a confident smile, but she didn't miss the worry in his eyes. "Hey, we'll figure this out, okay?"

Her bottom lip wobbled but she bit it to stem the tears and nodded. This was neither the time nor place for breaking down. But it was no easy feat. Her body was so heavy, her arms sore, and she didn't even have a bed to sleep in. The combination made everything ten times worse than it probably was.

"Wh-what are we going to do now?"

"Let's row to shore, then we'll go to the resort and see if someone can help."

She managed another nod, glad that he had a level head. She gathered enough strength to follow him to shore. When their kayaks banked, she got herself out this time and removed her tote bag from inside the bulkhead. Her only possessions.

Her heart stuttered as she followed Gavin. They dragged their kayaks onto the sand then made their way towards the resort. Her arms hung limply by her side and her legs trembled as she struggled to keep up with Gavin's long strides.

When they passed through the trees onto the resort property, Gavin stopped and turned to Nikki, taking her hands. "Alright, let's go in and find someone to talk to. I'm sure they'll be able to help. Everything will be fine. It's not the end of the world."

Nikki glared at him and ripped her hands away as her anxiety bubbled to the surface. "Not the end of the world? We wouldn't be here if it weren't for you! How exactly do you propose we get back now, hmm?"

He held his hands up and stepped back. "I didn't make this happen, you know? It's not entirely my fault that we lost track of time."

Nikki huffed but said nothing because she had no rebuttal. He was right. They'd both got carried away. She couldn't entirely blame him.

Gavin's expression softened. "This isn't ideal, I know that, but the plane isn't going to come back. The best thing we can do is ask for help."

Nikki followed Gavin into the resort through an archway and followed him around a corner to reception. There was seating with plush cushions and island-inspired décor for guests to relax while completing their check-in process or waited for their room. A terrace spread across the western side of the building. From Nikki's vantage point, she could just make out some houses and the ocean.

Guests came and went, staff and porters flittered about, and soft Fijian music played. It was all so welcoming, the staff greeting them with bright smiles.

"Over here," Gavin said, tugging on her hand.

She stumbled over her feet as she followed him to a massive hand-carved reception desk. It gleamed with its rich dark wood, polished to perfection and adorned with fresh tropical flowers and Polynesian artwork. Adjacent to it was a concierge desk staffed by friendly attendants.

As they approached the desk, the woman who greeted them when they arrived looked up. Her calm demeanour shifted when she saw them, her eyes widening in alarm.

"Oh my God, where have you two been? We've been looking for you! The seaplane left. It couldn't wait, and we couldn't get in touch."

"I'm afraid we lost track of time," Gavin explained. "I lost my phone and by the time I found it, it was waterlogged and unusable." Gavin shrugged as though it was nothing.

But it wasn't nothing, and Nikki's entire body hurt, and she was so tired and so damn emotional right now. When tears brimmed once more, there was no stopping them as her anxiety bubbled over. Her face flushed as they spilled down her cheeks, hot and fast.

"Hey," Gavin placed a consoling hand on her arm. "It's okay."

She shook off his hand and spun around. "No it's not! We're stranded! I don't have my phone, or clothes! What am I going to do without a change of clothes?"

She knew it sounded ridiculous, but all the little things suddenly felt huge and overwhelming.

Tenika rushed around the reception with a box of tissues and Nikki took one with a wobbly smile. She dabbed at her cheeks as Tenika slid an arm across Nikki's shoulders and guided her to a bench, getting her to sit.

"It'll all be okay," she consoled. "Take a deep breath and I'll grab you a glass of water. We'll help you figure this out, okay?"

Nikki nodded and tried to stem her tears without success. Tenika left the box of tissues, then rushed off. Gavin sat beside her and his arm replaced Tenika's across her shoulders. This time she didn't push him away and leant into him instead, welcoming his warmth and reassuring calm.

What a nightmare this had become! She drew in steady breaths and released them slowly. Tenika returned a couple of minutes later with a glass of water, a notepad and pen, and a middle-aged Fijian woman in tow.

Nikki accepted the water with thanks and took a sip. The coolness of it helped to calm her. Now that she was more composed and could see past the problem, she knew Gavin was right. It wasn't the end of the world. If they were on a deserted island, that would be a different story.

"This is Litia," Tenika said. "She owns the resort with her husband. She'll organise somewhere for you both to stay and I'll get in contact with your cruise company. Do you have their details?"

Nikki nodded and relayed all the information, which Tenika wrote down. Gavin gave his details too and Tenika disappeared.

Nikki glanced at Litia and asked, "Is there any chance I could borrow a computer? I should email my parents and let them know where I am."

She doubted they'd notice after the way her mum had reacted on the first day of the cruise, but she still wanted them to know. Katie? Well, Nikki didn't care enough to email her. Mum and Dad could tell her if they wanted to.

"Of course," Litia said. "Follow me."

They followed her into a little office behind a reception desk. A Fijian man around Tenika's age sat behind a small desk. He was insanely good looking and the blinding smile he sent her way made her cheeks flush.

"This is my son, Eroni," Litia explained. "Eroni, if you have a free moment, these guests need to borrow the computer to send urgent emails."

"I'm done now." He closed whatever application he had open and stood, squeezing past them. "You can leave it switched on when you're done."

"Thanks," Nikki said, sitting down at the computer and opening a browser.

"Eroni," Litia said, "I'll need your help getting a room ready..."

They left and Nikki logged into her email. Her churning stomach began to abate now things were in motion, but she'd feel better once they had a room, shower, and some clean clothes.

Nikki finished her email and clicked send. She looked up at Gavin with a small smile. "I'm sorry for snapping at you before."

"It's fine, really."

She stood and stepped back from the chair. "Your turn."

He frowned. "Why? I have no one to email."

"What about Sophie?"

He paused, shrugged, and they switched places. "I suppose you're right.".

His jaw was set as he logged in and wrote the email. What bothered him? They appeared to be close, at least from the outside. Sophie had never revealed much about what life had been like for them in foster homes.

"I'm done," he said a moment later, getting to his feet.

They made their way out of the office and back into the reception area. Tenika was on the phone and Litia was busy on a tablet.

Litia came over holding out two keycards. "All sorted, but we only have one room available. Will that be a problem?"

Nikki glanced at Gavin with wide eyes. Her face turned hot while he had a smug smirk on his face.

"Not a problem at all," Gavin said, taking a card.

Nikki shot daggers at him but he ignored her. Sharing a room with Gavin? She could still feel his mouth on hers, the way her body had responded in the cave. How on earth was she supposed to sleep next to him?

"Thanks," Nikki said reluctantly, taking the other card. "We really appreciate this, Litia. Um, are you able to help us with a change of clothes?"

Tenika, who'd hung up, also came over to them. "Leave it with me. Just let me know both of your sizes and I'll organise something. We have a laundry service if you want to wash the clothes you're wearing, too. Now, I've reached out to the cruise line, and they said you can meet at the next stop and re-board. The plane will return tomorrow morning and then we'll get you back on your cruise. Okay?"

Nikki nodded, relief washing over her. It was all falling into place. Surely, she could spend *one* night in the same room with Gavin.

Chapter 17

With Nikki by his side, Gavin followed Tenika's directions on a handwritten note. They stepped through the palms, across the sand and onto the long L-shaped jetty they spotted earlier. It extended out into the water, wood panelled bungalows with thatched roofs coming off it. Each had its own deck at the back with stairs that led into the water.

Gavin stopped at the first one and reread the note.

"Is this ours?" Nikki asked.

He nodded and unlocked the door, gesturing for Nikki to go through first. As she breezed past, her long ponytail brushed his arm and make him shiver. He drew in a long, slow breath before he followed her inside. It would be a real test of strength sharing a bungalow with this woman.

Since their adventure to the little island, his senses were heightened. One small smile, a twinkle in her eyes, her creamy coconut scent, made him want fall to his knees and beg for a simple kiss.

He shut the door and cast a cursory glance around the small bungalow. Directly opposite double doors opened onto the deck where Nikki stood, arms wrapped around herself, the gentle breeze lifting her hair around her shoulders.

The room was open plan with a small kitchen and mini fridge, dining area, and lounge. It was decorated with varnished floorboards, modern wooden furniture, and island decorations in browns, whites, blues and greens.

His eyes landed on the queen-sized bed and his breath caught. A frantic look around confirmed it was the only bed. The only privacy they had was the bathroom.

It was intimate. *Too* intimate. This might've been a fling, but Nikki wasn't like other women. He had to keep his hands to himself until she was ready. Not that he minded. At all, in fact. There was something enticing about the wait. Gave him something to look forward to.

Nikki came back inside, shuffling from foot to foot. Bathed in bright light from outside, she looked almost ethereal, her honey-brown hair shining golden.

"Give me strength," he muttered as his breath quickened.

Nikki cast a cursory glance around the room. Her gaze landed on the bed and she swallowed before looking at him. Even with her on the opposite side of the room, the air crackled with tension.

"I've got dibs on the bed," Nikki exclaimed, sprinting over to it and throwing herself onto it.

Gavin didn't hesitate, he flung himself beside her.

"Who says you get to choose?" he joked as he made short work of straddling her, so he was on top. He trapped her by placing his legs on either side of hers, holding her hands above her head.

"I need my beauty sleep."

She smiled up at him, such a blinding smile that his heart flipped inside his chest. For a long moment he drank in her beautiful features.

"No, you don't," he said on a growl. "You're absolutely perfect as you are," and he lowered his head to kiss her for all he was worth.

A little groan emanated from the back of her throat as she reciprocated. The gentle lapping of the water against the jetty, the occasional seagull squawk, and Nikki's coconut scent made his head spin. He released her hands, using his to run along her flanks, her clothes still slightly damp.

As his hands brushed against her soft skin, Nikki's gasp echoed around the room. Her arms came up and looped around his neck, pulling him flush against her. Her breasts were soft against his chest and her low groan vibrated throughout his body, awakening every part of him.

If he didn't stop soon, he didn't think he'd have the strength to stop later.

Goosebumps rose on his skin as Nikki ran her hands through his cropped hair.

The usual fears that would paralyse him were missing and he let himself float away in the moment. Just himself and Nikki in this hidden paradise. Out of everybody they knew, not a single soul knew where they were. There was something thrilling about that.

He broke away to trail kisses along her cheek, down her neck and across her collarbone. Her arms tightened around him, her breathing laboured as his name came out on a breathy sigh. *Good lord.*

A loud rap at the door had them pulling apart. Gavin rolled off onto his back, panting, as he covered his face with his hands. The bed moved next to him as Nikki got up. He silently groaned and sat on the side of the bed, scraping his hands over his face. Holy hell!

"I've brought some clothes for you both," came Tenika's voice. "Don't forget we have a laundry service if you'd like your clothes washed. You'll find laundry bags in the closet, and you can bring them over to the resort any time. There should be all the toiletries you need in the bathroom too."

"Thank you so much," Nikki said.

Gavin heard the door click shut and dropped his arms. Nikki held a pile of clothes. Her cheeks were flushed, and she wouldn't meet his gaze.

"I'll leave yours here. I'm going to take a shower." She placed some of them on a shelf near the door.

What just happened?

Gavin got to his feet and approached her. "Hey, did I do something wrong?"

She blinked once and glanced up at him, her grey eyes filling with moisture. "No, it's not you."

"You can talk to me, you know?"

She nodded, one tear slid down her cheek. He used his thumb to wipe it away. He wasn't sure *why* he wanted to help her, but something deep down told him to. A longing of some kind. Of wanting to kiss away her sadness and make her happy. Forever.

Unease threatened to spread through his veins, the usual fear that laid dormant. Would it ever go away? He squashed it down. This was neither the time nor the place.

Nikki dropped her gaze for a second, took a breath, then flicked it back up to him. "I-I'm embarrassed. About my body." She bit her lip and dropped her face again.

He raised his eyes heavenward and gathered her in his arms, silently cursing her sister to hell and back. He wished so much he could convince Nikki there was nothing wrong with her. There was a way, but she had to be ready and willing.

"Hey." He pulled back and held her at arms-length. "You have nothing to be embarrassed about."

"But... but you haven't seen everything."

He smiled and kissed her. "When you're ready, I want the opportunity to see for myself. I'm certain I won't be disappointed."

A coy smile tugged at her lips, her cheeks going from pink to red. She reached up and touched his cheek. "I just need a bit of time."

"Take all the time you need."

"Thank you." She held her clothes against her chest. "I'll have a shower, then we can discuss sleeping arrangements."

"I'll sleep on the floor, it's fine," he said.

She frowned and glanced at him. "That's not necessary. I trust you, Gavin. We can share the bed."

She disappeared into the bathroom.

When the shower switched on, Gavin groaned into the empty room and clutched his hair. He didn't know if he trusted himself.

❧❧❧❧❧ ❧❧❧❧❧

Once they'd both showered and changed into their Fijian style clothes, Nikki took their soiled clothes over to the resort to be laundered.

A couple of hours later, as nighttime set, they ordered room service for dinner, then sat in front of the TV once it arrived. Nikki chose the movie, Gavin happy with anything as he was content being beside her.

While they ate a fish curry followed by a tropical sorbet, Gavin couldn't pay attention to the movie. He was so fixated on the woman next to him. The way her eyes would light up at something happening in a scene, or when she'd shout out an exclamation, or give an opinion about the characters on screen. He honestly had no idea what was going on.

Nikki was so damn easy to be around, he could be himself, relax and not think about anything. He was *home*.

This is very bad.

It was so much easier being a nomad where he could avoid commitment and attachments. This current adventure proved exactly why.

The TV switched off and Nikki stretched her arms above her head. "I'm spent. I'm calling it a night."

Thankful for the interruption, his gaze followed Nikki as she stood and readied for bed. He appreciated her natural hourglass curves, her long legs, and that long hair he ached to run his fingers through. Oh yes. He couldn't wait to explore and worship her body when she let him. There was nothing not to love. She was new, exciting, and so damn enticing.

While she disappeared into the bathroom, he dressed down to his boxers and sat on the edge of the bed. Weird butterflies looped in his stomach, which was stupid. He'd slept with many women, something he used to be proud of. Now, not anymore.

This was different. It wasn't sexual. At least not tonight, it wasn't. They were simply sleeping in the same bed, and *that* was the problem. He could behave himself when he was awake. He had no control over what happened when he slept.

When Nikki emerged dressed in shorts and a t-shirt, he ducked in after her to use the toilet and brush his teeth. He came out a couple of minutes later to find Nikki sitting up in bed with the covers pulled up over her chest. If this situation wasn't so damn awkward, he'd almost find it comical.

He made his way around to the other side of the bed and slipped under the covers, fluffing up his pillow until it was comfortable under his head.

He glanced over at Nikki with what he hoped was an open smile. "I promise I won't try anything."

Her cheeks coloured and she laughed but shuffled further down so they laid side by side. Their arms didn't touch, but warmth radiated off her. He wanted to hold her. Nothing else, just holding until she fell asleep.

She rolled over with her back to him and he rolled the other way with a silent sigh of disappointment.

"Goodnight, Gavin," Nikki whispered in the darkness.

"Goodnight, Nikki."

Silence filled the bungalow apart from the gentle lapping of water against the bungalow. Nikki fell into an instant sleep, and Gavin stared into the darkness, too wired and unsettled to think about sleeping.

H e didn't know when he fell asleep, but when Gavin woke, he relished in the peacefulness of the island. The consistent water lapping at the bungalow combined with birds chirping and a gentle breeze caressing the wood panels.

He couldn't remember the last time he slept so well. Not only had he slept through—a rarity in itself—it had been solid. Usually, he tossed and turned. Was it because of Nikki?

He opened his eyes, letting them adjust to the light streaming through the gaps in the curtains. As he came to, he realised they'd gravitated to each other but were fully clothed, *thank God*. He was on his back while Nikki had her head on his shoulder and one arm around his middle.

Her face was relaxed and peaceful, her breathing steady. Gavin should've moved, but he selfishly didn't want to. Her closeness, the softness of her body pressed against his, was perfection. For a moment, he wanted to enjoy the simple, quiet intimacy of it. He didn't dare move an inch.

Images of waking up like this every morning flittered through his mind.

No. Bad thoughts. Don't go there.

His heart rate quickened the same moment Nikki stirred. Her eyes fluttered open and she glanced around first before looking up at him. She gasped and scrambled away reflexively, putting space between them.

"I'm so sorry. I didn't realise I moved."

Gavin sat up and rubbed his eyes, pretending like he'd just woken too. "Must be all my magnetism."

Even though his stomach tumbled with uncertainty, he managed a grin. She bit back a smile as she grabbed her pillow. He raised his hands to protect himself but was too slow and the pillow connected with his face.

He pushed it away, laughing, and got out of bed. "C'mon, let's hurry and get ready. Hopefully, we can get back on the cruise today."

Time to put the brakes on and slow this down. This is getting too intimate.

"I call dibs on the bathroom," he said, legging it across the floor.

"No fair!" Nikki called as he shut and locked the door.

He leant against it and closed his eyes, taking deep, calming breaths. He really needed to be back on that ship. Away from all this intensity. Away from all things Nikki.

The woman who was perfect for him. And that terrified him more than anything else.

Chapter 18

Nikki had a bounce in her step as she followed Gavin across the sand towards the resort. Who would've thought after such a tumultuous day yesterday, that today she could be so carefree? She still ached from yesterday's adventures, but otherwise, she didn't have a care in the world.

She'd had the best sleep and waking up snuggled up to Gavin was pure perfection. Even if it wasn't meant to happen, she would forever secretly call upon it to enjoy. Guilt free. And last night? She'd been *so* embarrassed at letting her self-consciousness become all-consuming, yet Gavin had been so understanding.

Yes, it was a wonderful morning!

Warmth from the sun kissed her skin, freshly lathered in sunscreen. The borrowed clothing, a tropical Fijian style dress, was comfortable and cool. She'd never worn anything like it.

They passed the pool where a handful of guests took a morning swim. When they entered the resort and headed through to the entry area, more guests flittered around as they went about their morning. The reception desk was unmanned.

"We should come back," Nikki said.

His cast his gaze around the lobby and nodded. "You want to grab some breakfast while we wait? There's a restaurant over there." He pointed to the door of the restaurant, past the reception desk.

Rich, earthy coffee and smoky bacon assailed her senses at the same moment and Nikki nodded.

"Come on." He slung his arm over her shoulders and steered her in that direction.

She leaned into his side with a quiet sigh. This fling thing was so difficult. How did normal people not get attached? It seemed an impossible feat!

Gavin seemed unaffected. Did he feel *nothing*? Sometimes she'd catch a glimpse in his eyes that told her he felt something, but it'd be gone in a split second. She honestly couldn't figure him out. Yeah, sure, he found her attractive and that was flattering as hell, but she wanted to know if his feelings ran deeper. It was a dangerous road, but it was a risk she was willing to take.

They entered the restaurant and navigated past table settings onto the terrace to enjoy the cooler morning. Everything glistened, as though they'd had rainfall overnight. The breeze was cool too, the air fresher and lighter, not so humid.

Once they ordered, Gavin reached across the table and laced their fingers together. "This is nice, isn't it?"

Nikki nodded, heat surging up her arm. Such a simple touch sent her heart racing. She hid the effect he had on her by casting her gaze over the rainforest. In the distance, the ocean was dark blue, a stark contrast to the sky.

"Is it weird that I'm not worried about when we leave?" she asked, turning back to him.

He kissed the back of her hand then let it go. Her heart did a little pitter patter inside her chest.

"Not at all," he said, smiling at the waitress who placed their food and coffees in front of them. "I feel the same," he added after she left. "There's so much here I want to explore."

"Me too." Which surprised her, but that was the side of her she wanted to embrace.

They ate breakfast and drank their coffee in companionable silence, only offering small talk here and there. It was nice and Nikki felt at peace. She didn't overthink about how or what she ate. She enjoyed her food, confident in the knowledge Gavin didn't judge her.

Nikki finished her coffee just as she heard, "There you are, I've been looking for you!"

She turned to find Tenika striding over. Her tight curls bounced around her shoulders as she approached, a warm smile on her face. That same inferior feeling from yesterday resurfaced. Would it ever end?

"Good morning," Nikki said, folding her hands in her lap.

"I hope you both slept well?" Tenika glanced from Nikki to Gavin.

"Great thanks," Nikki said, and Gavin nodded in agreement. She didn't miss the little smile and wink he threw her way. Her breath hitched. These were the little moments that made her wonder if he felt something. *Anything.*

"So," Tenika tucked her hair behind her ears, "I've got some not-so-good news I'm afraid."

Gavin's gaze met Nikki's across the table, his eyebrows raised.

"The seaplane is still in Suva," Tenika explained. "Fiji is experiencing bad weather and it's too dangerous to fly or sail right now. At this stage, the weather is avoiding us, so they'll wait it out and monitor it. We hope they'll be back in another day or two." Tenika's hands twisted in front of her as she gave Nikki an apologetic smile. "I'm *really* sorry, I know how much you want to get back on your cruise."

To Nikki's surprise, there was no anxiety. They had to get back at some point, but she wanted to enjoy this journey. Maritimo Island was paradise on earth, staying another day or two wasn't a bad thing.

"You can't control the weather, right?" Nikki said with a shrug and a smile.

Tenika's shoulders slackened and she nodded. "Exactly. Thank you for understanding. I understand your cruise will have moved on by then, but we'll be able to fly you to the island it's stopped at." She went to walk away, then turned back. "Oh, I nearly forgot. Your clean laundry has been placed in your bungalow, and if you're up for it, there'll be a lovo feast on the beach tonight for dinner. Guaranteed bonfire and Taito will tell one of his stories." She leaned in and added in a conspiratorial whisper. "If I'm honest, there'll be at least three."

She stood back with a chuckle and Nikki couldn't help but like her. She reminded her a little of Sophie.

"That sounds great," Nikki said. "Thank you."

With a nod and a wave, Tenika left.

"How about it?" Nikki asked, turning back to Gavin. "You want to go to the lovo feast tonight?"

Gavin drank the last dregs of his coffee, then stood. "I wouldn't miss it. Now," he held out his hand, "how about seeing what else Maritimo Island has to offer?"

She narrowed her eyes. "No kayaks this time?"

He laughed and reached out to grab her hand, pulling her to her feet. "No kayaks, I promise. Let's go on foot and explore."

"Alright, let's go." She linked her fingers through his and tugged him away from the table.

They stopped by their bungalow to change into their clean swimwear, then headed off. They followed the path through the island with no destination in mind. There was so much more to see on foot. Spotting a sign pointing to the peak of the island and waterfall, Gavin tugged on her arm and indicated they should go in that direction.

They followed a dirt path through dense tropical foliage up a steep incline, the air filled with the earthiness of vegetation, moisture, and soil. Nikki wasn't much of an exercise enthusiast and felt the strain in her calves after a few minutes. They were probably only walking for half an hour when she needed a break. She'd never been hiking before and *damn,* it was hard. Who actually *enjoyed* this?

She stopped and grabbed Gavin's arm. "Need... to... breathe," she gasped between pants, hands on her knees.

Gavin nodded and stood with his hands on his hips, taking even breaths. She needed to get fit!

After she caught her breath, her ears tuned in to her surrounds again and... was that water? "Do you hear that?"

Gavin listened, then nodded. "The waterfall?"

"Let's check it out."

They walked a little further until they found a narrower path with a sign pointing to the falls. It was only a short walk into the clearing. A waterfall cascaded from the highest cliff, showering into the emerald-green pond surrounded by lush tropical foliage, rock faces with moss, and creeping vines.

"Stunning," Nikki whispered.

Gavin slipped his arm across her shoulders and kissed her temple. "Yes, you are."

She turned to him, eyes wide, and he wasted no time in claiming her lips. Slow and sensual, making her heart race and head spin, but it was over as soon as it started.

"Come on," Gavin said in a rush. "Let's go swimming."

He'd disappeared by the time her eyes fluttered open, and she struggled to catch her breath. After a kiss like that, she needed to swim.

Fling. It's just a fling.

But as each moment passed, the lines blurred between it being a fling and something real, which both invigorated and terrified her.

"Come on in," Gavin called from the pond. "The water's great."

She hesitated, knowing she'd have to strip down in front of him. It was hard enough last night when she'd let herself think. At least right now she only had to strip down to her swimsuit. Katie's recent harsh words flittered through her mind, but she pushed them away. They were soon replaced with the memory of how Gavin looked at her when she'd emerged from the pool.

That was only a few days ago, but it felt like a lifetime. Still, that same thrill sent shivers down her spine. Drawing in a breath, she pulled her dress over her head before she could talk herself out of it, kicked off her shoes, and set one foot into the water.

She gasped and scuttled back again. "Oh my God, it's freezing!"

Gavin's laugh echoed around them as he flicked water. She shrieked and jumped back.

"Hey!"

"Then get in."

She held her breath and attempted again, this time making it to the middle of the pond where the water reached her chest. It didn't appear to go much deeper than that. To acclimatise completely, she ducked under and came up less chilly.

Under the water, Gavin took her hand. "You want to check out what's on the other side?" Gavin inclined his head to the waterfall.

She glanced at it, then back at him with wide eyes. The anxiety that was missing earlier hit her tenfold. She shook her head before she could think. "I-I'd rather not."

He frowned. "Why not? It's just a quick duck under the water to the other side. From here it looks like there's an opening."

A shudder ran along her spine. "But *what* is on the other side?"

Paralysis overcame her and she couldn't move. The fear of the unknown because what if there was... nothing? If they stepped through and it just... dropped. It sounded stupid, but sometimes this happened, and she didn't understand it.

"Probably a cave," Gavin said, having no idea of her thoughts.

This did nothing for her paralysis. He had no clue how terrifying it was for her, but she couldn't explain it either.

Her eyes darted to the waterfall, then back to him. "What if there's a serial killer hiding in there?" The words came out before she could stop them and silently cursed. Could she be any more ridiculous?

Gavin's eyebrows raised and he spluttered out a laugh. "A serial killer? Behind a waterfall? It would be a very wet hiding spot."

She folded her arms, stomach fluttering, legs refusing to move. This was so dumb. Why was she like this? Beside her, Gavin ran a hand over his head, and she winced. This whole thing was stupid. *She* was being stupid. She had to push through and stop letting fear take over.

Katie wasn't here. Nikki could be whoever she wanted to be, and she realised yesterday she wanted to be more like her younger self. That person would've ducked under that waterfall the second she entered the pond, no questions asked.

"Are you okay?" he asked, his brow furrowing as her body tensed.

She swallowed and nodded. "Alright, let's do this."

His gaze searched hers. "You sure?"

"As long as I can hold your hand."

He squeezed it under the water. "Suits me just fine. I won't let go." He tugged on her arm, and she stumbled forward, her legs finally deciding to move.

They trudged towards the waterfall. It grew louder the closer they got. Gavin slowed as they approached, probably for her benefit, but she embraced her old self, let go of his hand, and took three large steps straight under the water to the other side, shrieking as the water pounded over her head.

On the other side, she glanced around the small cave. Smooth rocks on the floor, stalactites hanging from the ceiling, and the walls covered in moss dripping with moisture. A small river flowed between sharper rocks and pebbles, stopping her from progressing further.

Gavin stepped through seconds later. His face lit up as he glanced around the small area. He turned to her, eyes alight and she fell a little more for this man. They had different goals in life, but they weren't that different. Not really. She enjoyed the same things he did, she was just a little stunted. They could be so good together.

Their gazes clashed. She reached up for him, cupping his face with her hands and moved in to press her lips against his. He wrapped his arms around her waist, pulling her flush against his warmth. The spray from the water dripped down her face and mingled with the kiss, a perfect combination of warm lips and cool water.

He started to move away but she chased his lips for more. She felt rather than heard his chuckle vibrate through her as he obeyed, kissing her so fiercely her head spun, and her heart raced. She would never be the same person again after this.

The spray of the water could've sizzled on her lips when he pulled away. Her eyes fluttered open and he smiled at her as he tucked her dripping hair behind her ears. Finally, she saw what she so desperately wanted to. Reciprocation. He shared her feelings. It was there in his gaze. The shutters came down, like he'd got lost in the moment, but it was there. She was *certain* of it.

"Come on," Gavin yelled over the water, taking her hand and tugging on it.

On trembling legs, she followed him out from the cave, under the falling water, and back to the centre of the pond where it wasn't so loud.

"What happened to me holding your hand when we went through?" he asked.

"Sorry," she said with a grin. "I realised I didn't need it."

He held a hand to his chest. "But what if *I* needed it?"

She scoffed. "Unlikely. I bet you're the type to go cave diving."

He smiled sheepishly. "There was that one time..."

"No!"

"If it's any consolation, I wouldn't do it again. It was sort of fun, but a little too claustrophobic for me. I nearly panicked."

She shuddered at the thought. "Okay, right here, right now in front of you, I vow to take more risks, but cave diving is *not* on the list."

"That's totally fair." He came over and wrapped his arms around her. "Hey, I'm not sure why these things scare you, but I'm proud of you."

She stopped and considered this for a moment. It wasn't just Katie, surely? This fear had been there for so long, and she couldn't remember the exact cause. Katie only exacerbated it.

"Thank you," she said.

"Come on," Gavin said, acting as though nothing had changed in the cave even though something *had*. "Let's keep exploring."

As they left the pond, Nikki's heart grew heavy. Gavin was so damned determined to feel nothing. Why? All she wanted was to understand, but she didn't think she ever would.

Chapter 19

The late afternoon sun sank in the sky as the hours passed. Gavin couldn't remember a time he'd been so relaxed, especially when he was with a woman. He wasn't proud to admit he'd been *that* guy. Appreciated a woman, her assets, and the pleasure they could both receive, but never anything further. Never deep enough to feel anything.

Nikki inadvertently forced him to slow down, genuinely appreciate a woman, not just the surface level. For that, he'd be forever grateful.

After they left the waterfall, they hiked to the peak of the island. From there they came back down and arrived at the western side of the island early. They settled on the sand under the palms as they watched the waves lap at the shore. The dock where the smaller cruise ships came was quiet with no boats due for a few days. He'd heard one was due today, but the cruise was cancelled due to the severe weather in Fiji.

Locals passed with a friendly smile and a wave, arms full of gear for the lovo feast. When another small group came out with more gear,

Gavin jumped up. "I'm going to see if they need help. You want to join?"

Nikki nodded and got to her feet also. He approached a middle-aged Fijian man who introduced himself as Litia's husband, Taito.

"Do you need help?" Gavin asked.

Taito looked surprised for a second, then smiled. "Thanks for offering, that's real nice of you." He pointed to a nearby path. "If you follow that, you'll find some locals coming from a storage shed. Everything from the shed needs to come out. As for you," he said to Nikki, "I have a different job for you."

Nikki nodded, grinned at Gavin and followed Taito. Gavin took the path Taito pointed out.

Over the next half an hour, he helped the locals carry heavy logs for sitting on, some solar torches to set up along the beach, a pop-up beach bar and associated drinks. Nikki was stringing fairy lights across torches then she helped to bring out food for cooking.

By the time everything was set up and the food was cooking in the pits protected by banana leaves, Gavin looked for Nikki but couldn't find her. While he waited, he found a log and sat, chatting to Taito as he built up and stoked the bonfire. Gavin offered to help a couple of times, but Taito shooed him off.

He liked the man. He was happy, easy-going but wise with a different world view to Gavin.

"You don't ever get bored out here?" Gavin asked when Taito finished and sat next to him.

"No way." He shook his head for emphasis. "Litia and I lived in Australia for a bit many years ago. While we appreciated the wealth of knowledge we received there, the hustle and bustle of the city was too much. This is our life, and we will die here."

He said it with such a large smile, there was nothing mournful about it. Gavin hoped one day he could achieve such peace.

"Speaking of," Taito said getting to his feet, "there's my lovely wife now. I hope you'll hang around for a story later." With a wave he strode off and met Litia coming off the path.

Gavin turned his attention to the horizon where the sun inched closer to it. Deep, rhythmic drumbeats vibrated through the air as the fire grew. He breathed in wood smoke mixing with the aroma of spices, vegetables, and roasting meat. The scent drew more people out, guests and locals spilling onto the sand.

Smaller drums joined the bigger drums, their beats quickening and adding a new layer to the rhythm. Soon they were accompanied by the melodious hum of Fijian chants with the occasional flute and wood instrument thrown in. Some locals danced fervently around the fire, tourists watching on in awe.

While Gavin watched, his thoughts drifted back to earlier and how he'd changed in a few short days. Strangely, it felt like a lifetime. Being with Nikki was so natural and he wanted to be an overall better person for her. Sophie had often berated him for the way he'd treated women and he'd never seen anything wrong with both parties receiving pleasure.

He'd been *so* wrong, and he had Sophie and Nikki to thank for helping him see that there was so much more to people... to *women*. If he could go back and apologise to every woman he'd treated badly, he would. Since he couldn't, the best he could do was be better in future.

Thoughts of Sophie brought on a strange feeling of homesickness. Was she okay? He hadn't thought to check his emails again, but she was probably too busy and wouldn't have checked them. He had faith she'd be fine though. Always the strong one, ever since their parents passed. He couldn't have got to where he was without her.

A gentle *ahem* caught his attention and he looked up, blinking a couple of times. A vision of beauty stood before him bathed in the golden glow of the setting sun. He could've sworn it was an angel, but his vision adjusted and he realised it was Nikki.

Her hair, appearing golden, hung around her shoulders, half of it pinned back with a yellow hibiscus flower behind her ear. She wore a new set of clothes, a bright, tropical two piece. She was stunning when he saw her at the restaurant on the ship, but tonight? Was there a word that was *more* than stunning? There was no way he'd be able to keep his hands off her.

This was *very* bad.

But did it have to be? What if it could be very good? He waited for the usual fear to rear its ugly head, but it didn't.

His heart did a little flip as he got to his feet. "Wow."

Nikki's smile was shy, and her cheeks turned pink. "You can thank Tenika. She dragged me away after I finished my assigned tasks."

The woman who'd been so helpful appeared by Nikki's side, grinning. "Doesn't she look amazing?"

All Gavin could do was nod, unable to take his eyes off her. Something shifted, but he wasn't sure what. All he knew was that the world as he knew it rotated on its axis. For once, he dared to hope that perhaps he wasn't entirely lost. What if someone like Nikki could love him? Maybe he *was* capable of love? He'd experienced that deep, scary feeling before but tonight it wasn't scary at all. That had to mean something... right?

"Told you he'd be smitten," Tenika said in a stage whisper and Nikki's cheeks grew redder. "Have fun tonight."

Tenika squeezed Nikki's arm. As Tenika turned to walk away, a tall man with red hair and a short beard came up behind her, wrapping his arms around her waist. She spun around, her face lighting up as she flung her arms around his neck and they embraced.

When they pulled away, Tenika looked flushed but she was beaming. The man looked at her with adoration and again, something flipped inside Gavin's chest. What would it be like to love someone so much? To commit to them and vow to be with them always, as was evidenced by the diamond sparkling on Tenika's ring finger.

A part of him wanted that with the right person.

"This is my fiancé, Hamish," Tenika said, her smile never leaving her face. "This is Gavin and Nikki."

"Oh, the ones who got stranded," Hamish said in a strong Scottish brogue with a wide grin. He stepped forward and shook Nikki's, then Gavin's hand. "Nice to meet you both."

"You too," Gavin said. "Which part of Scotland are you from?"

"Edinburgh. My brothers and me run a whisky distillery there. If you fancy tryin' some, we keep some stocked at the bar." He inclined his head to the pop-up bar.

The drums faded into the background as the music turned gentle. The vocal melodies continued with the addition of a soft flute and people started slow dancing.

"I'd love to, but maybe later." Gavin slung his arm over Nikki's shoulders. "Right now I've got a beautiful woman I want to dance with."

"What a great idea," Hamish took Tenika's hand and tugged on it. "I think we'll join you."

"Are you happy to dance?" Gavin asked, staring into Nikki's eyes.

She nodded, and they moved closer to the fire. She placed her arms loosely around his neck and he wrapped his around her waist, holding her flush against him. They swayed to the music, their hearts beating in time as the sun dropped below the horizon and set for the night.

"I wouldn't have minded you going for a drink," Nikki said. "You don't have to always be glued to my side." She rested her cheek against his chest.

He stroked her soft hair and tightened one arm around her. Something surged through him, a protectiveness of some kind. "Oh, but I want to be glued to your side." She lifted her head to look at him and he caught her lips.

Her contented sigh washed over him when they pulled apart and he rested his forehead against hers. He could stay in this moment forever. Anything seemed possible right now, and he wanted to relish every second of it.

The music stopped but then another slower number started. This encouraged some more couples to join them. After the second song ended, the music stopped all together.

"Sorry to interrupt such a cosy atmosphere," Taito announced in a loud voice, "but the food is ready, and I have a story to tell! Dig in and find somewhere to sit."

Gavin took Nikki's hand and they followed the crowd to where food was laid out on trestle tables, using banana leaves as serving plates.

The beach heaved with people now, easily over a hundred. Groups huddled around the bar, eating and drinking. Others sat on the sand or on logs around the fire. The sunset on the horizon faded as darkness encroached, stars popping into view. Silence settled while people ate, and Taito stood in front of the fire telling a story about two people from opposite shores, separated by a vast ocean.

"The man, a fisherman, lived on a small island in the east. He was brave and independent and spent his days at sea, though he longed for something more. For someone to share the sunsets with, to share a home with. But he believed that love was not for him. He was too wild, too untamed, just like the waves he rode."

Gavin shifted on the log he and Nikki occupied. There was no way Taito could know his situation, yet why did the words ring so true?

Taito's gaze swept over the crowd as he continued, "The woman who lived on an island in the west tended the gardens, helped people, and looked after children. She dreamt of finding a man to fall in love with, to build a family with, but she feared she was too tied to the land. She never wanted to leave her happy place."

Apart from the waves caressing the shore, the crackling fire, and the occasional gust of wind, the group was silent and hung onto Taito's every word.

Gavin glanced at Nikki when he sensed her looking at him. The shadows of the flames flickered across her face, making her eyes shine. She said nothing, but her wide, confused eyes confirmed she caught onto their likeness through Taito's fictional characters. He reached over to take her hand and she laced her fingers through his.

"One day, a storm blew in while the man was sailing. Winds howled, waves rose high, and he got lost at sea. When his boat succumbed to the waves and sank, he was sure he was dead, far from home, with so many regrets."

He paused for effect then continued in an animated voice. "The man awoke in a strange home with a beautiful woman tending him. She told him he was on the western island and would help him get home. They shared a deep connection, but he knew he'd never be the man for her. She looked after him so well, brought him back to health, but she'd never want to leave her haven."

Taito's voice softened. "But fate intervened and the two soon realised that love was about finding someone who complemented them and meeting them halfway. In the end, they built a home where the sea met the land and they both got to live their dreams and still have each other."

The words settled over the crowd as Taito closed his eyes and held his hands up to the sky. The fire popped, breaking everyone out of their reverie as they erupted into applause and cheers.

Gavin sat in stunned silence as he watched Taito across the crowd, thanking everyone as he made his way back to Litia, who sat on the sand a few feet away. Taito had unintentionally made Gavin wonder for the first time if it was possible that he and Nikki could meet in the middle and have a future.

The music started again. People started talking, dancing, and drinking. Nikki hadn't said a word and when Gavin glanced over at her, she was staring into the fire with a wistful expression on her face.

"That was quite a story, wasn't it?" Gavin said.

She nodded and hummed a response but said nothing else. He wished he knew what she was thinking, but in a way, he wasn't sure if he was ready to hear it. Things were changing so fast and he wasn't sure how to deal with it.

When Tenika came over to talk to Nikki, he took that moment to go to the bar to sample the whisky. As it happened, Hamish was tending the bar and they chatted while Gavin enjoyed the drink. It was smoky and sweet, apparently the last batch made by his late father.

As the hours passed, Gavin lost track of time as he and Hamish chatted. He only noticed it grew late when the crowd dwindled. Nikki and Tenika joined them at the bar when the music and dancing ended. Nikki looked so happy with her eyes shining, a smile never leaving her face.

When Hamish offered whisky to them, Gavin half expected Nikki to say no, remembering she wasn't a big drinker. To his surprise, she accepted with no hesitation and shot it down in one go. He shook his head in disbelief as Hamish and Tenika cheered.

Nikki pulled a face but held the glass in the air as though celebrating the achievement.

"This is great stuff, Hamish."

"Another?"

She slammed the glass down. "Maybe one more."

Hamish poured another shot but this one she sipped. "This is amazing, but so strong," she said with a giggle as she stumbled.

Gavin grabbed hold of her to keep her steady. "I thought it was just wine that made you tipsy too fast," he murmured.

She grinned and leaned into him. "Apparently not."

Before Hamish closed the bar at one a.m., Nikki had accepted one final shot of whisky. She certainly was a quick drunk and after bidding Hamish and Tenika goodnight, Gavin kept his arm around Nikki as she walked beside him.

"I had so much fun!" Nikki said gleefully, attempting a skip but stumbled instead.

Gavin chuckled. "I'm glad and you were beautiful out there."

She let go of him and ran ahead along the sand, arms outstretched. "I feel beautiful," she cried out as she fell onto the sand giggling.

He smiled and stopped in front of her, reaching down for her hands. "Come on, beautiful. Let's get you to bed."

Her gaze snapped up to his and she let him pull her to her feet. "Yes please," she whispered, grazing her lips along his ear. "Take me to bed, Gavin."

A groan escaped before he could stop and he dropped his head to her shoulder. "Oh Nikki, not tonight."

He lifted his head only to be met with a frown. "You don't want me?"

"Oh, I want you alright." He pulled her against him tighter. "But you've been drinking and I don't want to do anything you might regret."

That was always where he drew the line. If a woman was even slightly tipsy, he wouldn't sleep with her. He wanted a clear mind and consent on both sides.

She looked at him hard, her eyes glassy, and she nodded once. "You're a good man, Gavin." And she planted the softest, sweetest kiss on his lips that made him want to weep. "Come on, let's go."

After arriving at the bungalow, they changed, brushed their teeth, and slipped under the covers.

"Will you hold me?" Nikki asked in a sleepy voice.

"Of course." Gavin shuffled closer and wrapped an arm around her middle, planting a kiss on her shoulder. "Goodnight, beautiful."

She fell into an instant sleep while he laid awake, listening to her gentle breathing.

❧❦

Gavin barely slept. Too many 'what ifs' ran around his mind. He was already awake and holding Nikki when the bungalow grew lighter with the rising sun.

Maritimo Island had a magic about it. What Gavin once thought was impossible for him—a relationship, settling down—he felt like he could achieve it now. It was as though he'd been overcomplicating his entire life.

His biggest fear was that this would all go away once they returned to normality. He wasn't ready to lose that.

Nikki stirred and as he expected, she jolted awake with a gasp and tried to move away. Gavin chuckled and tightened his arm around her.

"Hey, it's okay," he said. "Let's enjoy this. What if today is the day we return to the ship?"

Nikki stopped fighting and laid on her back, squinting up at Gavin. She looked adorable with pillow creases on the side of her face.

"I hope not," her voice was barely a whisper, but in the bungalow's quiet, it was crystal clear.

I hope not either, but he kept this to himself.

"Remind me never to drink whisky again," she said on a groan. "It's worse than wine in getting me tipsy too fast."

He chuckled and pressed a soft kiss on her lips. "Hey, I loved that side of you. You were so carefree."

She smiled up at him. "It was a nice feeling. Maybe I'll limit it to one shot." A smile played at her lips, then she added, "I got Taito's message in that story."

Gavin stilled. "You did?"

She nodded. "Mmhmm."

And that was it. He wanted to ask what she thought the meaning was, but he bit his tongue. The fear that hadn't reared its head last night now hovered in the background. He wasn't ready to broach the unchartered territory about their future.

For a few minutes, they stayed in each other's arms enjoying soft, teasing kisses, their hearts beating in time.

A knock on the door had them hesitantly moving apart and this time, Gavin answered it.

"Good morning," Tenika said, "I'm sorry to bother you so early. I just wanted to let you know the seaplane won't be returning today. The weather is still too bad in Fiji, so the boats are out of action too, but they're forecasting it should start to clear later tonight, so the seaplane should be able to come back tomorrow. We can organise for your return then."

"The ship will be at sea all day tomorrow," Nikki said from behind. She sidled up next to Gavin and grinned at him.

Tenika frowned. "Hmm that does pose a problem. If you don't mind staying here a couple more days, I will make plans to get you back to your ship the day after tomorrow. I'm very sorry for all this."

"Don't be," Nikki said a little too enthusiastically. "We're loving it."

"Oh, I see how it is," Tenika said with a knowing smile. "The island is working its magic on you, too?"

Nikki nodded and Gavin just smiled, wrapping his arm around her waist. Her excitement was contagious, and he wasn't about to deny the truth. Since coming here, he'd felt more himself than ever. That had to mean something. There must've been some magic in this place.

"Well, as always please let me know if you need anything," Tenika said then with a wave, she turned and left.

Gavin shut the door and turned to Nikki, raising his eyebrows. "What happened to being desperate to get back on the ship, huh?"

Her eyes shone as she wrapped her arms around herself. "I'm not *that* desperate. I'm not going to complain about a couple more days here, are you?"

"A couple more days with you?" He pulled her closer, so they were flush. "I would never complain about that."

He moved in swiftly to capture her lips in a soft, promising kiss. A lot could happen in two days.

"Let's make every second count," he said when he pulled back.

Chapter 20

S *norkelling?*

She looked across at a grinning Gavin and managed a wobbly smile in return.

When she let Gavin choose the morning's activity after a light breakfast, snorkelling never crossed her mind. She remembered seeing the beautiful reef when they kayaked on their first day but hadn't thought about it again.

While her stomach fluttered and her heart raced a little faster than normal, Nikki's fears didn't overwhelm her. Something was different today. She was in touch with the carefree teenager she once was and was excited to try new things and live again.

"Hey," a voice called, "do you need lessons?" Eroni, the man they met on the first day in the office, approached.

"I'm good," Gavin replied, "but I think Nikki does." He looked at her for confirmation and she nodded.

"Easy." Eroni stopped in front of them with a wide smile. "Let me grab the gear, then I'll come back and show you what you need to know."

He strode off and Nikki turned to look at the turquoise ocean, the colourful reef visible beneath the water.

Suddenly a flash of memory had her spinning around to face Gavin, eyes wide.

"Are you okay?" he asked.

"It was a car accident!" she blurted.

Gavin's brow furrowed. "What was?"

She shook her head. "Me… I mean, I was *in* one a few years ago." Gavin's eyes grew concerned and she continued. "It wasn't that bad. I had some whiplash, but something changed *in me*. I lost all my confidence. I became terrified of driving, and it took me nearly a year to get over it. By that point, I'd started up my web design business, but my dreams had vanished."

"What were they?"

"Nothing big like travelling, but after I graduated from school, I'd planned to move out of home. I'd even looked at a few places to move into. It's likely I would have travelled at some point, but I desperately wanted my own independence. My own place, you know?"

She looked at Gavin urgently. He nodded as though he understood.

"But for some reason, after the accident, they seemed so overwhelming. The idea of moving out became terrifying. It wasn't long after that my sister changed and any plans I might've had were meaningless. I lost the desire to do anything, so I never moved out of home. Never travelled. Never *lived*."

"Until now?" Gavin asked with a smile.

She nodded. The accident had been minor, so minor she'd literally forgotten about it. But she'd never made the connection that it had impacted her life more than she realised. How much it had become a part of *her*.

"Then I came on this cruise," she continued with a grin. "I met you, I ran into Sophie again, I got to experience this place, go on new adventures, and, well, it's been terrifying."

"Until now?" Gavin asked again with a wink.

She laughed and nodded. "Yes, until now. Because today *I* feel different and I'm ready to do this."

Gavin draped an arm over her shoulder and planted a wet kiss on her cheek. "Thank you for telling me that. And for what it's worth, I'm proud of you for getting to this point. Now, we should get ready while Eroni grabs the gear. I hope you have sunscreen in that bag of yours?" He nodded at the tote bag over her shoulder.

She nodded and Gavin ripped his shirt off over his head. She kicked off her sandals but hesitated before removing her dress. There was still some lingering shyness, but she pushed it aside and removed it, relishing in Gavin's gaze of approval.

After taking out the sunscreen from her bag, she lathered a goodly amount everywhere she could reach, then handed it to Gavin. "Could you do my back, please?"

His eyes flashed. "It would be my pleasure." He twirled his finger and she turned so her back was to him.

She pulled her hair over her shoulder and Gavin's hands rubbed cool sunscreen over her back. Slowly, sensually, with the occasional heated kiss on her shoulder. She shivered and let her hair fall back into place when he finished. Turning, she found Gavin staring at her as he lathered sunscreen on himself.

"Your turn," he said with a smirk, handing over the tube.

She took the tube, their fingers brushing. Gazes clashed. Nikki's breath caught. They were only inches apart and the desire to kiss him was overwhelming. If Eroni hadn't returned with snorkelling gear at that moment, she would have.

Gavin turned and her heart pounded as she squirted a blob of sunscreen on her fingers, then began rubbing it in. His skin was soft and warm under the sun. As she rubbed his entire back, she briefly observed his tattoos by trailing her fingers over them. She had so many questions, knew they were there and had seen them many times, but she'd never stopped to look.

Their gazes met once more when Nikki stopped rubbing and put the tube back in her bag. Gavin threw her a smile, then strode away to grab some snorkelling gear as Eroni came over to give Nikki a lesson. He brought over a mask, snorkel, and fins to demonstrate how to wear and use them. It all sounded simple enough, but how she'd go once in the water was a different story.

After she'd found gear that was comfortable on her, Eroni said, "Let's take this into the water and I'll demonstrate the rest. All I ask is you don't touch anything, and Gavin, feel free to snorkel but stay close. We prefer it if people swim in pairs or groups."

Gavin grinned and entered the water, snorkelling like a pro.

"Any chance I can be that good?" Nikki asked as she sat on the sand to put the fins on.

Eroni stood beside her, casting a shadow. "What if I said I could make you better?"

She grinned and tugged on a fin. "Bring it on!"

He chuckled, then once she'd put on her other fin, fitted her mask to her face and added the snorkel, she followed Eroni's example by walking backwards into the water. It was cool enough to make her breath catch, but it warmed up quickly. They got to chest height, and she experienced the strangest sensation as though the water were embracing her. Like a comforting hug.

After Eroni demonstrated how to snorkel and blow any water out if it got into the snorkel itself, Nikki followed his demonstration. When she was confident enough to swim alone, she ducked her head partially under the water and was met with a whole new world!

Bright coral reefs in every shade of orange, red, and pink swayed with the current. Schools of fish darted through the water, their scales reflecting the sunlight, creating a dance of colour in front of her.

Spotting Gavin a short distance away, she swam up and past him before finding a safe place to stand away from the coral and pushing her mask off her face. He stood beside her. "Look at you go. It's like you had a good teacher or something."

Nikki laughed and turned to the shore where Eroni stood. She waved and he waved back.

"Funny that," she said. "Now you up for more?"

He nodded and they both ducked their heads under water to explore the reef some more. When a sea turtle glided past, its shell glistening, Nikki stopped and reached out to tap Gavin's arm, pointing at it. They followed it a short distance, not touching, before it disappeared. They resurfaced again and pushed their masks back.

"That was *amazing*!" Nikki exclaimed.

Why had she been even a little afraid? At long last she was no longer a spectator in her life. She was a part of the world, going on adventures, having fun, experiencing it firsthand. Oh, how she hoped so much this would continue once she returned to reality in two days' time.

⚘⚘⚘⚘⚘ ⚘⚘⚘⚘⚘

The evening air had a coolness to it as Nikki and Gavin walked to the resort's restaurant, hand in hand. After snorkelling, they'd had lunch and explored the island some more—the dense tropical rainforests, the village and meeting the locals, and finally, they joined the sunset cruise to watch the sun set from afar.

Nikki was exhausted but content, the kind of tiredness that came from a full day of adventure and experiencing nature. It saddened her to think how much she'd missed out on, but she was still young. It wasn't too late to start now and once she got home, she'd make some changes. Travel more, move out on her own, *have* a life.

They sat on the restaurant terrace for a late dinner, enjoying a delicious meal of grilled fish and vegetables with coconut rice. The conversation between her and Gavin was light and easy with moments of laughter and banter as they exchanged stories about their lives. He talked a little about Sophie, but mostly he spoke of his travels. She lived vicariously through his stories and a new dream formed. That one day she and Gavin could travel the world *together*.

She let this thought fester in the back of her mind as she relished the closeness forming between them. It appeared they'd come here for a reason. A mistaken adventure where all walls were broken down and they could be their real, true, authentic selves. The only thing Gavin hadn't broached was his past. The death of his parents. Nikki wanted to ask questions, she knew enough through Sophie, but the timing felt wrong.

They finished their tropical desserts when Tenika and Hamish came up to them.

"Hey you two," Tenika said. "We were going to hike up to the peak to stargaze. It's so clear tonight, the sky will be incredible. Would you like to join us?"

Nikki took one look at Gavin who nodded, and she grinned. "We'd love to, thanks!"

"Great! You won't regret it. How about we meet out the front of the resort in say half an hour?"

What could be more romantic and intimate than stargazing before returning to their bungalow and taking their relationship to the next level? That was her plan at least. She hadn't drunk anything alcoholic over dinner on purpose. She understood and appreciated Gavin's refusal the previous night and she wanted to be clear-headed tonight.

⁂

An hour later, the four of them hiked up the hill towards the peak. The path was lined with solar lights, but they still had torches because the tropical foliage was so dense. Gavin walked beside her with one torch, his breathing even compared to Nikki's coming out in hard pants. She was so damn unfit.

Tenika and Hamish strode ahead with another torch, barely breaking a sweat, but they'd stop at regular intervals and wait for them to catch up.

An hour into the hike, now closer to the top, Nikki stopped again to catch her breath. She struggled last time, and this time was no different.

"Are you okay?" Gavin asked.

"Yeah, I'm fine," she said with a grin, breathing in slowly and deeply. "I'm not built for hiking, I'm afraid."

"You're doing great and it's not a race."

She smiled in appreciation and they started walking again. It was only a few minutes later when they reached the top and turned the torch off. Nikki stopped, hands on her knees as she caught her breath. A few feet away, she heard the quiet murmur of voices. When she stood, she found Tenika and Hamish in semi-darkness next to a gravesite. Nikki didn't notice it last time. It must've been someone close to Hamish by the way he stood in front of it, hands clasped, head bowed. Tenika stood next to him, her arm looped through his.

Nikki looked at Gavin who shrugged and they quietly passed them to find somewhere to settle for stargazing. The light from the nearly full moon shone on the headstone, but all she could make out was the name 'McNeill', which meant nothing to her. Maybe it was a friend.

She turned to take in the open space, a three-sixty-degree view of the entire area. The moon's silvery light shimmered on the ocean, and the other islands dotted around were silhouettes.

"Come on," Gavin said, taking her hand. "Let's find somewhere we can lay back and look at the sky."

They found space on the ground and settled down. "Wow," they said at the same time.

Having grown up in the city, Nikki had never taken the time to look at the stars. There was no point with too much light pollution to really appreciate them. Here... definitely *wow*. The stars were like a blanket of millions of diamonds shimmering in the endless sky. The moon, as bright as it was, didn't drown out the magnificent view.

"It's amazing, isn't it?" Tenika said suddenly nearby, her voice barely above a whisper. "It's like the world slows down when you're up here."

Nikki just nodded, at a loss for words. Overwhelmed by such beauty, tears shimmered in her eyes, blurring the stars. She blinked them away.

She sensed Tenika and Hamish settling down nearby, their voices a whisper as they too enjoyed the view. Nikki wondered for the first time what it would be like living here. It would be such a change from the life she'd known, but she suspected she'd fit in so well. The quiet life suited her.

But not Gavin.

She silenced the thought, but now that it had entered her mind, it would come back again. A harsh truth she knew hovered in the background.

"Come here," Gavin whispered next to her, holding his arm out.

She didn't hesitate and shuffled closer so she could rest her head on his shoulder. He wrapped his arm around her. Their silence was comfortable... peaceful... only broken by the occasional rustle of the breeze through the leaves, the ocean below, or a nocturnal animal.

For a long while, no one said anything. Nikki enjoyed Gavin's warmth next to her as she committed this moment to memory. To call on when it was all over.

Sadness threatened to overwhelm her, but she pushed it away. Not now. Not here.

"I suppose you knew Sophie and I grew up in foster homes?" Gavin whispered, breaking the silence.

Nikki held her breath, not expecting him to talk but not wanting him to stop either. She nodded against his chest.

"I..." He paused and took a deep breath. "I think it has a lot to answer for why I travel so much. Why I can't commit to..." another pause, "anyone."

You. Was that what he was going to say?

Nikki's body tensed but she quietly said, "I'm so sorry, Gavin."

"I don't remember much about my past. All I've got is this bottled-up anger and... and frustration inside me. I don't know why it's there or even what to do with it. Then I see how relationships go, never good. Sophie and her husband are divorced, my parents died, look at your sister, too."

Nikki couldn't let him get away with that. "Yes, but my parents have been married for thirty years." She sat up and he followed suit, his eyes looking at the ground rather than her. "My grandparents on both sides, both sets still alive, over fifty years married. There are so many other good examples too."

Gavin looked up, meeting her gaze. He looked scared and her heart broke for him. "I know." He reached out and took her hand. "I guess I just want you to understand why I struggle. Why flings are more my thing. But…" He trailed off as though considering his next words. "I guess I just want you to know that if I ever get my head sorted out—"

He looked away, shaking his head.

"What?" Nikki asked, dying from anticipation.

After a long, agonising pause, Gavin said so softly she barely heard him, "It's you I'd want to commit to."

❧❧❧❧❧ ❧❧❧❧❧

The walk back to the bungalow was quiet, the moon above casting a dappled glow on the path in gaps of the tropical canopy. Tenika and Hamish were a few steps ahead, their laughter soft and light as they bantered back and forth. Gavin and Nikki followed at a close distance, not talking but comfortable in each other's company.

When they stepped out of the hiking path into a more populated area that had better lighting, they turned their torches off.

Nikki's head swam from Gavin's earlier admission. She wasn't sure her heart would ever recover. How bad was his trauma? Would he let her help him? Or did he need a professional?

What she did know was that she needed to be with this man. Needed to show him she was genuine, that her feelings were real. If he believed her, perhaps it would help in getting his head sorted. A new hope formed, drowning out the inevitable heartbreak.

A few minutes later, Tenika and Hamish stopped at the end of the jetty leading to the row of bungalows. Gavin handed the torch to Hamish.

"Thank you so much," Nikki said, accepting Tenika's goodbye hug while Gavin shook Hamish's hand. "That was amazing."

"Any time," Tenika said with a smile. "We'll see you tomorrow sometime. I should have more news on getting you back on your cruise by then."

Nikki's smile wavered but she kept it fixed to her face. Tenika meant well, but she had no idea how much pain those words caused. Now more than ever, Nikki didn't want to leave.

After bidding their goodnights, Nikki entered the bungalow with Gavin hovering behind her. She heard the click of the door and every nerve ending responded. She spun around, chemistry crackling between them. Gavin's eyes were heavy and hooded, his pupils dilated. Neither of them moved and Nikki knew she had to make the first one. *She* was the one who was embarrassed of her body, so she had to show him she wasn't anymore.

She stepped closer and grabbed the front of his shirt, pulling him to her until their lips met. His hands rested on her hips as she pressed her hands against his chest where she felt his heart beating steadily.

When they pulled apart, she whispered, "I want to be with you, Gavin. I'm not embarrassed anymore."

It was as though they were the words he needed to hear. Gavin's breathing hitched, then he closed the distance once more. His kiss was gentle at first, testing, as though making sure this was what she wanted. When she reciprocated by deepening the kiss, their tongues duelling, it became slow, deliberate, full of promise. The world outside faded away until it was just the two of them in this cosy bungalow with the gentle waves lapping at the stilts.

Nikki's hand found the back of his neck, pulling him closer, her body responding to his. She pushed against him, no longer self-conscious about how she looked, or whether she was good enough for him. All she experienced was the warmth of his embrace and the touch of his hands as they moved from her hips around to her back.

"Are you sure?" Gavin asked when they pulled away for air.

"I've never been surer of anything." Nikki took his hand and led him to the bed.

Chapter 21

Balmy breeze, chirping birds and the gentle lapping of water woke Gavin. He jolted and squinted in the bright light. A quick glance around confirmed where he was. On the deck of their bungalow.

A smile touched his lips as he glanced down to where Nikki was in his arms. Her head on his chest, one arm over his middle, her breathing steady and warm on his skin. Her beautiful body melded so perfectly with his.

After their first love making session last night, they'd gathered the bedclothes and camped out on the deck for round two under the stars. They laid on the soft duvet with a sheet over their bodies. There was enough privacy to not be seen by anyone in the other bungalows.

He sighed and looked up at the bright blue sky, a couple of fluffy clouds floating across it. Having no protection on him, he'd made a mad dash back to the resort to ask if they had any. The late-night receptionist didn't even blink as he handed over a handful. It might've been awkward as hell, but it was worth it.

So worth it, because last night had been...

He blew out a breath and tightened his hold on her, planting a kiss on the top of her head. No words could do it justice. Wonderful. Magical. Mind-blowing. The best night of his life. His heart clenched and an overwhelming sensation overcame him. It wasn't a bad feeling. In fact, it was pleasant.

Calm. Yes, that was it.

Even his admission last night, confessing she was the one he'd commit to if he could, didn't change this. He was happy he'd said it. Needed her to know his feelings were genuine. It wasn't just about sex, as amazing as it was. It was about connection. Something he thought was a myth but now had experienced it himself.

Was Nikki right? Was it possible for two people to be happily married for years and years? Yes, she'd given examples, but he still hadn't seen it himself. It was difficult to comprehend.

He let these thoughts float around his mind as he laid there, running his fingers through her long tresses and relishing in this strange contentment. Usually he'd wake with racing thoughts, always focused on the next adventure. But here, with Nikki in his arms, time slowed down. Life made sense.

A rogue gust of wind and a seagull flying overhead with a loud squark made Nikki stir, a soft moan escaping her lips as she shifted. Her eyes fluttered open and she squinted up at him, disoriented at first, and then she smiled. A smile so brilliant it somehow made the morning even brighter.

"Good morning," she murmured, her voice sultry from sleep.

Gavin's heart thumped as he leaned in to kiss her. "Morning." He pulled back and brushed a lock of hair from her face, his fingers grazing soft skin.

Nikki blinked, her eyes coming into focus as she met his gaze. "I can't believe we stayed out here all night." She sent him a coy smile and sat up, taking the single sheet with her to cover her chest. Her long hair hung down her back. "I also can't believe it's our last full day here," she added.

Her words popped the bubble Gavin had been in. Reality began to seep in. Soon this calm contentment would be gone. There was no escaping it. As much as he wanted to stay here, he couldn't. Neither could she. His chest tightened at the thought, but he pushed it away, wanting to enjoy this moment.

"Well then," he said, "we must make the most of it."

He pushed the covers back with a grin, and dove into the water stark naked. The coolness on his skin took his breath away until he surfaced.

"Are you *insane*?" Nikki whisper-yelled so as not to bother anyone else, getting to her feet.

Treading water, he spun around and ran his hands down his face to remove the water. She stood on the end of the deck with the sheet wrapped around her.

"Come on," he said. "You should join me. It's exhilarating!"

She shuffled from foot to foot. "It'll be cold, and people might see us."

"It'll only be cold for a second or two and if you're quick, no one will know." He sent her a mischievous grin. "Come on, Nik. What happened to that adventurer I witnessed in bed last night." He added a wink for effect and her cheeks turned pink.

He loved that she didn't hold back last night. She became so confident and carefree, which just made her even sexier.

She stared at him for a long moment.

"What's wrong?" Gavin asked. "Why are you looking at me like that?"

A slow smile spread across her face. "You just called me Nik."

He did? "You don't like it?"

"I do, but only those close to me call me that."

He swallowed at the enormity of her words but had no idea what to say. Instead, he said, "Are you joining me or not?"

"Oh fine," she said, then dropped the sheet, displaying the sexy, curvy, hourglass figure he'd spent hours worshipping last night, before diving into the water.

Fat? Far from it. Absolutely perfect, more like it.

After an exhilarating swim, Gavin ordered room service and enjoyed a quiet, lazy morning with Nikki in their bungalow. He wanted to fool himself a little while longer that this life could be possible. That he was allowed to be this blissfully happy.

On the way to the resort in search of one last adventure, Gavin was struck with an idea. He grabbed Nikki's hand, and she turned to him, eyebrows raised in question.

He inclined his head to the kayaks lined along the shore. "I've got an idea."

Her eyes widened. "You promised no more kayaking!"

"That was a couple of days ago." He grinned mischievously. "We won't go far."

She looked unconvinced.

"Look, it'll be quicker and easier to show you rather than explain," he said. "Please trust me. I promise we'll stay on the island. It's just where I want to take you will be quicker by kayak."

She paused for a long moment. "Fine, I trust you."

Those words were music to his ears, and he grinned as he led her away.

They kicked off their shoes and stored them in the bulkheads, then dragged their kayaks closer to the water.

Minutes later they were on their way towards Coral Cove where they snorkelled the day before, past the cliffs, then veered toward the wild rainforest with the aquamarine lagoon visible through the trees. It was mostly in shade apart from some dappled light through the canopy of foliage. He glanced over his shoulder to make sure Nikki followed, then they banked a moment later and stepped out of their kayaks.

"This is the place?" Nikki asked, coming over to him.

"Yep." Gavin slung his arm over her shoulder. "I saw it when we first went kayaking and wanted to check it out. Fancy a dip?"

She nodded without hesitation, and they trod carefully over tropical foliage and rocks. Nikki was the first to strip down to her swimsuit and slide into the water. Gavin watched, admiring how far she'd come since they'd arrived here. How confident she was now. He only hoped it would last once they were back on the ship.

He joined her and they spent the next couple of hours swimming, playing, laughing and talking... so much talking. Each of them revealing bits about themselves. Nikki talked about life before her sister changed. How happy their family had been and how she wanted to fix their relationship. He loved how much she cared for her family, even her brother-in-law Monty. Gavin loved his sister, Sophie. She was all he had left, but he'd never felt that same sort of love for her ex-husband, Richard.

Even though Gavin couldn't clearly recall his past, he spoke about his travels. He'd been travelling since he turned eighteen. Ten years of seeing the world and he had been on a lot of adventures. His tattoos acted like a journal of his travels, one for every place he'd visited. Some had a story while others were more of a memento.

When they emerged from the water, they sat on some rocks to dry off and Nikki took a keen interest in them.

"What about this one?" Nikki asked as she ran a finger across the eagle on his right forearm. "I spotted this when I first ran into you."

She met his gaze and smiled. Where would he be now if they hadn't run into each other that day? Probably still on the ship and having a lousy time.

He studied the tattoo and smiled fondly. "Alaska. I went on a hiking trip with a group of people. It was one of those transformative trips where we push ourselves to the limit." He smiled wryly. "Not usually my thing, but it was in the early days of travelling when I was... dealing with stuff. Towards the end of the hike, I was looking down over a valley from the top of a cliff when an eagle soared above me. It reminded me of freedom, and for the first time in a long time I felt free." He grimaced and glanced at her with a chuckle. "Stupid, huh?"

"No, not at all." She ran her finger up his arm and traced a Japanese geisha. "Let me guess, Japan?"

"Of course."

"And the story?"

He shrugged. "There isn't one. This is just a memory of an awesome place. Japan is stunning and its culture is amazing."

She nodded and continued admiring the tattoos on his arms, chest and back. "Oooh, I like this one." She said from behind, tracing the large Chinese dragon on his back. "China, obviously?"

The Chinese dragon was his personal favourite. The body was black but the scales all along it, and the pointed end of its tail, were a representation of red-hot flames. Its head was shaped like a lion with a wild, yellow mane and its jaw was open wide with orange flames coming out of its mouth.

"Yep, although this one..." He cleared his throat. "Well, it's symbolic, I guess. It reminds me of a fire within. That I'm not completely broken, and I have some strength in me." He glanced at the ground.

Nikki moved back and looked at him, her expression serious. "I think that's beautiful, Gavin." Her eyes flicked across his chest and settled on a lion tattoo over his heart. "What about this?" She placed her hand over his heart and his eyes fluttered closed.

"South Africa," he said, his voice hoarse. Her touch made his heart race, and he was sure she could feel it. "Reminds me of strength and courage. The two qualities I try to show but sometimes fail."

"Nobody's perfect," Nikki murmured. "I really admire that you even have those qualities. I'm not strong *or* courageous, I'm afraid."

"Hey." He opened his eyes and turned to her. "You're a lot more courageous now. You've come a long way. I also think you're much stronger than you think."

She smiled shyly and shrugged one shoulder. They fell into silence and Gavin admired the scene before him. Now that they weren't swimming, the water had stilled. The reflection of the lagoon and tropical foliage was so clear, the water acted like a mirror.

Beside him, Nikki rested back on her elbows. He moved in closer and feathered kisses along her shoulder. She shivered under his touch and he smiled, continuing up her neck until he captured her lips. God, he loved the taste of her.

He gently pushed her back onto the rocks, deepening the kiss, loving how she melded so perfectly with him. Loved every inch of her and hoped she could see it. He pulled back, breathing hard, and stared down at her, admiring her round face, flawless skin, beautiful, grey eyes, everything that was inherently Nikki.

She stared up at him with wide eyes. This new look, one he recognised as *love*, shook him to the core. The one thing that wasn't meant to happen. She was falling for him and the way his heart pitter pattered inside his chest made him fear he was on that same precipice.

She opened her mouth to speak, "I—," but stopped and snapped her mouth shut, her cheeks turning red.

Gavin pulled back, putting distance between them, eyes narrowed. "What were you going to say?" he asked.

Her mouth opened and closed wordlessly as she tried to recover. "I... I think we should leave." She sat up and scrubbed her hands down her face. "The sun has moved, and I didn't bring sunscreen with me."

She averted her gaze and when he glanced around, the sun *had* moved, but they were still mostly in shade. He didn't correct her though, only nodded and got to his feet. He helped her up, then they made their way back to their kayaks in silence.

After a blissful few hours, reality continued to seep in. The end was close. Less than a day until they left this island. Probably a good thing too. This was getting dangerous.

This island had changed him. Made him soft in the head. Had him believe that love was possible. That *he* was able to love. For heavens' sake, what was wrong with him? There was no possible way he could make her happy. She deserved the world and that was the one thing he couldn't give her. All he'd be able to give was half-hearted commitment while the shadows of his past hovered overhead.

What had he done?

Stupidly convinced himself this could be a harmless fling. Thought he was invincible and not susceptible to those feelings. Oh, how wrong he'd been. Nikki wasn't like the other women he'd been with. She was special. Innocent. Had her own scars. She didn't need new ones from him, but she would get them whether she liked it or not.

On the row back, the silence between them was heavy. Gavin's entire body was tense. Tomorrow, he had to make sure it was all over as amicably as possible. It had gone too far.

After dragging their kayaks back onto the shore and slipping on their shoes, Tenika came over.

"I was looking for you two!" She stopped in front of them. "The seaplane is back, and you can catch the ten-thirty flight to Suva in the morning. From there, you'll catch another seaplane which will take you to the island where your ship will be docking. You'll be back in time to board before it leaves later tomorrow afternoon."

Gavin experienced a strange sense of relief mixed with anxiety. "That's great news," he said with forced enthusiasm. "Thank you for everything."

"It's been my pleasure. Pop by reception when you leave so we can settle accounts. And if you feel like celebrating, the tidal restaurant is being set up for tonight's dinner. Hamish and I are going and would love it if you joined us."

Gavin glanced at Nikki to gauge what she wanted to do, but she wouldn't look at him. He held back a sigh and answered for her. "That sounds great, we'll be there."

He wanted to enjoy one last evening together before he broke both of their hearts.

Chapter 22

The last thing Nikki wanted to do was go out again. Dinner at the tidal restaurant would've been amazing any other time. But now, after that humiliating moment, she wanted to hide away.

The end of the freefall was fast approaching and soon she'd plummet to the ground.

She and Gavin trudged back to the bungalow in silence after running into Tenika and agreeing to meet in an hour.

She'd vowed not to fall in love and now look what she'd done. The last four days had been so wonderful and given her a true glimpse into Gavin's real self. He hid behind his nomadic existence, but he was so much more than that. He was kind. Courageous. Knew exactly how to help her feel good about herself. He had deep feelings, but he also had a tragic past, which he clearly didn't know how to deal with.

Back at the bungalow, she didn't say a word as she grabbed a change of clothes, then disappeared into the bathroom to get ready for dinner.

Her heart thumped as she stepped into the too warm shower. For a long while, she leaned against the wall and let the water cascade down her body. Tears threatened, but she refused to let them fall. She'd gone in with eyes open and knew this would end badly if she wasn't careful.

Sleeping with Gavin had been stupid. It complicated *everything*, but she couldn't bring herself to regret it. Last night... it was all she'd hoped for and more. She'd been *so* certain it could lead somewhere. That Gavin might've been ready to take a leap of faith. Of course, she didn't expect a full-blown relationship from the get-go. She was happy to go as slow as he wanted. All she wanted was a chance.

But the way Gavin clammed up after her slip of the tongue proved she wouldn't get that chance.

She ducked her head under the water, giving her hair a quick wash, then washed herself and turned the water off. Once dried and changed in fresh clothes, she stepped out of the bathroom. Gavin, who'd been sitting on the end of the bed waiting for her to come out, stood.

"Sorry for taking a while," she said, moving past him without a second glance.

"It's alright."

She kept her back to him, shoulders tense, waiting for the click of the door that never came. She felt his presence rather than heard him stop behind her. His hand was on her hip and her entire body burned. She closed her eyes, holding back tears.

"Nikki," Gavin said, "are you okay? You seem a little quiet."

Of course I'm freaking quiet, she wanted to yell. *I'm bloody heartbroken because I stupidly fell for you!*

She was a stupid, lovesick fool.

"I'm fine," she forced out in a fake chirpy voice. "Too much sun I think."

She cringed. Apart from kayaking to the lagoon, which had only taken ten minutes tops, she'd been mostly in shade.

"Uh huh," he said in a disbelieving tone. He said nothing else, just leaned in to kiss the spot between her neck and shoulder, causing a violet shiver to run down her spine.

The click of the bathroom door sounded, and she let herself breathe. While she waited, she made her way onto the bungalow's deck and sat on the edge with her legs hanging over the side. She stared out over the aqua blue ocean growing darker as the sun dropped lower in the sky.

Her heart raced and her emotions were all over the place. Tears threatened to fall again but she kept them at bay. Gavin would notice and that wasn't a conversation she was ready to have. Ever. One slip up was enough. She couldn't risk saying those three special words aloud. That would definitely scare him off for good and she wanted to have a bit more time with him before the inevitable separation.

A few more days might help her understand *why* his past held such a hold over him. Last night while they'd stargazed, he'd admitted as such but she didn't know the specifics. She only knew a little through Sophie about what they'd been through. In and out of foster homes and that their parents had died. Nothing else.

A few days in paradise wouldn't miraculously heal whatever trauma Gavin had hidden away. It certainly wouldn't make him ready to commit to her, or anyone for that matter. That made her feel a little bitter though, because if she couldn't have him, she didn't want anyone else to either.

Selfish? Yes, but for once she didn't care. She only hoped that he didn't walk away with a simple "Seeya, it was nice knowing you." That would hurt more than a proper goodbye. If they were transparent and honest, she would recover.

Somehow.

"Nik, you ready?" Gavin called from inside the bungalow.

She got to her feet and forced a smile as she turned. "I sure am, let's go."

Gavin looked at her hard, as though trying to read her soul. Make sure she wasn't lying, and he hadn't completely broken her. She kept her smile in place and held out her hand. He took it and they left together.

❧❧❧ ❧❧❧

When they reached the tidal restaurant, Nikki took it all in. It was literally a mini restaurant set up on the beach. They stopped at a podium where a hostess instructed them to remove their shoes and leave them higher up on the sand. They were then shown to where Tenika and Hamish sat at a four-seater table waiting for them.

"I'm glad you could make it!" Tenika came around to embrace Nikki while Gavin and Hamish shook hands.

Nikki loved this new budding friendship and hoped they'd stay in contact. She'd never made friends easily and had always stuck with the same ones since school. While this wasn't a bad thing, it was also nice making new friends.

They sat and placed their orders, then chatted like they'd known each other for years. For a while, Nikki's worries disappeared as she enjoyed this final moment in paradise. It was her first time at a tidal restaurant and loved the concept of setting up and packing up the same day. Solar lights were dotted around with strings of fairy lights attached to each one. A couple of lovo pits had leaves over them, delicious aromas wafting out of them. There were also a couple of spits with roasting meat, and a barbeque with vegetables and seafood.

The water lapped at the shore as the tide came in and according to Tenika, if they stayed late enough, the water would lap at their feet.

Entrees arrived as the sun kissed the horizon and began its descent, casting a golden glow over the water and sand. Tropical drinks were served, alcoholic for those who wanted it, but Nikki chose non-alcoholic. She didn't know where this evening was going after the blunder at the lagoon, but she wouldn't take any risks. Besides, if Gavin was up for round three in bed, she wasn't going to say no. She'd take all he was willing to give. If this was the only time in her life she got to experience something so wonderful, she wanted it all.

"So, you and Gavin," Tenika said in Nikki's ear after they finished their entrees. "How long have you two been together?"

"Oh, it's not like that." She sipped her drink.

Tenika raised a disbelieving eyebrow. "Isn't it? You could've fooled me. You two look like the perfect couple."

Nikki spluttered on the drink and coughed, grabbing a serviette to wipe her mouth and chin.

"Sorry," Tenika said with a chuckle.

"Don't be." Nikki put her drink down, ignoring Gavin's curious gaze before he resumed talking to Hamish. "We met on the ship," she continued in hushed tones. "It was meant to be a fling."

"Meant to be?" Realisation dawned on her pretty face, and she nodded. "Oh no, he doesn't feel the same way as you?"

Nikki sighed, her shoulders slumping. "Oh, he does alright." She glanced over at him where Hamish poured them a shot of whisky each. "But he's a commitment-phobe. He can offer flings but nothing more. I'm doomed to be a spinster."

Tenika pulled a face. "That sucks, but maybe it won't be as bad as you think?"

If only she knew, Nikki thought but didn't say it aloud. She wasn't about to air all their grievances. All she did was pull an 'I doubt it' face and Tenika nodded, receiving the unspoken message loud and clear.

"Hey," Tenika added, "this island's thriving so if you feel like being a spinster on a tropical island, you'd be welcomed with open arms!"

Nikki thanked the waitress as she set her main meal in front of her. "Yeah, sure, perhaps I'll take you up on that," Nikki said with a laugh. She picked up her knife and fork to dig in when she sensed Tenika staring at her. "Wait, you weren't joking?"

Tenika shook her head. "Not at all. I meant it when I said we're thriving. We were even thinking of doing some kind of campaign, calling for anyone willing to relocate. We especially need young blood, so you'd be perfect."

"Wow. Honestly, I don't even know what I want to do right now. I've got a lot to figure out in my life."

Tenika's smile was soft as she started eating. "Well, just know it's an offer that will always be there. Remind me to give you my email tomorrow so we can keep in touch."

Nikki nodded enthusiastically and cut off a piece of white fish. She added some barbequed vegetables and popped it in her mouth. "So," she said in a normal tone after finishing her mouthful, "tell me about how you and Hamish met."

Tenika's grin told Nikki this would be a hell of a story, and she was thankful for it. She didn't want to think any more about saying goodbye to Gavin.

But as Tenika told her own story, about how they met here when she was finding herself and Hamish and his brothers were following a journey set by their mother, Nikki found herself craving that same connection, where two people know they belong together and make it last.

It seemed Gavin didn't even want to try, and that hurt more than anything.

⁂

On the way back to their bungalow, with the silvery moon lighting their way and waves lapping at the shore, Nikki came to a decision.

She wouldn't let Gavin go without him knowing *exactly* how she felt. Tonight she would make it very clear she wanted to make love to him and she'd use actions rather than words to express herself.

Whether he realised it or not, Gavin was going to be as heartbroken as she was. It might be the kick he needed to face the emotions he always ran from. Realise once and for all that running did nothing but delay the inevitable breakdown that came with bottling up feelings.

Once back in the bungalow, Nikki went in first and Gavin came in behind her. She took a couple of small steps inside. At the click of the lock, she spun around. Closer than she thought, she had to stop herself from ramming straight into him.

His eyes widened at her closeness, and she pressed up against him, resting her hands on his chest, feeling his heart race under her palm. She kissed him but he didn't kiss her back. *Oh no you don't, mister.* She moved away and nibbled at his ear lobe, feeling him shudder beneath her.

"Nikki," he murmured, his voice coming out in a shaky breath. "It's late."

"I know." She trailed kisses from his ear down his neck and sucked on the sensitive spot between his neck and shoulder, loving the goosebumps appear on his skin. "Then we better be quick."

"It... it's not a good idea." His hands came up to rest on her hips, his fingers biting into the soft skin.

"Why?" She yanked his button-up shirt open, a button pinging across the room, and ran her hands along his smooth chest, using one finger to trace the lion tattoo over his heart.

"It... it just isn't," he said lamely.

She gave him a disbelieving look and pressed her lips against his again. This time he reciprocated, but she still sensed reluctance.

She pulled back, resting her hands on the waist of his shorts and looked him square in the eye. His pupils were dilated, their hearts beating in time. Her entire body was on fire, she needed this man, but she wouldn't force it either.

She took one step back to put space between them.

"Alright," she said calmly, even though so many scenarios ran through her mind. He'd lost interest. He didn't want her anymore. She was too fat for him after all. Now that he'd seen her naked, anything was possible, wasn't it?

"Do you want this?" she asked.

He nodded without hesitation, which at least put her biggest worries to rest and she breathed a little easier.

"Do you want *me*?"

His brow furrowed. "What type of question is that?"

"I need to know you're not just doing this for a quick shag."

His frown deepened and this time *he* stepped closer and wrapped an arm around her waist, pulling her to him again. "Don't ever think that," he said on a growl. "You're more than that, Nikki." He huffed out a sigh and rested his forehead on hers. "I just don't want you to fall for me."

Ah. There it was. Little did he know it was too late, but she wouldn't tell him that.

"Hey, those are some big tickets you've got on yourself."

He pulled back and smiled but it didn't reach his eyes. "I mean it, Nik. You know I can't offer forever, and I feel like things have changed. *You've* changed."

"I could say the same about you," she fired back.

He shrugged. "Perhaps I have, but I still can't give you what you want."

"I know, and I never asked for it."

"What about what happened at the lagoon earlier?"

She sighed and shrugged. "Okay, you got me." Since he was being open, she would be too. "I got caught up in the moment, but you gave off some pretty strong vibes yourself, you know?"

He nodded and she noticed fear in his eyes. What was he so afraid of?

"But I know where we stand," she added, reaching out to stroke his cheek. Her fingers brushed his jaw where stubble had formed from not shaving for a few days. "I'm a big girl, Gavin. I can look after myself. You're not going to break me."

Yet as she said that her heart cracked open a little. He would break her alright, but she'd recover in time because life was exciting again and she wanted to experience it.

"So, I'll ask again," she whispered, wrapping her arms around his neck. "Do you want *me*? No strings."

Because damn it, she was a glutton for punishment, and she still needed as much as he could give. When desire replaced the fear in his eyes and he closed the gap, kissing her with so much passion it made her head spin, she gave in to it all.

Chapter 23

Kryptonite.

That's exactly what Nikki was to Gavin—his kryptonite. His weakness. The one thing he should resist but couldn't.

In the early hours, after sleep eluded him, he left Nikki asleep in the bed, donned his underwear, then sat on the deck of the bungalow. Still dark, the stars were studded like diamonds in the sky and the moonlight shimmered on the water.

His legs dangled over the edge of the deck, his feet skimming the water of the high tide. It was cool and refreshing on his soles. A balmy breeze caressed his skin and whispered possibilities of what could be if he just took a leap of faith.

But he couldn't. That fear simmered low, ready to reappear the moment he stepped on that plane. The island had only silenced it for a few blissful days.

Resting his hands on the deck behind him, he leant back and angled his face to the sky, breathing in the fresh, salty air. He shouldn't have given in when Nikki seduced him. And she had, damn it! Of course he'd wanted it, but this was all getting too complicated and messy. Once they were back on the ship, that had to be it. No more nights together. Because every time he made love to her, he fell deeper.

For a long time he stared at the sky and the twinkling stars. He even spotted a shooting star at one point but didn't make a wish. Load of rubbish, that was.

A memory came to him out of nowhere. The last time he wished on a star. He was a child, only ten years old. His parents had been gone for two years, and he'd wished so hard they'd come back but they never did.

Of course, he knew now why they hadn't, but it had tainted the magic.

Rattled by the unexpected memory, he stood, dried his feet on the mat at the door and returned to bed. The moment he laid down again, Nikki gravitated to him in her sleep, a soft smile on her lips. She snuggled against him with her arm across his middle, her head on his shoulder. She mumbled something he didn't catch.

Tears stung his eyes and he blinked them away. His heart hurt so much, like someone was ripping it out of his chest.

When his bottom lip trembled, he drew it between his teeth and bit hard. The taste of blood sobered him up and he breathed slowly and deeply until the emotions passed. They always did.

***

Banging on the door had Gavin sitting bolt upright in bed. "Wha—?"

Nikki yelped and sat up too, looking shellshocked as she looked from him and around the room. "What's going on?"

"Nikki? Gavin?" came a familiar voice followed by an urgent knock. "Are you awake?"

The urgency in Tenika's voice had Gavin scrambling out of bed with a curse.

"Guys, come on!" Tenika yelled. "I'm going to give you to the count of three and if you don't answer, I have a key."

Nikki squeaked and pulled the sheet up over her chest. "We're awake!" she called.

"Well, hurry up then!" came Tenika's urgent cry. "The seaplane leaves in fifteen minutes. I am not letting you miss another flight. Now hurry!"

Realisation dawned on Nikki's face and she scrambled out of bed too. Neither of them spoke as they rushed to get ready. There was just enough time for a quick toilet stop, but no time for anything else.

As Gavin rushed to the door about seven minutes later, Nikki stood holding one of the dresses she'd borrowed.

"What should we do with the clothes?" she asked.

"I left mine on the bed," he said, pulling the door open.

She hesitated and sighed.

"Nikki," Gavin pleaded, "we don't have time."

She started, nodded, and laid the dress over the bed and followed him. They broke into a sprint down the jetty, past other bungalows and across the sand. Tenika stood on the path next to a cart, gesticulating wildly to hurry them up.

"What is it with you two and missing flights?" Tenika said as they approached, her brow creased with worry. "Take this cart and hurry!"

Gavin jumped in the driver's side as Nikki said, "We haven't checked out or settled—"

"Forget about it for now," Tenika said, grabbing Nikki's arm and all but manhandling her into the cart. "Here." She pulled out a rectangular business card from a pocket in her dress and handed it to Nikki. "I promised you my email address so here it is. Reach out to me once you're back and we'll get everything settled."

Gavin lowered his head so he could see Tenika through the window, and said, "Thank you for everything."

"You're welcome, now go!"

Nikki and Tenika managed an awkward hug before Gavin put his foot down and set off as fast as the cart could go. Neither of them spoke, the tension too high, as Gavin sped down the path, beeping as he approached people, villagers and guests, all of them moving out of the way with a wave and a smile. When he reached the seaplane dock, the plane spluttered to life.

"Shit." Gavin forced his foot on the brake, coming to a sudden stop and jerking them forward. "Come on, we've got to run. I'll race ahead to stall him."

Gavin barely noticed Nikki's nod as he jumped out of the cart, darted across the sand and onto the pier leading to the dock. He waved his hands over his head as he approached the plane where Ratu checked off a list. He spotted Gavin, tipped his cap, and moved from the cabin through the plane.

Gavin glanced hurriedly behind him, relieved to see Nikki dashing towards him, holding her tote bag over one arm. Even in their rushed state, she was still a true vision and didn't even realise it.

"Cutting it a bit fine, eh?" Ratu said, stepping out of the plane.

"Sorry," Gavin said between pants. "Thanks for waiting."

He almost said, "Thanks for not leaving without us... *again*," but held his tongue. After all, it wasn't Ratu's fault. Gavin bit back a smirk. Despite everything, he had zero regrets.

Ratu nodded once and inclined his head to the plane. "Jump on board. We're leaving in two minutes."

Nikki stopped next to Gavin, panting, and smiled at Ratu. "Thank you so much."

Ratu boarded and made his way to the cockpit, Gavin following with Nikki on his heels. They found two seats opposite each other. Other passengers, which meant a full flight, took the other four. Settled, Gavin stared out the window and focused on his breathing. That was *not* the wake-up call he'd expected. The last couple of mornings they'd woken early, so he didn't think to set the alarm.

A couple of minutes later, the plane took off, leaving Maritimo Island behind them. It grew smaller the further away they got. A heaviness settled in Gavin's chest as reality crashed back in like a wrecking ball. The fear that had been hovering rose and taunted him, reminding him of what he was missing out on because he wasn't good enough.

Would that negative voice ever stop?

G avin stood in front of the large white ship, Nikki by his side, shoulders drooped.

Masses of people chattered and laughed as they made their way back from the island, barely paying them any attention. The sun dropped in the sky as evening approached.

They'd been travelling and waiting for a few hours and made it back with two hours to spare. It all felt so surreal now being amongst so many people. He'd never lived in a small place before, had always thrived in cities, but Maritimo Island was different.

Now that he was back, the same feelings came with it. The overwhelming desire to travel and explore new places. And for the first time in days, he remembered his upcoming trip to Las Vegas and that familiar thrill skirted along his skin. It had been his plan for so long, it was so strange he'd clean forgotten about it.

Now it couldn't come soon enough.

Beside him, Nikki sighed. "Well, that's it."

They hadn't spoken much since they left. It was as though they had nothing to say, which saddened him when they'd had lots to say before now. A canyon had formed between them, but neither were prepared to acknowledge its existence.

When her words sunk in, his heart flipped. Did she mean—?

"Maritimo Island," she elaborated, gesturing behind her as though it was only a few feet away. "It feels like a dream, doesn't it?"

He took her hands. "We'll always have the memories." He kissed her knuckles. "And remember, out of all these thousands of people, we were the only two who got to experience paradise."

He winked and she smiled. That was what he wanted to see. Her beautiful smile that lit up the entire world. If he had to live life without her, he hoped he'd forever remember her smile.

Yes, he was keen to get back to travelling and running from the past, but he'd miss this amazing woman.

His insides trembled. Panic formed and rose into his throat. Lungs suddenly couldn't get enough oxygen. There it was. The fear had returned with force. And to think he'd almost believed he was capable of being loved and *loving* someone! Who was he fooling? Not only himself, but Nikki too.

It was time to end this. *Now.* He gave Nikki's hands a squeeze and let them go.

"Nikki, I think—"

"So, I was thinking," Nikki said at the same time.

They laughed awkwardly and Gavin hated that it had come to this.

"How about we meet for dinner tomorrow night?" Nikki asked before he could talk.

One look confirmed it. Her eyes shimmered but no tears fell. Lips were pursed, shoulders tense, spine rigid. She knew but wasn't ready.

"Nikki—" he started but she shook her head.

"Not yet," she whispered. "Please. Just... just one more night."

He ran his hand over his head, huffing out a breath.

Kryptonite. Definitely. He couldn't say no because he had to face the truth. He didn't want this to end either. And that terrified him.

He really needed some space to think. To get his thoughts straight. To figure out what was going on because so much had changed.

"Okay, let's do dinner," he said before he could talk himself out of it. "Tomorrow night. I'll pick you up at your room at six."

A day of thinking and planning how to do this right while limiting the heartbreak as much as he could, should do the trick. Maybe he'd get his sister involved or at least get her advice. She was good at common sense.

Nikki's shoulders relaxed. "That sounds perfect."

He leaned in to kiss her cheek, letting it linger longer than necessary, so he could savour the softness and sweetness that was wholly her.

"I'll see you tomorrow, Nik."

She nodded in a daze, her eyes fluttering open. Her beautiful grey irises looked almost blue today and it took all his willpower not to kiss her again. But no, it was time to put some space between them.

With a final squeeze of her hand, he left her standing on the wharf as he approached the gangway and joined the queue of people waiting to board.

Chapter 24

S he *actually* begged.

Not Nikki's proudest moment. She wasn't that type of person, but Gavin made her do things she wouldn't normally do. Like kayaking, and swimming behind waterfalls, and snorkelling, and—

Begging.

Ugh. She was an idiot. She'd agreed to this stupid fling on the proviso she wouldn't fall in love, thinking she was smarter than that. Now look where she was. In love, heartbroken, and begging for one more night. The problem was, she hadn't prepared for the worst-case scenario and now she was flailing. Had no idea what to do with herself when it all ended.

"Idiot," she muttered to herself as she stepped into an elevator with a handful of other passengers and pressed the button to her deck.

She swallowed and blinked away the threatening tears. This was self-inflicted, and she didn't have the right to cry.

When she reached her room a few minutes later, she stopped outside the door and rummaged in her tote bag for the keycard. It was probably buried at the bottom since she hadn't needed it on Maritimo Island.

Her insides trembled. Yes, she'd secured that one more night with Gavin, but what good would it do? Bloody nothing. He wouldn't change his mind, of that she was certain, but she'd grab every last bit she could so she had something to remember him by. Greedy, that's what she was.

Her freefall had ended and she'd fallen… hard.

"Found it," she muttered under her breath, pulling the keycard out and swiping it.

The door unlocked with a click and she pushed on it. She took one step into her room when she heard her name called. The hairs on the back of her neck stood on end and she bristled. All thoughts of Gavin vanished. Four days without Katie's insults had been bliss. She was *not* ready for them now.

Turning, she opened her mouth to speak but snapped it shut again. Katie did not look her usual prim and proper self. Dark bags under her eyes. Oily hair that was stuck up in all directions. Shabby and stained clothes.

"You're actually here," Katie said, a wobble to her voice. "Where have you been?" Her eyes grew wide, and she stepped closer as though not believing Nikki was real.

"Why does it matter to you?" Nikki snapped.

Katie flinched and stopped. "I haven't seen you for four days. I was worried. I knocked on your door so many times." Her jaw twitched.

Nikki scoffed. "*You*," she pointed at Katie, "were worried about *me*?" then pointed at herself.

Katie's brow creased. "Of course, I was. You practically vanished."

Who was this person and what had they done to her sister? Nikki opened her mouth a couple of times but had no words. Shock had rendered her speechless.

"Mum and Dad weren't even worried," Katie said, affronted. "Said you were responsible and wouldn't do anything stupid." She shook her head. "Where *have* you been?" she repeated.

What the hell was going on? This whole situation was bizarre. Nikki wasn't prepared to deal with this side of Katie, so she did what she did best. Defaulted to defensive mode.

"Why does it even matter to you?" Nikki said. "Are you going to make fun of me again? Scoff at the things I do and the people I spend time with? Because that's what you usually do and having four days without your constant nagging and insults has been bliss."

The moment the words left her mouth, she pressed her lips together and looked away. It was like the sensors in her brain switched off. Standing up to Katie once had blocked them and now she blurted out whatever came to her.

"No." Katie's voice was barely above a whisper. "I told you I was worried."

Nikki looked back, confused, and nearly fell over. Katie was *crying*? It didn't make any sense.

A ball of guilt formed in her chest and Nikki sighed in resignation. "I'm sorry, I didn't mean to snap."

Katie ran her hands down her face. Her shoulders even slackened a little. "No... it's okay." She shook her head, her usual confidence gone. "Um... do... do you want to have dinner together? Like... tonight? Just... just the two of us?"

Nikki's jaw dropped. Had her disappearing off the face of the earth somehow made Katie a normal human again? Or perhaps it was from her standing up for herself? Maybe both. She didn't want to jump in and accept the metaphorical white flag, but she wasn't the old Nikki anymore. The new Nikki wanted to reconnect with her sister again, but on *her* terms. It would take a while to trust Katie again.

"I can't do tonight," she lied. "But perhaps we could do breakfast tomorrow?"

Breakfast was casual. It was their last island stop so Nikki had a perfect excuse for a quick escape if she needed it.

Katie nodded, a small smile on her lips. "I'd really like that."

Nikki nodded once then disappeared into her room without another word.

❧ ❦

After a shower, Nikki dressed into fresh clothes and sat on the edge of her bed. She took her phone out from the bedside cupboard drawer. The battery was flat, unsurprisingly. She put it on charge and waited a few minutes before turning it on. There was only one message from Monty with a photo of his identical twin daughters.

She sent a reply and sighed. Was this who she'd become? Until this cruise, her only real friend was her sister's husband. She had some school acquaintances, but they weren't friends as such. Meeting Gavin and reconnecting with Sophie had confirmed she hadn't been in a good place mentally. Rarely going out, never experiencing new things, living like a hermit. It was no wonder her life had spiralled out of control.

As much as she loved web design, it was probably the worst career path she could've chosen. It was isolating. Well, as of now she'd make her business mobile. It was time to branch out more. Meet more people, make new friends while maintaining current friendships, and she could do that *while* working.

Something shifted inside her. She felt... free?

This reminded her of Tenika, and she dug out her business card. Even though they still had to settle accounts, Nikki hoped this was the start of a new friendship. After sending an email, she checked the time, then put her phone away. Five p.m. The ship would depart in half an hour.

What to do now? She stood and paced the floor, jittery all of a sudden. Four days outside of her comfort zone had her eager to do more. Maybe she'd explore the ship. Find somewhere to eat. Nikki *had* missed out on four days of the cruise after all. She could drop in and say hi to her parents on the way. She hadn't seen any email reply from Mum, so it was likely they were none the wiser to her adventures.

Nikki was still baffled how Katie had noticed but her parents hadn't.

Slipping her feet into sandals, she left her room. First stop was her parents' room but they exited as she arrived, on their way to a fancy dinner. They greeted her exuberantly with cheek kisses and promises to catch up soon, then they were off as fast as they exited. Nikki's head spun as they disappeared, engulfed by other passengers.

She was thrilled for her parents, but this left her... lonely?

"Nikki? You're back?"

She turned to see Sophie coming out of a room. "Oh, hey! We got back about an hour or so ago."

Sophie grinned and came forward. They embraced. "I'm so happy to see you! I really want to hear all about it. Gavin's email communication skills are caveman level, and his email was so cryptic. Something along the lines of 'Phone waterlogged. Plane not here. Stuck. No big deal.'" Nikki laughed and Sophie just rolled her eyes. "I'm still on the clock, but are you free later? Like six-thirty?"

"Yeah, I'm free. I've got lots to tell you."

"Alright, got to run. I'll pop by your room." With a wave, she dashed off.

Left with her thoughts once again, Nikki continued walking and stepped out onto the deck to get some fresh air. They were still docked but the ocean stretched out before her. The late afternoon sun dropped in the sky. Nikki always loved the longer days of summer. The breeze was balmy, the sun warm on her skin.

It should've been beautiful, but all she could feel was sadness. It had dulled for a while, but now it returned with force. The reality of being back on the ship, the end of the cruise fast approaching, only made it grow heaver. It wasn't just because the holiday was ending, either.

It was because she'd lose Gavin too.

She'd been fully aware of the impending heartbreak but didn't realise *how* painful it would be. But she couldn't blame him. He'd laid the cards out and she'd accepted. Knew he was a traveller. A nomad. Afraid of love, afraid of staying in one place for too long. Afraid of *her*. Of the weight of the promises she wanted him to make, the promises he couldn't return.

Stepping up to the rail, she leaned over it slightly. The water lapped against the hull, reminding Nikki of the bungalow she'd shared with Gavin. Making love to him the first time in bed. Then the second time on the bungalow's deck.

She thought of his laugh. His smile. His golden-brown eyes. How happy and carefree he'd been on the island. Like he also experienced the same magic she had. That anything was possible. He'd held her like she was the only thing that mattered. He'd touched her as though worshipping every single inch of her.

But it'd been fleeting. He'd promised her one more night—*tomorrow night*—and she'd make it count. This heartbreak had to be worth something.

❧ ❧

Nikki sat back in her chair and sipped her cider. She'd just finished telling Sophie everything—yes, *everything*—and was exhausted.

"It sounds like a lovely place," Sophie said slowly, as though choosing her words carefully.

"It really was, you should visit." She took another sip of her cider and eyed Sophie over the bottle. "I can hear the 'but', Sophie."

She shook her head and tutted. "It's not a 'but' as such. It's just, I worry about you, Nik. I warned you about Gavin—"

"Must you do this?" Nikki asked with a sigh even though she'd brought up the 'but'.

"I'm your best friend, so *yes*." She held her hands up. "Fine, I get it. You're a grown woman and you can make your own decisions, even if they end up in devastating heartbreak."

Nikki nodded once. "Exactly. Thank you. And don't be mad at Gavin. I made this decision. He didn't force me."

"Hmm." Sophie narrowed her eyes but said, "So Maritimo Island, hey? You really think I should visit?"

Relieved to be moving onto safer topics, Nikki jumped on this. "Definitely *yes*." She sat up straight. "I happen to remember a certain *very* hot Fijian man there. Probably similar age to you." She smiled and drained the last of her cider. "Eric... Enrico..." She shrugged. "Sorry, I can't remember, but it definitely started with an 'E'."

Sophie raised her eyebrows but shook her head. "That's a big fat no. I've got baggage in the form of trauma, an ex-husband, and two kids. No sane man wants that and I'm not about to get involved with an *insane* man."

It was Nikki's turn to hold up her hands. "Okay, I hear you loud and clear. Men aside, I still think you should go when you can wrangle some time away again. Even just for a holiday. I hope to go back and see Tenika and Hamish. We could always go together."

Sophie hummed a response. "We'll see. So anyway, what are you up to tomorrow? I'm not scheduled to work until late afternoon and we have the final island stop. Perhaps we can do something together?"

"I'd love that, but it'll have to be after breakfast. I'm meeting up with Katie." A cold dread ran down her spine. Why did she have to choose the one thing Katie could criticise? Food. Ugh.

"Ooh, you're brave. Fill me in tomorrow." She yawned and checked the time. "I'm spent, Nik. Would you mind if we met at say ten-thirty? I wouldn't mind a bit of a lay in. My first time in months."

"That's fine. Let's meet on the wharf."

They said their goodnights and Sophie disappeared.

As Nikki made her way back to her room, the weight of the conversation with Sophie rested heavily on her shoulders. The excitement from the past few days had faded and was replaced with the dull ache of reality.

Gavin was slipping away from her and nothing would change that.

Chapter 25

Gavin had spent the last few hours wandering the ship, the hum of returning passengers buzzing around him like static. He was desperately trying to ignore the storm raging inside. His jaw ached from clenching it so tight, his stomach twisted in nauseating knots at the weight of everything. The memories, the emotions, the unspoken things between him and Nikki pressed down on him.

For the first time in his life, the thought of being tied down, the very thing he'd spent the last decade avoiding, seemed *right*. Maritimo Island had been the best few days of his life. He'd been everywhere, seen everything, but nothing compared to Nikki. The way she made him laugh, the way she lit up when she talked about things she loved, the way her eyes softened when they were together. She had him thinking thoughts he'd shut out for years.

He didn't do love. *Couldn't* do love. Yet, the word kept resurfacing like a splinter he couldn't pull out, but still deep enough to ache.

How did he tell her that? How could he be the man she deserved when he couldn't even figure out how to love himself? He'd spent years running from the ghosts of his past, memories that would haunt him more than he could bear. The last thing he wanted was to put Nikki in that line of fire.

And yet, she kept popping up in his thoughts. He wanted to reach for her, wanted to be near her, but the closer he got, the more his fear morphed into something darker, something that threatened to swallow him whole. Leaving was the only way to make it stop. He'd been stuck in one place for too long.

Only three days left. The rhythm of the countdown soothed his anxiety for a few blissful seconds. But then he noticed the familiar rush of excitement was gone. In its place was a cold dread. He didn't want to leave, and *that* terrified him more than anything.

He stepped out onto the deck, the ship's horn blasting as it set off. The sea stretched out endlessly before him, the warm, balmy air caressing his skin. The freshness of the ocean cleared the fog from his mind, but he still couldn't shake the unease gnawing at him.

He needed to talk to someone. Sophie was the only one who might understand, and she'd been waiting for him to face all of this for years. Could he really do it? Face the truth? Stop pretending everything was fine? Stop *running*?

His feet carried him toward his sister's room. His mind a whirlwind of uncertainty, but he couldn't ignore it anymore.

When he reached her door, he knocked once. Twice. But there was no answer. She'd be at work, he realised, so he sat on the floor, back against the wall, and let the minutes pass.

What had he become? Stuck, emotionally frozen, and the longer he stayed like it, the harder it was to break free. But that's what he did best, right?

Time passed in a blur as he sat with the weight of his own decision. When Sophie turned the corner and saw him, looking every bit as dishevelled as he felt, she stopped short.

He stood, a small smile tugging at his lips. "Hey, sis," he said, trying to sound casual.

Sophie's eyes narrowed as she strode towards him. "Don't 'hey sis' me. You got yourself stranded on an island?" She stopped in front of him, hands planted on her hips, wearing the face she reserved for when her boys were in trouble.

Gavin winced. "I sent you an email."

Her glare intensified. "You call that an email? Seriously, Gav, you're making me want to send you an instruction manual on how to communicate like an adult."

The tension grew in his chest. "You could've replied," he shot back, even though it was a pointless argument. He hadn't even checked his emails since.

Sophie didn't buy it either. "Why would I bother when I'd just get a similar response? You're the world's worst communicator." She tugged at her ponytail. "I've been worried sick about you." She poked his chest.

He winced and rubbed at the spot, guilt twisting in his stomach. Sophie's words stung. She was his only family, the only one who tried to help him, and all he did was shut her out.

He opened his mouth to apologise when Sophie looked at him hard. "What about Nikki? What's going on with her?"

He froze. The question hit him like a slap to the face. "What about her?"

"Don't play dumb. I saw her. We had dinner, and she told me everything."

His heart stuttered. "Everything?"

"Yes, *everything*. We're good friends, we do that. Maybe not all the details, but I know the gist of what happened."

His hands balled into fists. "Then you don't need to hear it from me."

She threw her head back in exasperation. "You're infuriating! I'm not just talking about what you did on the island, I—" She held her hands up and shook her head. "You know what? Don't worry about it." After taking a deep breath, she asked, "So what was it like then? The island, I mean."

"I thought Nikki told you everything?"

Her eyes hardened and she pinched the bridge of her nose. "I want to hear it from you, dumbo. So?"

He sighed and shook his shoulders of their tension. "It was nice. We had a great time, and I promise we didn't do anything stupid. I really think you'd like the place."

Sophie stared at him for a moment, then inclined her head to the door. "I need to shower and change. Come inside and tell me more."

He followed her into her room and sat in one of the two chairs next to a table as she disappeared into the bathroom. When she came out in fresh clothes ten minutes later, she sat on the chair opposite him.

"Alright, start from the top. I don't care if I've heard it, everyone has a different version of a story and I want to know your version of everything." She tucked one leg underneath her and turned to him.

He started from the top and as he did, he even opened up about his feelings for Nikki, a first for him. It was a relief to get it off his chest.

Still, he didn't reveal his deepest fears. The ones that told him he wasn't capable of loving anyone romantically. Or that they could ever love him. He honestly believed he was one of the minority who'd forever be lonely.

Once upon a time that life would've appealed to him, now it only made him sad. Oddly enough, he wanted to have a normal life, and he began to see that spending his life travelling and running from problems was far from normal.

"Wow," Sophie said when he'd finished. "That's quite an adventure."

"Tell me about it."

She eyed him sceptically, opened her mouth to speak but didn't.

"What is it?" he asked with a sigh.

She paused, then, "I'm worried about Nikki, Gav." She said it softly. "Please don't avoid my question. What are you going to do? You must think about it. I presume you won't declare your love and commit to a relationship?"

He glared at her, seeing exactly what she'd done. Trapped him into talking about his feelings before pouncing.

"That's not fair, Sophie," he snapped.

"It's very fair. This is *Nikki* we're talking about. We both care about her, and she deserves to be considered in all this. So?"

He let it hang in the air as he contemplated what to say. Sophie was right, but how was he supposed to answer?

"Is the idea of a committed relationship really that abhorrent?" Sophie asked when he was silent too long.

"It's not like we've had any shining examples. Mum and Dad deserted us and look at what Richard did to you?"

He tried not to think about what Nikki had said the night they stargazed.

Sophie's eyes softened and she shook her head. "Oh, Gav. Richard and I, we were so young. I don't think it was ever going to work. He was what I needed at the time, but we shouldn't have jumped into marriage the way we did. I don't regret having my boys, but I hate that they're being shuffled between two homes. As for Mum and Dad, they didn't desert us, they *died*. It wasn't their fault, you know that." She looked at him hard. "You *do* know that, don't you?"

He blinked. "I-I..." He shook his head and stood, running a hand down his face. This was why he'd come, to talk to Sophie, but now... he couldn't do it. "I don't want to talk about it," he whispered.

Sophie gave a sharp nod and sat motionless, her lips pursed in a thin line while he paced the small room with the walls closing in on him.

He needed to get out.

"I know what you're doing, Gav," Sophie said before he could leave. "With Nikki."

Cold fear clawed through his veins as he slowly turned to her. "Sophie, please drop it."

She didn't. "You're pushing Nikki away because you think you're not good enough."

He flinched as her words hit him square in the chest. She wasn't wrong but hearing it spoken out loud made the weight of it more suffocating.

"I'm not good enough for anyone." He flexed his fingers and started pacing again.

"Don't say that. You're plenty good enough, but you've got stuff to deal with."

Heaviness settled in his chest, and he stormed to the door. "I have to go."

"You can't keep running from this," Sophie said behind him.

He turned and smiled bitterly at her. "Watch me."

He heard her heavy sigh as he opened the door and disappeared into the hallway. Running, yet again, from a past that would haunt him if he didn't do something about it.

He'd come here to start on that path, but he failed at that too, just like he'd failed at everything else in his life.

Chapter 26

Early the next morning, Nikki knocked on Katie's door, fighting the desire to flee. She wanted to bridge the gap that had stretched between them for so long, but it was so much easier to stay angry than to be vulnerable again. Still, she planted her feet firmly on the ground. She wouldn't run away. Not this time.

The door opened and Katie appeared in her pyjamas. Her hair was dishevelled, her face had creases from sleep, but there was something different in her eyes. The challenging look Nikki had come to expect was gone. She looked more... human. Vulnerable.

This was *their* moment. They had an opportunity to wade through the debris of their tattered relationship and rebuild it. Family was important to Nikki, and even if she hadn't shown it in recent years, Katie was the same.

"Hi," Katie said, her voice softer than usual, almost tentative, like she didn't know how to speak to her anymore. Her smile was small, tight around the edges, but it held no bitterness. "I'm so sorry, I overslept." She rubbed her eyes. "How are you?"

Nikki hesitated, the weight of everything between them pressed on her chest.

"Um, I'm okay. You?"

Katie shrugged one shoulder. "I'm a little better than yesterday." Tears filled her eyes. "I, um… I need to get ready, and I need to message… Monty… uh, I mean Montgomery." Her brow furrowed, confusion clouding her face.

Nikki's heart lurched. It was the first time she'd ever heard Katie call him Monty. It was a small thing, but it spoke volumes.

"How about I meet you at the buffet?" Nikki offered, her voice unsteady.

Katie nodded. "Yeah, I should only be a few minutes behind you."

Nikki nodded and turned to leave, her mind racing, but then was struck with a thought. She spun around as Katie was closing the door. "Katie, wait. Do you want to check out Noumea for a bit after we dock? I've got plans from ten-thirty, but maybe we could spend an hour or so doing… stuff?" She shrugged and rubbed her nose.

It was so strange to stumble through small talk with someone who used to know her best. They weren't enemies anymore, but they weren't quite sisters again either.

"I'd really like that," Katie said.

Their gazes met and they shared a smile. Nikki breathed a sigh of relief. This may not be so bad.

With a wave, she turned and left.

At the buffet, the usual morning chaos of passengers filled the room. Smoky bacon and fresh bread filled the air, mingled with the conversation and clinking silverware. Nikki grabbed a plate, trying to ignore the nerves eating away at her stomach. The buffet line stretched in front of her, and she noticed the familiar pressure in her chest. Katie's voice, always criticising, echoed in her mind.

A part of her wanted to pull back, afraid of getting hurt again. But she had to take this risk if she was ever to get anywhere with Katie.

When she reached the Bain Marie she served herself bacon, eggs, hash browns, mushrooms and beans. Her mind wandered back to the last time Katie had made her feel small. Could they really move on from this? She tucked the thought away for now. That could only be answered once they'd made some progress. *If* they made any.

A moment later, with food in one hand and coffee in the other, she searched for a table. She wandered around for a few minutes, the smell of bacon wafting to her nose, making her stomach grumble. When no tables came free, Nikki gritted her teeth.

She seriously considered sitting on the floor when she spotted a couple a few feet away standing. She hovered close by as they dithered a bit, grabbed their dirty dishes, then walked away. Nikki ran to the table and slid into a seat before anyone else could steal it.

Grinning triumphantly, she placed her food and coffee down as her stomach gave another undignified growl. She picked up her cutlery when a voice next to her ear said, "Nice work. I saw someone else eyeing this table, but you left them for dust."

She turned, her gaze meeting Gavin's. He smiled and straightened. He looked good in snug-fitting jeans and a casual t-shirt hugging his muscled form, but he had bags under his eyes. And those eyes... there was something different about them today. Always happy and bright, today they were dim. Like he had the weight of the world on his shoulders.

"Hi," she said with a smile. "What are you doing here?"

"I was about to grab some brekky when I saw you. Mind if I join you?"

Before she could answer, Katie appeared with a bowl of oats, yoghurt and fruit, sitting opposite Nikki with a nod to Gavin.

"Sorry," Nikki said with an apologetic smile at Gavin, who looked confused. "The seat's already taken. Gavin, this is my sister Katie."

Katie nodded, her gaze distant, but she didn't offer a greeting. She merely dug into her food, casting a quick glance at Gavin with a cold expression.

Gavin leaned close, his breath warm against her ear as he whispered, "Do you have a sec?"

Nikki nodded, excused herself and followed Gavin out of buffet area.

"What's going on, Nikki?" Gavin asked once they were out of earshot, his voice tight. "You're not going to let her walk all over you again, are you?"

Nikki folded her arms across her chest. "I'm trying to fix things, Gavin. I have to give her a chance. I'm not giving up on her." Her voice wavered, but she cleared her throat. "I know she's been awful to me, but I need to know what's going on with her. I can't just walk away anymore."

Gavin ran a hand over his head. "You're too nice. You're putting yourself in a position to get hurt again. I don't like it."

Nikki felt a pang of hurt at his words, but she stood her ground. "How can someone be 'too nice'? She's my sister, and family means a lot to me. I'm not going to let this ruin us. I must try."

He stepped closer, his knuckles brushing her cheek. "No one should ever treat you like that."

Nikki closed her eyes, leaning into his comfort and the warmth of his touch. He always made her feel safe. "She never used to be like this," she whispered, looking up at him. "I just want my sister back."

Gavin gathered her in his arms, and she basked in the closeness, the security of his arms around her. But she knew that tomorrow it would all be over. The reality of their situation hung over them, unspoken but understood.

They pulled away. "Just don't let her get away with the insults anymore, okay? Be *you*. The beautiful, confident woman I know you are." He hesitated, then added in a softer voice, "Do what *you* want for a change. Experience life. Have fun. Even when it's hard."

His words hit hard, like they were his unspoken goodbye. Like he needed to get them out now in case he lost his nerve later.

Nikki's throat clogged and she nodded. "I'll see you tonight?"

Gavin nodded after a brief hesitation. "Yeah, I'll see you tonight." He leaned in to kiss her before disappearing into the restaurant.

When Nikki returned to the table, her heart heavy, Katie was still there, her food half gone.

She looked up when Nikki sat. "Where'd you get to?"

"Just chatting." She picked up her fork and speared a mushroom, popping it in her mouth, not caring that it was cold.

"That guy... he's the one from the first day, right? You seem close."

Nikki's spine stiffened and she managed a quick nod before continuing to chew so she wouldn't have to speak. When Katie didn't say anything else, she relaxed.

Cutting off some bacon, she added some egg and mushroom to it and popped it in her mouth.

"I don't know how you can eat that stuff," Katie's tone was accusing. "It's extremely fattening. You won't ever lose weight."

Nikki stopped mid-chew and glared at her sister.

Katie gasped, her face reddening. "Sorry." She dropped her gaze.

She just apologised for insulting me? This is progress! They ate in silence for the rest of breakfast, but Nikki couldn't stop smiling.

Chapter 27

Nikki had a skip in her step while she and Sophie walked in silence back to the ship after a day in Noumea. She still buzzed from the excitement, mingled with the quiet anticipation of what the night would bring. Even the impending heartbreak with Gavin didn't dull her mood. She would enjoy every single second of their last night together. She was high on life and the memories they'd made.

The ship came into view and Nikki glanced across at Sophie but noticed a worried frown on her friend's face. Sophie had been her happy-go-lucky self all day, so this change was unexpected. Sophie's gaze dropped to the ground, and she sighed.

"What's wrong?" Nikki asked, concerned.

"Nothing," Sophie said.

Nikki didn't believe her for a second.

Sophie suddenly came to a halt and grabbed Nikki's arm, forcing her to a stop too. "I forgot to ask you how this morning went with your sister."

"It went really well," Nikki said, surprised by *how* well. "We didn't talk a lot but when we did it was easy. No arguments, no tension, a few laughs even. It felt good. I feel like she's beginning to accept me as I am for the first time in years."

The time spent with Katie had been a turning point. Her sister, the person who'd been so critical of her for so long, was beginning to thaw. The fear and uncertainty were going nowhere fast, but Nikki lowered her walls a little. Just enough to give her the confidence to think about spending more time with Katie.

Sophie smiled but it didn't reach her eyes. "I'm glad to hear it, Nik. I hope she's genuine, because family's important." Her frown returned and her voice was flat.

Nikki felt the weight of Sophie's words and pressed once more. "C'mon, Soph, what's wrong? You can talk to me."

Sophie looked up at the sky before turning to Nikki, shoulders slumped. A tear slid down her cheek.

"It's not your ex giving you grief, is it?" Nikki pushed gently. "Or the kids?"

"No, they're all fine. I mean I miss the kids, but—" she sighed. "It's just Gavin. He's been back home for a year and after this cruise he'll leave again for God knows how long. He hasn't told the kids either. They love him and they'll be so shattered. He thinks they'll be better off without him."

Nikki's stomach twisted. She'd already known that Gavin's wanderlust and restlessness were part of him. She just didn't realise how they'd affected Sophie and the kids.

Sophie wiped a tear from her cheek. "I miss my brother so much, Nik. We used to be close, but he's so distant now. When he started travelling, it was like he stopped caring about me. He was so desperate to run away and forget about his life." She rubbed her temples. "He's got all this rage bottled up inside him and refuses to talk about it. I don't know what to do anymore." She tugged at her ponytail so hard she winced and rubbed her head.

Nikki slid her arm around Sophie's shoulders. "He hasn't forgotten you, Soph. If he had, he wouldn't have come home."

Sophie scoffed and shook her head. "He comes home because he has to. Not because he wants to. And when he's here, he's not really *here*, you know?" Her voice broke, emotion lacing every word.

Tears stung Nikki's eyes as Sophie's pain hit home. She was afraid of losing her brother the same way Nikki was scared to lose him, but for different reasons.

"Even this time," Sophie continued, her voice wavering, "he only came home so he could save for Las-bloody-Vegas. If he could spend the rest of his life travelling and not have to come home, he would. I wouldn't even be a passing memory."

Neither would I. Nikki winced at her own thoughts but shoved them aside. This was about Sophie, not her.

"Hey, don't be like that, Soph," Nikki said. "I don't believe it for a second. You might not remember your parents, but I can imagine losing them would affect you in ways you wouldn't expect. I think he runs because he doesn't know how to deal with it."

Silence. Then a small smile tugged at Sophie's lips. "That actually makes a lot of sense. I married too young, and you know how that turned out, but I think that was my way of coping at the time. Gavin's way of coping is to run away so he doesn't get hurt again." She sighed and rested her head on Nikki's shoulder. "I don't know how I've coped these last few years without you."

"Will you be okay?" Nikki asked.

Sophie sat up and shrugged. "I have to be, I just wish I could help but he's got to do this on his own terms and in his own time." She looked at Nikki, her brow creased. "What about you? I know his behaviour is the reason he's not committing to you. And let's face it, I'd love it if you were my sister."

Nikki's heart ached but she forced a smile. "We can still be sisters, Soph. And don't worry about me, I'm stronger than you think. I just want Gavin to be happy and if that's while he's travelling, then so be it." After a breath, she added. "You need to tell him how you feel."

Sophie scoffed. "What's the point? He's the most stubborn person I know, he'll just shut me out."

"I still think you should try. If he doesn't hear it now, he may never hear it. He deserves to know the truth. You're the only family he has."

Sophie shook her head and stood. "I don't think family means anything to him anymore, Nik." She shrugged. "Anyway, I better go if I'm going to make my shift on time."

Nikki nodded and stayed put while Sophie walked away.

After a few minutes, Nikki wandered back to the ship. The day's buzz had faded. So had the excitement for the night ahead.

At the gangway, she stopped when someone called her name. She saw her parents approaching, who looked so relaxed, carefree, and happy. Her spirits lifted at the sight of them and they greeted each other with hugs. They chatted about their travels so far, including Nikki's own adventures on Maritimo Island. She mentioned she visited with Gavin but spared any details about how involved they were. They didn't need to worry over something she had complete control over.

Do you?

She silenced the inner voice and boarded the ship with her parents, talking and laughing. When they reached their deck a short time later and stopped outside their room, Nikki was struck with an idea.

"Do you want to go out for dinner tomorrow night? I'll see if I can get Katie to join us. One last family hurrah before we dock."

Nikki had wanted another opportunity to spend time with her sister and this was the safest option. Hopefully this would be more successful. A do-over from their disastrous anniversary dinner. She winced at the memory.

"We'd love that," Mum said, and Dad nodded in agreement.

Nikki promised to organise a place and let them know. They parted ways and, on the way back to her room, Nikki knocked on Katie's door.

Katie appeared seconds later in a black one-piece swimsuit with a lime green, tie-dyed sarong around her waist. Her smile was bright, genuine even. "Hey, how was your day?"

"It was great, yours?" Nikki studied her sister closely.

Katie gestured to her attire. "Quiet, I just lounged by the pool."

Nikki nodded, smiling. "Do you want to join me, Mum and Dad for dinner tomorrow night?" She kept her tone light.

Katie's smile faltered, the familiar defensiveness Nikki had come to expect crept into her eyes as her gaze dropped to the floor. "Well, I don't know. I mean after—"

"Let's forget about last time, okay?" Nikki said and Katie's head jerked up, a hopeful look in her eyes. "This is a redo. No more awkwardness. Just family."

Katie's lips parted, the flicker of hope breaking through the mask she'd worn for so long. Then she smiled, stepped forward and wrapped her arms around Nikki in the first hug they'd shared in... *years*.

For a second, Nikki was frozen in place. Then she moved her arms and returned the embrace. Her mind raced with memories of the years they'd wasted, time they'd never get back, but the embrace wiped them away. This was a new beginning, and they were finally... *finally*... on the same page. Tears stung Nikki's eyes as she experienced a renewed closeness to her sister.

When Katie stepped back, she wiped underneath her eyes and Nikki blinked to stem her tears, albeit unsuccessfully. There was still an element of awkwardness between them, but it was different. No longer filled with bitterness or resentment.

"Thanks," Katie said, her voice trembling, "I'd really like that."

Nikki nodded. "I'll let you know the time and place." She almost said more, about how much this moment meant to her, but the words lodged in her throat.

Instead, she waved then turned and entered her room, her heart lifting with hope. She might not go home with the man she'd fallen for, but she might go home with a sister and she was more than okay with that.

Chapter 28

In the end, Gavin had done very little at the final island stop. He'd wandered through Noumea for a while, but it all felt hollow. Nothing new to see, nothing to capture his attention. He spotted Nikki and her sister at one point. They appeared more at ease around each other. There was warmth in their interactions and their body language was more relaxed.

He didn't interfere again. He'd had Nikki's best interests at heart when he found them at breakfast, but she claimed she knew what she was doing, so he gave them space.

Why did he care anyway? If Nikki got hurt, it wasn't his problem, right?

But deep down, he knew the answer. He *did* care so it became his problem because he didn't want her to get hurt.

She'd got under his skin, and he didn't know how to handle it. He'd spent the last few days with her, feeling things he'd never experienced before. His pulse quickened just thinking about her. Every second they'd spent together had been perfect, except for the parts where he'd tried to push her away.

Back on the ship, he wandered aimlessly around the decks, trying to shake the feeling of dread that had settled over him. Sophie's words from the night before looped in his mind. He tried to silence them, but they taunted him, reminding him of what he had to do.

One more night with Nikki, then it would all be over. He'd walk away. She'd understand. It was the right thing to do—for her sake, not his. If he stayed with her, their relationship would fail, and he'd only hurt her more.

Back at his room, he entered the shower. The thought of their last night together gripped him harder. What did he think would happen? One more night of passion, then disappear like he had with all the others before her? It had worked in the past. He'd always made it work. Erased them like they never existed. But the guilt now? Relentless. What a dick he'd been!

The reminder, yet again, of how his actions hurt others, hit hard. Women to him had been nothing more than pleasure toys. He never cared how they felt so long as they both got the pleasure they desired.

How many women had he hurt? Had he dismissed them rudely? Made them feel like trash? If he could go back and apologise to them all, he would.

And that was why Nikki was different. She was the first one to make him feel like this. Who made him question everything, to see his wrongs and want to be a better man. Do it right this time, even if it hurt like hell.

She deserved more than he could give—a flawed man running from his past, leaving a trail of hurt behind. Sophie was right! How had he not realised it sooner?

He had to speak to his sister again. Had to stop running from his emotions. She and her children were the only blood relatives he had left, and he had to nurture those relationships. Sophie wasn't happy and it wasn't just the breakup of her marriage. Gavin was certain he, too, was a factor, and it killed him to know he'd done that.

Family was important. Nikki had taught him that.

With a shake of his head, he finished showering and stepped out. His head spun with so many thoughts and emotions.

Once dressed, he left and wandered to Nikki's room. With each deck he navigated, the dread only grew. When he arrived, his hand hovered in the air, ready to knock but his resolve weakened. The thought of walking away and leaving her behind gutted him. But his sister had been right. He couldn't go on like this.

Nikki had changed him. Maritimo Island had changed him. Hell, even his own sister had changed him. In the beginning, he convinced himself there wouldn't be any heartbreak he had to feel guilty about, but he'd been so damn wrong. The guilt would never leave him. It was his punishment for all his past wrongs.

His mind was still clouded when he knocked, his thoughts racing a hundred miles an hour. He tried to focus on the words he had to speak. If he didn't, he'd cave. As much as he wanted that one more night like she did, he couldn't. Not this time.

Seconds later the door opened. Before losing his nerve, Gavin opened his mouth to speak, but the words died on his tongue.

Kryptonite.

His jaw slackened and he stood open-mouthed, staring at the beauty before him wrapped in a towel. Her hair had been piled messily on her head, but some long strands had escaped and clung to wet skin from a shower. Droplets of water glittered in the light, some dripping onto the carpet. This was *not* fair.

The world seemed to slow and all he could focus on was her.

Just one more night. The words came from somewhere deep inside him, a whisper of a hope he knew he should ignore.

"I'm so sorry!" Nikki's knuckles turned white from gripping the towel. "I lost track of time. I'll only be a few minutes. Do you want to come in?"

Kryptonite.

Gavin barely heard her. His mind had gone blank, his body betrayed him, heart pounding harder with every passing second. All rational thoughts disappeared. His fingers itched to touch her, to feel the warmth of her skin under his fingertips. He swallowed hard, trying to focus, but failing.

When Nikki called his name, he blinked and snapped his head up. She held her bottom lip between her teeth, a light blush colouring her cheeks. Gavin became all too aware of what he so desperately wanted to do.

When it registered what she'd said, he gave a single nod in response. Nikki released her lip and smiled, stepping back. His eyes never once left her when he stepped past, his breathing shallow.

She closed the door and turned back. "Are you okay?" Her voice was laced with concern, her grey eyes studying him.

His tongue refused to move, and his mind failed to form coherent words or thoughts.

"How about we start off with dessert?" he asked when he found his voice.

He saw the way her eyes sparkled, the subtle way her lips parted, heard her breath catch as her pupils dilated. She wanted him as much as he wanted her.

Gavin stepped closer and wrapped his arms around her, pulling her flush against him and breathing in her sweet coconut scent. She was intoxicating. He placed a soft kiss on her neck and she moaned, her body pressing against his.

He pulled the towel away and let it drop to the floor. Hands touching soft skin, he placed a kiss on the crevice between her neck and shoulder, causing her to shiver. She wrapped her arms around his neck.

Something inside him pushed through the haze, made him pause. He pulled back a fraction, his eyes searching hers, glinting with desire and want. "We shouldn't be doing this." The words came out in a whisper before he could stop them.

The brightness in her eyes dulled but she shook her head and held a finger against his lips. "Please don't say that. Just one more night. I promise I won't chase you."

His heart stuttered. Resolve crushed. There was no hope for him. He crashed his lips against hers and promised, without words, to give her what she wanted... what *he* wanted... one last time.

She was his kryptonite, but tonight he would break the addiction.

⁂

In the darkened room, Gavin lay awake with Nikki pressed up against him, the heat of her skin almost unbearable. He ached for her in ways he couldn't explain.

He could make out Nikki's curvaceous body, the sheet only covering her bottom half. Gavin remembered all too well how she felt and tasted, already craving her again. He'd forever crave her.

With the curtains to the balcony open, her milky skin was luminescent from the waning moonlight. Gavin's fingers twitched, wanting to wake her so they could make love one more time. But he didn't dare.

This time, one more night *had* to mean one more night.

He moved away, coolness filling the space between them. He should walk away *now*. Leave her during the night like he'd done with so many others.

Although it was different this time. He didn't want to leave, but he had no choice. He was way too broken for her.

Gingerly moving his legs over the side of the bed, he glanced around for his clothes. Once he'd identified where everything was, he rose slowly, careful not to move the bed and grabbed each piece.

While he changed, he took one last look at Nikki. Couldn't help himself. Her long hair splayed across the pillow. A slight flush coloured her cheeks as she slept, lips parted as she breathed slow and steady. His gaze lingered, tracking the curve of her body.

He forced himself to turn away. The weight of what he had to do settled like lead in his stomach. He slipped on his shoes then stood and advanced to the door. Stopped.

It wasn't right leaving like a ghost in the night. He couldn't offer her a future, or stability, but he could at least say goodbye.

Spotting a pen on the desk, he grabbed it, then sifted through the information folder until he found a pamphlet with a blank back page and started writing. He'd never been one to leave notes. Wasn't the best at writing his thoughts down, as Sophie herself could account for after his terrible emailing skills. But tonight, the words flowed easily.

When he was done, he placed the pen back on the desk and sat for a long moment. The note was heavy in his hand. He didn't reread it, not ready to come face to face with his raw emotion. Just placed it on the pillow next to her, then stopped. Stared at her one last time. The ache in his chest tightened. Her peaceful face was a cruel reminder of everything he was walking away from. It felt like abandoning something precious, something that had made him feel alive for the first time in years.

The reality of what he had to do crashed over him like a wave, leaving him breathless. A lump formed in his throat. Tears burned at the back of his eyes, but he refused to let them fall. He didn't have the right to cry for himself, not after all the damage he'd caused. He'd changed so much because of Nikki but accepting the changes was the hardest part. Gavin still wasn't sure if he would. Or *could*.

Swallowing hard and blinking rapidly, he gathered up enough strength to turn and leave. Didn't once look back. It was the hardest thing he'd ever done. With each step closer to the door, his feet grew heavier, dragging on the carpet, and his shoulders hunched further forwards. When he made it into the hallway, he became all too aware of his pounding heart, heavy in his chest, almost like it'd been replaced with a millstone.

But at least he'd done it. He'd walked away.

Chapter 29

The next morning when Nikki woke, she knew Gavin had left. Sensed there was no one next to her and her heart was heavy. For a few seconds, she indulged in the daydream that perhaps he was in the shower. Or maybe he'd snuck out for breakfast and would come back.

But she was a realist. Still, she kept her eyes closed, wanting to relish in those last memories for a few more minutes. Of their last mind-blowing night together.

And, oh it was. Mind-blowing, that is. It was as though they were both saying goodbye without words.

She had no regrets.

Despite the heaviness in her heart, it still raced at the memory of their night together. His touches were soft, gentle, electrifying, leaving her skin to sizzle like a wildfire. She memorised his tattoos again, never wanting to forget them. She'd never been a tattoo gal, but she loved that all of Gavin's either had a story or a memory of a place.

Would he get a new one after this trip?

Do. Not. Go. There.

She stretched her arms and legs with a groan, then let her eyes flutter open as they adjusted to the morning light. A loud growl emanated from her belly, reminding her they'd skipped dinner, too caught up in each other to care.

Half sitting up, she checked the time first—eight-thirty a.m. Not too bad. With only two days left, both at sea, she couldn't wallow. Lots to do and so little time.

She fell back and splayed her arms out, replaying everything. Not just from last night, but from their time on Maritimo Island too. She felt like a new woman, like she'd transformed somehow. Old Nikki was a thing of the past. Oh, she knew her insecurities and self-deprecation wouldn't disappear that quickly, but she had better control over them.

Thanks to Gavin. And Sophie. Two people who took up so much space in her heart. She loved them both on different levels. One she'd remain friends with forever. The other, well, there was nothing else to say.

Something fluttered down off the second pillow and touched her arm. She turned, her heart skipping at the empty space even though she knew it would be, then she spotted the pamphlet. It was an advertisement for a restaurant. Did he want to meet her there? Then she noticed the indents from a pen.

Sitting up, she pulled the covers over her chest, her heart leapt into her throat as she turned it over and read his messy scrawl.

Nikki,

This is the hardest thing I've ever had to do. This was meant to be a fling, but it turned into so much more. Way more than I can handle, but I need you to know how much I care about you. How much I wish I could give you what you deserve.

You see, you and me, we're oceans apart. I'm a man who likes to travel, who breaks out in a cold sweat at the word 'commitment' and who gets bored staying in one place for too long. You're a woman who wants to settle down with the right man and start a family and you should be allowed to live that dream.

While we were on Maritimo Island, I felt alive for the first time ever, and even wondered if I could be that man. Dreamt of it even. I've never let anyone get this close. It was both terrifying and thrilling in ways I never thought possible. You made me feel things I didn't think I was capable of.

But I've got too much baggage, Nikki. I'm broken. I've spent my adult life running from things that scare me and I don't know how to stop. If life could stay as simple as it was on the island, I wouldn't be walking away right now. But reality isn't that simple and I'm not the man you need.

Don't think I regret a moment of our time together because I don't. You made me so happy, and we had fun. Thank you.

Goodbye, Nikki, and again, I'm sorry.

Gavin

Nikki held the note against her chest as her eyes fluttered closed, tears escaping from beneath her lashes. She knew this was coming. Had even begged for one more night. *Twice* if she counted last night when he arrived at her room.

Yet it didn't ease the pain. His note cut deep because from what she understood from Sophie, this was unlike Gavin. He'd even admitted that he ran from things that scared him, and Sophie had said he lacked communication skills. So, this had to mean something. He cared. She knew that without a doubt.

But not enough to make things work. That was what hurt the most.

An ache in her chest grew, the heartbreak already tearing her apart, bit by bit. She didn't have time to wallow. She had a table to book for dinner and a relationship to fix with her sister, but she'd allow herself an hour. After placing the pamphlet on the bedside cupboard, she set the alarm and laid back down pulling the covers over her head.

Her earlier hunger pangs disappeared and instead, an uncomfortable knot settled in her stomach. Her body shook with silent sobs as endless tears cascaded down her cheeks, wetting the sheet beneath her. She pulled her knees up to her chest and wrapped her arms around them. Their fling was always going to end. She *knew* getting involved would hurt, but she had no idea it would be this bad. It was as though someone had reached into her chest and ripped her heart out.

If this was what love was meant to feel like, she didn't want it.

※

T he alarm's snooze sounded for the third time. Nikki slid her arm out from under the covers and reset it again.

Come on, girl, you need to snap out of this. Things to do remember?

Nikki snuggled further into the darkness of the bedcovers. Gavin's scent lingered, breaking her heart all over again. She'd convinced herself she'd be fine, that she could deal with the heartbreak like all the others she'd endured. Oh, how naïve she'd been. This was *nothing* like the others.

First, she and Gavin weren't in a relationship. Second, she'd never been in love with any of her previous boyfriends. She'd never understood the difference between loving someone and *being* in love with them. Now she did, and the pain was bordering on unbearable.

Her eyes were sore from crying but she'd long since stopped. It'd been a long, self-pitying hour, but now she really needed to get a move on.

Her stomach growled again but the thought of food nauseated her. She squeezed her eyes shut again but her mind played a cruel trick by replaying every heated and sensual moment she and Gavin had shared. With a groan, she pushed the covers back with force and lay on top of them, staring at the ceiling.

To torture herself further, she questioned his fear of commitment. What if his travels allowed Gavin to do some soul-searching? What if he saw a therapist and got some help? What if, after getting help, he came back to her and they could have a life together?

She clutched her hair in frustration. The 'what ifs' would kill her. She was only fooling herself. Sophie had made it clear Gavin could forget anything he didn't want to confront.

The alarm sounded again, and she forced herself into a sitting position. She swung her legs over the side of the bed and turned the alarm off. Progress. She tapped the screen to check for any calls or messages. Nothing. Monty was awfully quiet, but Nikki suspected he coped the best way he knew how. Working and spending time with his daughters. She flicked off a quick text to say hi, then checked her emails.

There were three from Tenika. One was in reply to her email and an invoice of monies owed for their stay. Tenika had asked if she and Gavin were going to split the costs, and that she could split the invoice if needed. Nikki didn't even think about that, and after viewing the invoice, which was not as extravagant as she'd expected, Nikki chose to pay the full amount.

The second email was an e-vite to Tenika and Hamish's wedding in three months' time. Nikki's heart stuttered but she RSVP'd immediately. It was a no brainer. She wouldn't miss it for the world. Who knew where she'd be in three months, but she wasn't intending to still be wallowing.

Then the third email made Nikki's breath catch.

Do you have Gavin's email address? Hamish wants to invite him to the wedding too, but in the mad rush of you two leaving, he missed seeing Gavin.

Nika

"Damn it," Nikki muttered under her breath.

She *didn't* have Gavin's email since they'd never exchanged contact details. This wasn't a problem per se as Tenika knew the basics of their not-really-a-relationship. Nikki could reply saying she didn't have his email and that they couldn't invite him, but that would be mean and petty. Which brought the real issue to the fore: she had to find Sophie to grab Gavin's email, which meant telling Sophie what happened. *Then* she had to see Gavin in three months' time. Presuming he accepted the invite. Either way... *awkward.*

She shook her head. That was something her future self would deal with. For now, she put her phone away. She'd reply to the email later too. As she stood, her eyes landed on the pamphlet that Gavin had written on. The Italian restaurant looked nice, so she followed the instructions to book a table. Since she left it so late, she half expected all the tables to be booked but was surprised to snag one for later in the evening.

With that sorted, she phoned her sister's room, then her parents to share the details for the evening. Finally, she made it to the shower. Under the hot needles, her mind cleared and her lethargic body gained some life. Her heavy heart, while it would always have a piece missing, gave a little flutter of excitement. She had a whole future ahead of her now.

Steam filled the bathroom, swirling as it was sucked into the exhaust fan. It reminded her of freedom, something she'd lost but found again. It was likely her heart would never fully heal. Gavin would always own part of it, but she wouldn't die. After all, she'd experienced true love, something a lot of people never did.

⟡⟡⟡⟡ ⟡⟡⟡⟡

After a day exploring the ship, even making time for a Broadway-style live show, she returned to her room rejuvenated to get ready for dinner. There was still heaviness in her heart but keeping busy helped.

While she dressed and redid her hair, nerves fluttered in her stomach. The memory of the failed anniversary dinner was fresh in her mind. To prove she didn't hold a grudge, she even wore the same dress. This did nothing for her nerves. Katie's harsh words still floated through her mind sometimes, but Nikki refused to let it control her. It was a test of sorts, to see how genuine Katie really was.

Once ready, she made her way to the restaurant, weaving in and out of people who were enjoying the last couple of days onboard. A smile tugged at her lips, and she had a bounce in her steps. Excitement surged through her veins at great things to come.

She continued walking, humming under her breath. On the deck where the restaurant was, she slowed and kept her eye out for it. When she spotted the sign, she moved towards it but stopped suddenly when, a few feet away, she saw Gavin. He saw her at the same time and also stopped. She shivered as his gaze took her in from head to toe.

In her mind, she ran into his arms and kissed him senseless. In reality all she could do was stare. Her breath hitched, fingers itched in anticipation, wanting to repeat their night together.

She snapped out of her reverie when Gavin stepped closer, stopping in front of her. There was something different about him. Mouth downturned in a deep frown. Shoulders slumped. Eyes lacking their usual shine. All in all, he appeared downright miserable.

Her hands balled into fists at her sides. He was so damn stubborn. There were so many things she wanted to say, but she couldn't form words. Nothing she said or did would change a thing.

"Hi," he greeted, his voice hoarse.

"Hi." Her own voice sounded a few octaves higher.

Silence.

"You look great," he said.

"Thanks." She twirled a strand of hair around her finger. "I'm meeting Mum, Dad, and Katie for dinner." *Why are you telling him this?* Backpedalling, she asked, "Uh, are you going somewhere?"

Gavin ran his hand along his head. "Yeah, I am." He glanced at his watch and smiled apologetically. "I'm actually running a bit late."

Another woman?

She gritted her teeth. Why did her mind think such things. He wouldn't be that heartless, would he?

She shook the thoughts from her head and stepped aside. "Sorry, I won't keep you."

Maybe you should tell him how you feel. This could be your only chance.

Gavin forced a smile, then walked past. She breathed in his woodsy scent, the same one that still lingered in her bed.

Tears stung her eyes, and her shoulders sagged. She couldn't think of anything sensible to say. When she went to proceed to the restaurant, something occurred to her.

She spun around and called out to Gavin. He turned.

Walking over, she said, "You should speak to Sophie."

His eyebrows drew together. "Why?"

Nikki considered how to answer without betraying Sophie's trust. "It's not my place to say." Pushing him in the right direction would have to do. "But please trust me on this. She really needs to talk to you."

Gavin nodded slowly. "Okay, I'll chat to her soon."

Nikki released a breath of relief. "Thanks." Another awkward silence followed.

"Nikki!"

Katie and her parents appeared next to her and Nikki's heart leapt into her throat. Could this get any more awkward? Although the first thing Nikki noticed was that Katie was beaming like a weight had lifted off her shoulders. She wore a beautiful red dress and her hair was immaculately styled.

"Oh hi," Nikki said, smiling awkwardly at Gavin, who stood just as uncomfortably a couple of feet away. "Um, I'll be there in just a moment, okay?"

Her parents nodded and left but Katie hung back, glancing from Nikki to Gavin a couple of times. "You okay?" she asked for Nikki's ears only.

Nikki swallowed and nodded, willing the threatening tears not to spill. She wasn't used to Katie's concern. "Y-yeah, I'll be there in a moment."

Katie studied her once more, then nodded, casting one last glance at Gavin. "You look beautiful, Nikki," Katie said, then hugged her briefly and dashed off to the restaurant.

Oh God. Nikki blinked away tears. Her chest ached from holding them back but she had to do this. Just for a couple more hours.

"Sorry," she said, turning to Gavin and forcing a smile. "Um, I guess I'll see you around?"

As soon as she said it, she realised how stupid it was. With only a day left, he'd be leaving for Las Vegas soon after their return to Sydney.

Gavin winced. "Probably not."

"Oh. Right. Of course." Nikki hung her head to hide the pain she knew was in her eyes.

The note was clear: this was goodbye. She'd already promised she wouldn't chase him, but she hadn't considered they might bump into each other. Now that she had, she didn't know how to act. The ease of being around each other was gone.

She forced one more smile, then turned back toward the restaurant, shoulders straight, head held high, eyes brimming with tears. Her mind screamed at her to do or say something. It was her only chance to say her own goodbye, but the words in her head were a jumbled mess. Instead, she continued walking, sensing Gavin's eyes on her.

The closer she drew to the restaurant, further away from him, the heavier her feet became. Her body told her to say something, but her mind refused. Eventually, she came to a complete stop. Slowly turning, she found he hadn't moved, a strange look on his face. It was almost like he too was having an internal battle.

Just do it.

She pushed all her doubts aside and ran up to him. Without a second thought, she threw her arms around his neck and kissed him with all the passion she could muster. Gavin's arms wrapped around her waist and he reciprocated. The world around them disappeared and it was just the two of them. Her body vibrated with emotion, every single nerve ending sparking alive.

Even though this was their goodbye kiss, it strengthened her. He became her air and this the breath of life. While they'd never be together, he'd always be a part of her. That tiny part of him would keep her alive and encourage her to do things she was once too afraid of. He'd taught her to live again.

Finally pulling away, Nikki stared into his eyes, now shining brightly. Breathing heavily, she whispered, "I love you," then fled to the restaurant.

Chapter 30

Gavin couldn't move. Hell, he could barely breathe. All he could do was watch Nikki disappear with his mouth hanging open.

I love you.

The three words Nikki almost spoke on the island were out in the open. Three words he'd always thought were meaningless. In an instant, they changed his entire life. Shattered his heart. Left him wanting to blubber like a baby.

No one had ever said them to him before. Not even his sister. For so long, he didn't think he was capable of being loved or able to love anyone. Even now, he didn't know if he loved Nikki. He wanted to, so damn much, but was so messed up he had no clue.

After a few moments, he realised he hadn't moved. People walked around him, some bumped into him, but he was numb. He blinked a couple of times, slowly coming back to reality. He didn't really have anywhere to go. He only said so because he didn't want to come across as a pathetic loser.

In the end, he wandered until he found a bar. He sat there for hours drinking neat whisky, trying to forget about Nikki.

It didn't work.

Her beautiful features were fixed in his mind and those three words continued to ring in his ears. By the time he left at midnight, he felt like a steamroller had run over him. He didn't have the energy to lift his shoulders, so they stayed slumped. The dull ache that'd formed only grew, and when he walked, he couldn't lift his feet.

He rubbed his tired eyes. Perhaps a good night's rest would help. Although when he reached his deck and found Sophie standing by his door, he knew sleep would be a long way off. For once, he didn't mind. He'd bottled his emotions up for too long, he'd reached bursting point. It was time to offload onto someone he trusted.

Sophie looked his way when he approached. She didn't look happy either. She hadn't for... a long time.

"Bloody hell, you look like crap," Sophie said when Gavin stopped in front of her. She held a palm against his forehead. "You don't have a temp." She leaned in closer, eyes narrowed and sniffed. "You've been drinking, haven't you?"

"She loves me."

Sophie stared at him. "What? Who?" Her eyes widened. "Ooh, you mean Nikki."

Gavin nodded.

Sophie released a breath and ran a hand through her hair. "You're in deep now, Gav."

"I've ended things."

Sophie's eyes turned dark. "If you've hurt her, I swear I'll castrate you."

Gavin smiled weakly and shrugged. "I ended things last night. I saw her today and that was when she told me she loved me. She can't be too hurt, right?"

Sophie gave him a deadpan look. "You men are so oblivious." She glanced down the hallway and mused. "I should see if she's okay."

"She'll be asleep."

Sophie turned back. "So, what? I can wake her."

Gavin smiled. That was exactly what Sophie would do. "Speaking of which, why aren't you asleep? Why are you here?"

"I was bored and I'm not tired. Besides, it's not every day I travel with my brother." She heaved a heavy sigh, then turned away. "Anyway, I guess I'll see you—"

"Wait," Gavin grabbed her arm. "I want to talk to you."

Sophie turned back, her eyebrows raised in surprise. "You want to talk to... me?"

Gavin winced. "Yeah. Well... it's just, when I saw Nikki before she said you needed to talk to me. She didn't elaborate but I got the impression something was bothering you. And, well, I've noticed you've been a bit off." He rubbed the back of his neck. Usually, it was Sophie who brought up these topics and he'd ignore her.

"Oh." Sophie's eyes widened, and she turned painfully quiet.

He wished so much he could change how he'd handled things. Taken more time to be a supportive brother, the same way she'd always been so supportive of him. For so long he took her for granted. In his eyes she was Super Woman, the go-to person, a pillar of strength. She did everything without complaint. Even when she and her husband split, and then divorced, Sophie still held everyone up.

Then he recalled that one day, only a few months ago, when he'd stumbled across her crying in the kitchen after she lost her job. Richard was paying child support, but it wasn't enough to cover all expenses.

As she was still out of work, she'd hidden away so as not to upset her sons. Gavin could've consoled her, *helped* her, but he hadn't. He'd walked on by, not wanting to get involved. Not *caring*.

How many other times have I seen her like this but ignored it?

It was time to fix this. But how? Despite all his years of travelling he still had little life experience. Never had to deal with this sort of thing before. Now he'd been thrown in the deep end, and it was *his* turn to take control and be the rock Sophie had always been.

"Sophie," he said when she remained silent, "talk to me, please." He placed a hand on her arm. For the first time ever, he *wanted* to talk to her. Help her if he could. It was the least he could do after all the times he'd ignored her.

Her eyes filled with tears. One dripped down her cheek, followed by another, and another. Then she burst into tears and fell against him. Gavin wrapped his arms around her. Once upon a time, he wouldn't have known how to console her. It seemed Nikki had taught him something else.

Gavin looked up when he heard voices. A group of people walked towards them. He gently prised Sophie away. "We should go inside."

She looked up and nodded, wiping her cheeks. Gavin unlocked the door and let her in. He followed and locked up behind him.

"Do you want to talk about it?" Gavin coaxed.

Sophie's shoulders sagged in defeat. "I don't want you to go to Las Vegas."

Gavin didn't know what to expect, but not that. He tried to speak, but all he could do was open and close his mouth.

"What can I say?" Sophie gave him a watery smile. "I've got used to you living with us. The kids will miss you terribly." She laughed weakly and wiped fresh tears away. She sighed and threw her arms up in the air. "I'd hoped Nikki wouldn't say anything to you. I was going to leave it."

Gavin frowned. "Why?"

"Because I didn't think you'd listen. You don't pay attention to anything that doesn't affect you. All you're worried about is your next travel destination. I'm just a convenience. Free accommodation, free food, free Wi-Fi. It's like I'm not even your sister, but *I* was the one who held your hand when Mum and Dad died."

Fragments of memories came back in snippets while Gavin stared at his sister, speechless. His heart broke knowing she felt this way and he'd never known. Never took the time to find out. Deserted her and only focused on himself.

Years of travelling had eroded away any memory or emotion he might've once held around his parents' death—exactly what he'd hoped would happen. But those snippets turned into full-fledged images of that fateful day.

He and Sophie were only eight years old. They were at school, and he remembered being called into the principal's office. He didn't know what he'd done wrong, and other kids laughed at him. When he saw Sophie there too, next to an older woman, the social worker, he knew something was wrong.

The social worker was tall and imposing. She told them their parents had been in an accident and died instantly. Sophie had stood next to him, holding his hand. He was terrified but his sister's strength had sustained him. Through all their years in foster homes, she'd never left his side. Yet *he'd* disappeared the moment he had the opportunity.

It was a painful reminder of who he'd become. Sophie had lost parents too, but *she* hadn't run away. He had to speak, had to say *something* to prove he'd changed. That he cared about her.

"Am I not good enough?" Sophie asked when he'd been silent for too long. She gave him a pleading look, tears trickling down her cheeks. "Do I mean nothing to you? What is it, Gavin?"

What could he say? She was his sister. Of course he cared, but putting his feelings into words was impossible. They never came when he needed them.

Sophie being in such a state reminded him once more of how important family was. After his parents' death, he'd assumed family held no meaning anymore. A sister never seemed to have the same importance. He'd been so wrong.

Memories of Nikki returned for what felt like the millionth time. She'd changed him so much and probably didn't even realise it. The three words she spoke only hours earlier ran through his head again, making his heart pound. Despite his flaws, she'd still fallen in love with him. He didn't deserve her love, but having it made him want to be a better man.

He stared at Sophie. Her crestfallen face shattered his heart. If he didn't speak soon, he'd lose her too. He couldn't lose Nikki *and* his sister in one night.

He opened his mouth to speak, but the words lodged in his throat. His chest heaved up and down. He ran his hands down his face, trying but failing to talk. His eyes stung and seconds later big, fat tears dripped down his cheeks. Real, full-blown drops. It was the first time he'd cried in... Hell, he didn't know. Had he cried after his parents died?

Like a dam bursting, he gave way to them. He felt like the biggest sissy in the world. His knees gave way and he landed in a heap on the floor, sobbing like he'd never done before. Leaning against the door, he pulled his knees up and buried his face, embarrassed at his weakness. He sensed a presence next to him but didn't move. A moment later, the consoling arm of his sister rested across his shoulders. He leaned closer and placed his head on her shoulder, his tears unrelenting.

He had no idea how long he cried for, or how long they sat together. By the time he stopped, silence filled the room and his backside was numb. He couldn't move, though. All he could do was stare into his room, lit by a lamp on the bedside cupboard.

When Sophie shifted next to him, he looked across. Her eyes were rimmed red and shone with tears. Had they ever cried together? Again, he didn't know. What he *did* know was that this moment had drawn them closer.

"I'm sorry," he whispered. Everything was so eerily quiet, normal voices felt too loud. "For everything."

Sophie removed her arm from across his shoulders and instead looped it through his and rested her head on his shoulder. "Don't be. I'm sorry I made you cry."

He gave a weak laugh. "I'm glad you did. I had no idea you felt that way."

She shrugged "I never wanted to tell you. You're extremely stubborn, you know?"

He breathed out and laid his legs flat in front of him. "Yeah, I know." He wasn't proud of it. He added it to his growing list of things to work on. Stubbornness wasn't always a good thing. His own sister couldn't confide in him and that was wrong.

He moved away and stood. Sophie stood, too, and they stared at each other. He was so fortunate to have her in his life.

"I don't know what's wrong with me." He looked away. "I must have a screw loose."

Sophie laughed. "No, you don't. I think you just need to stop bottling up your emotions. Did you know, you never once cried after Mum and Dad died?"

He turned back to her. That answered his earlier question. "I didn't?"

She shook her head and smiled sadly. "Neither did I."

They were the only words Gavin needed to hear to realise her strength and the portrayal of being able to do everything was a façade. An act, so Gavin wouldn't have to worry about her. His heart squeezed tighter. He was so proud of her. He pulled her into an embrace. Breathing in her scent, he caught a faint whiff of lavender. It reminded him of their mother. How had he never noticed it before?

He tightened his arms and said, "Maybe it's time to listen to your own advice. You shouldn't bottle up your emotions, either."

Sophie pulled away and looked up him, a large smile on her face. "Maybe you're right."

"I know I am." He grinned but it felt forced. Instead, the ache in his heart grew.

Nikki.

Her name was a whisper in his mind. Even though he'd seen her a few hours earlier, he missed her already. There was no way he'd ever forget her, no matter how much he told himself he should for the sake of his sanity.

As if reading his mind, Sophie said, "I was worried, you know?"

He looked at her curiously.

"About you and Nikki. I was worried you'd hurt her. Perhaps you still have, but she's strong. I know she'll pull through. Now I realise you two were meant to meet."

Gavin's heart leapt. "Why?"

"She made you human again." She laughed. "And you gave her the confidence she'd lost. Even though it hasn't worked out, you've helped each other."

Gavin mulled this over. "I suppose you're right."

"I know I am." Sophie said with a wink and puffed out her chest.

"Don't get too inflated." Gavin poked her arm.

Sophie grew serious. "Can I give you some advice?"

Gavin looked at her warily but nodded.

"I can't believe I'm about to say this." She sighed. "I don't want you to go away but I think you need to. You're a good guy, Gav but you need to figure yourself out. You've been running for too long."

"I'm not running—" He heaved a sigh and ran a hand down his face. "Well, damn, old habits die hard."

Sophie burst out laughing and Gavin joined her. They laughed until their sides hurt and tears leaked from their eyes. It was the hysterical sort of laughter that only came about after a good cry.

"Oh, Gav," Sophie said a few minutes later with a wistful sigh. "I'll miss you when you leave."

"Me too." They were the most natural words he'd ever spoken.

Sophie left not long after, declaring she'd cried too much and needed to sleep.

Left alone, Gavin was faced once more with the agitation of leaving for his holiday. His stomach churned. He had always been drawn to Las Vegas because of bright lights, the women, the gambling. It was supposed to be the holiday of a lifetime. But now, it was like a new person inhabited his body because none of those things appealed anymore. He wanted to be close to his sister, so he could support her and her family. He wanted to be close to Nikki and, to his astonishment, build a life with her.

So, that was exactly why he'd take Sophie's advice. He was sick and tired of being terrified of the future. Of running from reality. He wanted to know if he could love a woman romantically. Hell, he wanted to love Nikki. But what if he was a lost cause?

There was only one way to find out.

Chapter 31

When Nikki woke the next morning, her eyes were bleary, and her entire body was heavy. Dinner had been lovely. They'd been a *real* family for the first time in years, but Nikki still held onto so much emotion she couldn't release.

No regrets though. Gavin needed to hear those words, and she was happy she could tell him how she felt. It had been torture holding it back. She'd run because she couldn't bear never hearing them said back to her.

Sleep was restless. Dreams filled with Gavin, reliving their beautiful moments.

It took enormous strength to pull herself out of bed, but it was the last day of the cruise and she wanted to make the most of it.

After a shower and changing into fresh clothes, she readied to leave when there was a knock at her door. Sophie stood on the other side, dressed for work. The look on her face told Nikki she knew what happened.

"Yes, I'm fine," Nikki said before Sophie could ask.

"How did you know what I was going to ask?"

"Because I'm not stupid. If you've spoken to Gavin, he would've told you everything."

Sophie's eyebrows drew together. "Are you sure you're okay?"

Nikki plastered on her most believable smile. "Of course, I am. It was only a fling, right? I'm a better person for it."

"Bull crap. I agree you're a better person, but don't pretend you're okay when I know you're not."

"But I really am. I'm not cooped up in my room for days on end, am I?"

"No, but what about telling Gavin you loved him last night?"

Nikki's eyes widened. "He told you?"

"Yes." A large smile spread across her face. "We had a really good chat for the first time in forever."

Nikki couldn't be happier for her friend. "What happened to his stubbornness?"

"He's still stubborn, but he listened." She paused, then added, "Look, Nikki, I want to thank you for suggesting he talk to me." Sophie's eyes shimmered. "We both needed it."

"Is... is he still going away?" Nikki had to ask even though she didn't want to know the answer.

"Yes."

Nikki's shoulders slumped. She'd selfishly hoped he wouldn't go. Even if they had no future, at least if he lived in the same city she'd see him from time to time.

"I told him to go," Sophie added.

"Why?"

"Because he needs to figure himself out, Nik. I think he's beginning to see he has bigger problems. Going on this holiday will give him time to think."

"Didn't you tell me he could forget anything he wanted to?"

"Yes, but I don't think he will this time."

Nikki's emotions were all over the place. Sorry for Sophie because she didn't want her brother to go. Angry at herself for pining after him. Miserable because she missed him. And, most of all, she loved him so damn much it hurt.

There was nothing else Nikki could say. After convincing Sophie she was fine and wouldn't lock herself away, Sophie turned to leave. She reached the door, then stopped and turned back.

"Actually, I just realised I won't get to see you again before we dock in Sydney tomorrow. Let's exchange details now. I'm not losing contact with you again."

"Yes definitely! And while I'm thinking of it, can I grab Gavin's email too?"

Sophie raised her eyebrows.

"It's for Tenika," Nikki said with a sigh. "The woman we met on the island. She's getting married and wants to invite Gavin."

Sophie looked sceptical but nodded. After exchanging details, they embraced, promised to stay in touch, then Sophie left.

Nikki sent a quick email to Tenika then, after checking she had her keycard, left her room for breakfast.

Katie stepped out of her room as Nikki passed.

"Oh, hi," Katie said with a smile. "I was just coming to see you." She hesitated, then said, "I-I think we need to talk."

Even though dinner last night had been successful, and it was clear Katie was really trying, they couldn't go much further without discussing what tore them apart in the first place. Nikki couldn't fully trust her sister because fear still lingered. The only way they could move forward was by taking every opportunity to reconnect.

"I'm off to grab some breakfast," Nikki said. "Do you want to join me?"

Katie nodded and together they set off for the buffet. It was quieter than usual because they'd arrived later, so they found a table easily. Nikki dug in, no longer caring what Katie thought. Although, to give her credit, Katie hadn't said a word when Nikki had ordered pasta and a glass of red wine last night.

Halfway through her meal she sensed eyes on her. She glanced up only to see Katie staring, eyes shimmering with unshed tears. Food remained untouched.

Fine, if Katie wasn't going to start the conversation, Nikki would. She placed her knife and fork beside the plate. "What did—?"

"I'm sorry," Katie blurted at the same time. Then continued, "For everything. I've been a crappy sister—"

Nikki rolled her eyes. "That's an understatement."

Katie's face dropped. "Please don't do that, Nikki. I'm trying here."

Nikki winced. "I'm sorry. Go on."

Katie rubbed her temples. "No, I'm sorry. I didn't mean to snap. It's just... I'm ashamed, Nikki. This whole thing has gone on way too long over a stupid, petty thing that happened years ago."

"What petty thing?" She didn't remember them falling out. It'd happened so suddenly.

For a long moment, Katie didn't speak. She looked down at her food, using her fork to push it around. Nikki had lost interest in her meal and waited for her sister to continue.

Katie looked up and said so quietly Nikki strained to hear her clearly. "I was jealous of you."

Nikki gawped at her sister. She remembered wondering if Katie was jealous on the first day of the cruise. Turned out she was right.

"Jealous? Of... of me?" Nikki said.

"You have no idea." She gave a disbelieving laugh. "You have this natural allure. Everyone is drawn to you! They come to you first for advice or help. Men are drawn to you. And it's not just appreciation, it's instant attraction! Remember the night of Mum and Dad's anniversary dinner?"

Nikki shuddered at the memory and nodded.

"I saw you when you entered." Katie looked away guiltily. "You were so beautiful. All eyes were on you, men *and* women."

Nikki's cheeks heated. She hated being the centre of attention so never noticed that sort of thing. Too focused on getting from A to B. It *did* explain Katie's mood that night though. Nikki thought it was the argument with Monty, but that might've only been a contributing factor.

"And look at the guy you ran into on our first day. Gavin, right? He was struck the moment he caught you. You can get any man you want just by being you. You've got this sweet, innocent, girl-next-door thing going on. You're practically perfect." She said the last three words in an almost whisper.

Nikki's mouth opened and closed wordlessly as everything slotted into place like a jigsaw puzzle. Then, she burst out laughing. *Perfect?* Far from it! It was so absurd. Years of insults all because of bloody jealousy? It was too much to get her head around, but still she laughed until tears trickled down her cheeks.

When she calmed down, she glanced across at a bewildered Katie.

"I am far from perfect," Nikki spluttered between giggles. "And men are *not* drawn to me. If they are, why am I still single?"

Katie raised an eyebrow. "What about Gavin? You introduced me to him the other day, remember? He seemed pretty into you."

Nikki looked away to hide the pain she was sure was still in her eyes. "It was only a fling." She looked up and forced a bright smile.

"Nothing major. He's a traveller and I'm a woman who wants to settle down."

Katie didn't look convinced, but she pounced on what Nikki said. "But you see my point, right? The fact you could so easily have a fling. If I was single and I tried something like that, I'd only make a fool of myself and have a lousy time in the process. Before I met Monty, do you know how many boyfriends I had?"

Nikki shrugged. Katie had always been private about her relationships.

"One." Katie held up her index finger. "Men just weren't interested in me. If we went out together, all their eyes were on you. Remember Jason? The guy you dated after my twenty-first birthday party?"

Nikki pulled a face and nodded. She couldn't remember what she ever saw in him. They only lasted for two weeks.

Wait. Katie's twenty-first. Things changed after that party. Nikki hadn't long turned nineteen and even though she'd been of drinking age for over a year, drinking in public was still a novelty. She drank more than normal and only vaguely remembered meeting Jason. Everything else was a blur. What had happened?

"Before you arrived," Katie continued, "Jason and I were flirting and having a great time. He was the first guy in a long time who'd paid me any attention. The moment you arrived though, *voilà*," she did a fancy wave with her hand, "he was smitten. He didn't even look at me for the rest of the night and I got stuck with Monty. The only guy who didn't look at you."

"That's a bit rude, isn't it? You make it sound like he was a leper."

Katie had the decency to look embarrassed. "It's how I felt at the time. I hadn't intended to sleep with him, but—"

Nikki's eyes widened and she sat back in her seat. "Wait, wait, wait." She shook her head. "Monty was at your birthday party and you had a one-night stand with him?" How wasted was she? "I only remember meeting him a couple of weeks after your birthday."

Katie shrugged. "You know how shy he can be around new people."

Nikki hummed in response. That was true. It was as though he had two modes—business mode where he was an exceptional, confident businessman, and personal mode where he was awkward and introverted. Only a select few got to know the true Montgomery Dalton.

"Mum didn't tell you any of this?" Katie sipped her orange juice. "I thought she would have. The twins were conceived that night. Why else do you think we got married so fast?" She placed her glass back on the table.

Nikki's mind was blown. She'd been so out of the loop she didn't even know this juicy detail about her sister's life. "So, you're telling me it was a shotgun wedding?"

"Yes. You know what his family in the UK are like. They're aristocrats and it would've been a scandal to learn he'd knocked up an Aussie girl, so he did the right thing and married me. When the twins were born, we said they were premature. They were sickly babies anyway, so they never questioned it."

Nikki stared off into the distance, her head spinning with the revelation. It was no surprise she didn't know any of this after the way things changed so rapidly.

"This still doesn't explain your sudden change though. Okay so you and Monty had a one-night stand, which resulted in the twins. Clearly you didn't love each other when you married, but how's that my fault?"

"It's not but I didn't realise that at the time." She ran her finger around the rim of the plate. "I think what happened with Jason tipped me over the edge. It was just one more guy I lost the chance with because of you. I was fed up and I snapped. I blamed you for something that wasn't your fault."

"So you decided to treat me like crap and make me feel worthless instead? It made you feel better, right? Seeing me lose confidence in myself." Nikki's voice trembled. The memory of all those horrible words still hurt so much.

Katie's face softened and she reached over to take Nikki's hand. "I'm sorry. I know it wasn't right, but I couldn't seem to control my actions. It was like someone else inhabited my body. I couldn't seem to move past it. Then, when Monty and I got married, you and he got on so well, it only fed the green monster. I thought you were trying to make a play for him."

Nikki shook her head. She had every right to be angry, but she wasn't. If anything, she felt sorry for Katie. Her self-esteem was so much lower than Nikki's, which was something she never thought possible.

"I would never do that," Nikki said. "I didn't even intentionally take Jason away from you. I had no idea you were interested in him. He just came up and introduced himself. I never saw you two talking."

"I know. When you told me recently about how much Monty loves me, it made me think. A lot. I realised if you really wanted to make a play for him, why would you tell me that? And you had plenty of chances to do so, too, but you never did. Then when I watched you with Gavin, you were so taken with him." She smiled tightly. "I realised how wrong I'd been."

"Have you ever spoken to Monty about this? I mean, your jealousy has affected your marriage."

Katie looked guilty. "I know, and no, I haven't. I haven't spoken to him for a few days. The last time we spoke, we argued. I told him I wanted a divorce."

"What did he say?" Nikki didn't let on she'd already spoken to Monty about it. She wanted to hear it from Katie.

"He doesn't want one." Katie's eyes filled with tears. "He insisted on working on the marriage, but I told him not to bother." A tear dripped down her cheek, but she wiped it away. "I've been so horrible to him, Nikki. Now I can't help but wonder if I should go through with it just so he doesn't have to put up with me anymore."

"Do *you* want that?"

It took a moment for Katie to respond, but she did with a very faint shake of her head.

Nikki's breath caught. Anticipation built in her chest when she asked the next question.

"Do you love him?"

It took Katie even longer to respond this time, a range of emotions flitting across her face. Eventually, she said, "Neither of us loved each other when we married. We did what we had to for the babies. Obviously, Monty grew to love me but I was blind to it. I was convinced I didn't love him..."

"But?" Nikki held her breath.

"But sending us on this holiday, it's made me realise that..." She smiled shyly. "Well, I do. I don't even know when it happened, but it did." She smiled a real, beaming smile. It lit up her whole face.

Nikki let out the breath she'd been holding and grinned. "Hallelujah!"

Light blush coloured Katie's cheeks. Her smile dropped when she asked, "What if it's too late?"

"You won't know until you ask him, will you? Why don't you phone him? Today, even." When Katie gasped in horror, Nikki added, "He needs to hear how you feel. If you want moral support, I can be there while you make the call."

Relief flooded Katie's face. "Thank you. He doesn't need to know you're there. Just having you in the same room will give me strength."

Nikki smiled at her sister, the wall between them shattering into smithereens around their feet. She still wasn't angry. Holding onto pent up anger was pointless after working so hard to get to this point. It would only widen the rift between them.

Katie interrupted the sudden quiet between them. "Nikki, I'm really sorry. All the horrible things I said—" She shook her head. "I don't think I can ever forgive myself. All I wanted was for once to have the attention you always got and I lost control. I wasn't myself."

"But you've always had the attention of Monty. Isn't that more important than having the attention of many people? He loves you so much, Katie. Why else would he have stuck with you for so long?"

Katie gave a watery smile and wiped away the stream of tears running down her cheeks. "I realise that now." She laughed dryly. "It's pretty pathetic, isn't it? Jealousy, that is. We're all guilty of it, but it's pointless. We should be happy with who we are and what we have."

Nikki smiled. "Exactly. And it's time we both took that on board."

Katie nodded. "I want you to know I truly think you're beautiful. I'm proud to have you as a sister, even if I haven't shown it in a long time."

Nikki's bottom lip quivered. To go from years of insults to this, was a stab to the heart. But a good one, because things were looking up.

"Oh, you." A tear escaped from the corner of Nikki's eye. "Stop it."

They both laughed, then stood and embraced. Food forgotten, they agreed to spend the day exploring the ship.

"Now will you tell me where you disappeared to for four days?" Katie asked as they left the buffet. "I've been dying to know."

With a coy smile, Nikki took another leap of faith and told Katie everything.

Chapter 32

They didn't end up exploring the ship for long. Jumpy and on edge about calling Monty, Katie wanted to go back to her room so she could ring him. Now, Nikki sat on Katie's bed as her sister paced back and forth with the phone against her ear.

"He's not answering." Katie turned to Nikki, her face etched with worry. "What if he's avoiding me?"

"How about I call him?" She removed her phone from her jeans pocket, which she'd brought with her on purpose, pre-empting this exact scenario. Then she gently added, "He might be more willing to talk to me."

Katie's face paled but she nodded and plopped down on the sofa. she was finally learning the implications of her actions.

After five attempts to call Monty, Nikki frowned and put her phone aside.

"Nothing. Perhaps he's busy?"

Katie gave a half-hearted shrug, then moved to sit beside Nikki. "Perhaps." She didn't sound convinced. "What should I do?"

"Not much. Wait until he calls back, I suppose."

"And if he doesn't?"

Nikki mulled over the question. With a diplomatic answer at the ready, she said, "Then we—" but then her phone rang. She winced when Monty's name flashed on her screen.

Katie's face fell. "This is my punishment, isn't it? I've pushed him away so it's only natural he comes to you instead."

Nikki placed a consoling hand on Katie's arm. "Don't talk like that. We'll figure this out, don't worry. Let me answer and we'll go from there."

Katie nodded weakly and Nikki swiped her thumb across the screen.

"Did you call?" Monty answered, sounding short tempered.

"Yes, is everything okay?"

"Not really." His voice broke. "I'm packing my things. I figured it'd be best to leave once you get home. I'll leave the kids in Katie's care, but only until I have my own place, then I'll sort out a shared custody arrangement."

Nikki's heart dropped and she blurted, "I don't think you should."

"Why?" Monty's tone was sharp, but Nikki forgave him. He'd been under an enormous amount of stress.

"Because Katie needs to talk to you. She called you earlier, too."

"I wasn't intending to call her back. If we're only going to argue, I'd rather not bother."

"Please don't be like that. Look, Katie and I have talked and—"

"I'm so happy for you." His tone was bitter. "But I don't really want to hear how chummy you are with her when—"

"Oh, will you shut up?" Nikki raised her voice otherwise he'd never listen. She put the phone on speaker and gave Katie a look that meant business. "Monty, you're on speaker. Katie's here. Now, talk."

"Nikki," Monty growled, "I told you—"

"And I told you to talk." Nikki refused to take no for an answer. She glared at her sister, who'd suddenly frozen to the spot.

"There's nothing to talk about." Monty wasn't giving up without a fight either. "She's made it clear—"

"Monty?" Katie said, her voice trembling.

Nikki breathed a sigh of relief.

"Are... are you there?" Tears dripped down Katie's cheeks.

Silence.

After what felt like an eternity, he spoke, "Did you just call me Monty?"

Katie half laughed, half hiccupped. "Yes." She wiped away her tears. "I need to tell you something."

When Katie looked at Nikki with a worried frown, Nikki nodded encouragingly.

"What is it?" Monty sounded tired. "If it's to do with the divorce, it can wait until you're home."

"It's not about that. I-I mean, it is, but... well... it's just, I don't think we should do it."

"What?" Was that a spark of hope in his voice? "But I thought you—"

"I love you," Katie blurted, then burst into tears.

Nikki grinned and blinked away her own tears. She never thought this day would come. Taking this as her cue to leave, she left the room. She'd pick up her phone later. For now, it was time for Katie and Monty to have a long talk without her involvement.

Nikki was so happy for her sister and Monty. They deserved this second chance, but it did nothing for her heavy heart. She kept herself busy for the rest of the day taking part in activities and even fit in a sunset swim, but Gavin was never far from her mind.

Her sleep was restless and when she woke the next morning, she was numb. It was hard to believe the cruise was over. Just like that. And reality loomed before her.

An hour later as she lined up to disembark, heaviness settled in the pit of her stomach. The holiday had been more emotional than she'd planned but there were so many good moments, too. She would call it a success, but rather than coming away refreshed, she was ready for another one.

As they shuffled along with the crowd, the idea grew. If she was serious about making her business mobile, nothing had to stop her taking another trip away. Alone. No men, no family drama, just her own company. Take the time to think. Reflect. Embrace this new side of herself. Perhaps she could tie it in with her upcoming trip to Maritimo Island for Tenika and Hamish's wedding.

"What time's our flight?" Dad asked behind her as they moved closer to the exit.

Nikki turned her head slightly to address her father. "Eight-thirty. We'll have plenty of time to get there and check-in."

Dad nodded in thanks. Nikki turned to Katie next to her and said, "When we arrive in Adelaide, Mum, Dad and I are taking a taxi home. Do you need a ride, or is Monty picking you up from the airport?"

Katie beamed. She'd been on cloud nine since she and Monty spoke yesterday. "He's picking me up. I can't wait to see the girls." She bounced on the spot.

"Me either." Nikki missed her nieces a lot and couldn't wait for their excited cuddles. She grinned at Katie and added, "But I'll let you have Mummy cuddles first."

Katie laughed. She had transformed. Seven years of jealousy and resentment had lifted from her shoulders. She and Monty agreed to have another go at their marriage. They'd see a marriage counsellor to deal with the underlying issues once and for all, wanting a fresh start.

They stepped out onto the gangway, the warm, early morning breeze catching on Nikki's hair and whipping it around her face. She tucked strands behind her ears as she scanned the length of the gangway. Her spine went rigid when she spotted Gavin on the harbour, a few feet away from the ship.

Her heart leapt. Was he there for her? Until she realised he would've been waiting for Sophie to finish.

"Are you okay?" Katie asked. "You look like you've seen a ghost."

Nikki nodded but couldn't take her eyes off Gavin. As though sensing someone looking at him, he caught her gaze and her breath hitched.

"Oh, I see," Katie said. "Do you need me to kick him in the balls?"

Nikki chuckled. "No!" But she was thankful for the interruption. "He didn't do anything wrong."

Katie raised an eyebrow. "I beg to differ, after what you told me."

Nikki frowned. "We had an agreement, Katie. This is all my doing. He made it clear what we had wasn't long-term. I was the one who fell for him."

To her relief, Katie dropped it and looped her arm through Nikki's. The gesture was appreciated and it gave her the strength to make the descent without breaking down. It was only when they neared the bottom that she looked up again. Gavin had stepped closer, so he was now only a short distance away.

Their gazes met. Time stood still. Nikki drowned in his golden-brown depths, wanting to remember every single detail. The way they shone so brightly when he was happy. Or how they turned a muddy chocolate when he was sad, like they were today. She ached to reach out. To touch him one last time, kiss him, tell him again that she loved him.

She didn't.

Then the moment was over, and she was whisked away with the hordes of excited people, eager to get home.

She didn't see Gavin again.

Chapter 33

The memory of Nikki's sad, grey eyes would forever haunt Gavin. Knowing he was the cause of her sadness killed him. He'd hurt her and all because he was an idiot who had no idea how to love.

After the crowd swallowed her up, Gavin stepped back and waited for Sophie. She ended her contract early and would fly back to Adelaide tomorrow after he left for Las Vegas. It turned out cruise life wasn't for her like it was for him. He understood her better now though. She didn't like being away from her family.

Last night she received an email from a previous colleague who'd heard of a job opportunity that she might be perfect for. Gavin really hoped it led to something permanent so Sophie could settle into her new normal.

The last two days for Gavin had been torture. He'd tried to keep busy so he wouldn't think about Nikki, but nothing helped. He was an emotional wreck, the ache in his chest a permanent companion since she walked away. The dread of flying to Las Vegas never left him.

What he really wanted was to rewind a few days to when he was with Nikki on Maritimo Island. If he could spend the rest of his life stuck in that moment, he'd be forever happy.

I love you.

Her words were a whisper on the salty summer breeze. His heart sped up. Every day they ran through his mind. When he slept, he dreamt of her saying them while they made sweet love.

The urge to say them back hadn't left him. Was this what it felt like to be in love? But what could he do about it? Not a damn thing because he'd missed his chance. To run back now and beg for forgiveness would label him a hypocrite. Besides, that fear still lingered, the same one that stopped him saying them in the first place.

No, he had to get himself sorted first. And he would. Whether Nikki would ever want him again, that was yet to be seen, but he'd do this for himself. He wasn't living life. Not really. He was running and it had to stop.

Today.

Later the next day, Gavin stood staring out the large airport window. When a plane touched down, the knot of dread in his stomach grew heavier. He used to get a thrill watching planes come and go. Not anymore. He now associated it with sadness and heartbreak.

His boarding call sounded. With a heavy sigh, he picked up the backpack at his feet and slung it over his shoulder. He turned to his sister and plastered on a smile, pulled her in for one last embrace. When they broke apart, he chuckled when she wiped away her tears.

"Don't laugh," she said. "I'm going to miss you, okay? And don't be a stranger. You have a new phone now. You have *no* excuse."

He took hold of her upper arms and said, "I promise I'll do better at keeping in touch." He looked into her eyes, so she knew he was serious. "And if I ever fail, you can hound me as much as you like."

"And I will." Sophie stuck her chin out defiantly.

"I should go, the plane won't wait for me." He turned and started to walk away, then stopped and turned back. "I'll miss you too, Sophie-Bug."

He grinned at the childhood nickname and even from a few feet away, he saw a couple of tears drip down her cheeks. She ran up to him and flung her arms around his neck. He held her, experiencing a new closeness to her. Their chat a few nights ago had changed a lot between them.

"Dad used to call me that," Sophie said.

"I know." He tightened his arms around her.

This was another thing that'd changed. He thought about his parents more. For a while he'd forgotten about them, but the memories were only locked away, waiting for the day he was strong enough to face them. He always thought they'd be too painful. If anything was difficult to come to terms with, it was the reality of never seeing them again.

One other thing he'd remembered was that they'd had a good relationship. A great one even, full of love and happiness, that had been taken too soon. A freak accident. A driver who'd suffered a heart attack at the wheel. No survivors. It would take Gavin a while to come to terms with it, but it gave him hope that perhaps not all was lost. That good and long-lasting relationships *were* a thing, and maybe he'd have a chance at one, one day.

Another boarding call sounded, and Sophie pulled away, wiping her tears on the back of her hands. "You really should go."

Gavin winced. The temptation to stay was strong. His heart screamed at him to do the right thing. He didn't have to go. There were other paths now, ones he hadn't dared to consider before he met Nikki. But Sophie was right. This was a chance to figure himself out. He'd been travelling for so long with no real purpose, he had no clue what to do with his life anymore. Apart from bar work, he had no skills to offer. If he was going to become a mature adult, it was time to figure out *how*.

Gavin nodded then turned and walked away. He hadn't made it far before Sophie called after him, "I love you, Gav."

He stopped mid-stride, his heart tripping inside his chest. For years, no one had said those words to him. Now, in less than a week, two people had. A part of him, knowing he wasn't a complete lost cause, blossomed to life. He turned back. Sophie stood a few feet away, her face creased with anxiety. Her long, dark brown hair tumbled around her shoulders, and her eyes shone with tears. He'd never taken the time to notice the similarities they shared before.

"Love you too, Soph." The words tumbled out so easily, he didn't even have to think.

A large smile spread across his sister's face and this was the last image he saw before he turned and joined the queue.

While he boarded, all he could think about was how easy it'd been to tell Sophie he loved her. The words flowed without any fear or restraint. Yet, when it came to Nikki, he turned stone cold with terror. It made no sense.

Rather than dwelling on it, though, he settled down in his seat for the long, twenty-hour journey. Nikki was gone, he couldn't do anything about it. But he *could* do something about changing himself as a person.

For once, he wouldn't flirt with the stewardess or use charm to mask his emptiness. He was done being that man.

Chapter 34

Three months later

The seaplane skidded along the water and glided towards the dock. Maritimo Island looked as stunning as ever before Nikki's eyes. It was hard to believe three months had passed since the cruise ended. So much had happened, but she felt like a new person.

Two weeks after the cruise, Katie and Monty dropped the bombshell that they were moving to England. With Monty's father about to retire, as the oldest son, Monty was set to take over the family estate. Add to it everything that had happened between him and Katie, and finally on a new trajectory, it seemed like the natural path to take.

For Nikki, this set off a chain of events that had her following them to England. After two weeks between London and touring the UK, she set off on a seven-week European tour. Not only was it a perfect antidote for her bruised heart, but she tasted freedom and adventure. She refused to let heartbreak take over, not when she had a life to live and a whole world to see.

She balanced her web design and travel, exactly as she planned. It had been a busy but wonderful experience. She would spend the next week in Maritimo Island, then return to Australia and make a plan to move out of home. After that, well, she wasn't sure. Either way, she had a new lease on life and was eager to live it to the fullest.

Oh, she missed Gavin. That went without saying. Every single day he was in her thoughts and dreams. Now that she was back on the island, the memories returned with force.

She had no idea if he'd be at the wedding. Sophie hadn't said anything, neither had Tenika, and Nikki didn't ask. Either way, she was prepared and would act like a civilised adult if they came face to face.

Jolted out of her thoughts by Ratu welcoming them to Maritimo Island, Nikki picked up the tote bag at her feet and followed the other five passengers as they disembarked. She stepped onto the dock, the warm island breeze tousled her hair and kissed her skin. It was autumn, so the heaviness of the humidity was gone but was still pleasantly warm.

A few feet away she spotted Tenika on the pier, waving. She was glowing, the excitement of the wedding coming off her in waves. Nikki grinned and waved back. She turned to pick up her case, thanked Ratu, then wasted no time in racing down the pier to meet Tenika halfway in a tight hug. They'd kept in contact almost daily and had become great friends.

"I'm so glad you're here!" Tenika exclaimed when they pulled away.

Nikki breathed in deeply, tasting the tang of salt on her tongue, and admired the stunning island view. "It's so good to be back!"

The sun shimmered on aqua blue water, the island was as lush and vibrant as she remembered, but busier somehow. Probably because of the wedding. Her heart swelled and she relaxed. Despite her travels across Europe and visiting so many amazing places, nothing stirred her heart like Maritimo Island.

It was like coming home. Except one very important person was missing.

Don't start that.

Less than five minutes and already her chest ached for Gavin. *Ugh.* This was going to be harder than she expected.

"Come on," Tenika said, looping her arm through Nikki's and leading her away. "Lots to do and so little time. When is your friend arriving?"

"Sophie arrives tomorrow." Nikki looked at Tenika curiously. "What else is there to do? You said you were organised."

Tenika's face grew grim, and a knot of dread settled in Nikki's stomach. "Yeah, about that... Nikki, I have a *huge* favour to ask."

That knot grew and Nikki shook her head on autopilot. She didn't like where this was going.

"My best friend, Brenda—you haven't met her yet, but you will soon—is sick. Like, really sick and can't be my maid of honour. I've asked Skye, my sister-in-law, to step in but now I'm short a bridesmaid and... will you be my bridesmaid?"

Nikki stopped walking and stared at Tenika. "You're kidding, right?"

Tenika stopped too, her brow crinkled. "I know it's last-minute, but Brenda's been throwing up since yesterday."

"It-it's not... contagious, is it?" That was the last thing anyone needed, a bout of gastro to spread across the island two days before the wedding.

"No, thank God. She's eight weeks pregnant and suffering from morning sickness, the kind that lasts all day. We almost flew her to Suva yesterday when she couldn't even keep water down, but she's improved today after finding some food and drink she *can* keep down. She's devastated, but since she can't guarantee she'll be well enough for the wedding, she made the hard decision to back out. So now I'm in crisis mode." She wrung her hands, glancing at Nikki expectantly. "Please? It would mean the world to me."

"But... me? Of all people!"

Tenika stared at her agape. "Why not?"

Old self-deprecating thoughts came to the surface, danced on the tip of her tongue threatening to spill, but Nikki swallowed them. Every day was a struggle. The thoughts never disappeared but she was doing better at controlling them. This was a privilege, a chance to pay it forward for someone who'd helped her in the past.

Besides, she'd never revealed that side of herself to Tenika. Didn't want to, either. Even if Nikki was still coming to terms with her new self, this *was* who she was now. A traveller. A woman who took calculated risks that she once wouldn't have. Someone who refused to let negative, derogatory thoughts take over.

"I-I just thought maybe you'd have other family or friends who you knew better," Nikki improvised. "I'd love to step in."

Tenika breathed a sigh of relief hugged her again. "Oh my God, thank you so much! You just saved my wedding."

"What if I mess it up?" Nikki asked. This had nothing to do with those pesky negative thoughts, and everything to do with the fact that she'd never been a bridesmaid before.

"You won't, and even if you do, which is *extremely* unlikely, it'll be another memory we can laugh about years from now."

"I'll remind you of that if something goes wrong."

Tenika grinned, then started walking again, Nikki following.

Once on the path, they grabbed a free cart and Tenika drove toward the resort where everyone was based. "So, tell me everything," Tenika said as she sped off, waving at the locals who passed. "You're coming from London, right?"

"Yes, I stopped off to see Katie, Monty and the girls one last time, then came straight here. Europe was amazing, but I wished I had longer. There was so much to squeeze into seven weeks and so much I couldn't see."

She regaled Tenika with stories of her travels and was so proud of what she'd done. Stepping out of her comfort zone and going on new adventures had been so good for her soul. Although, it didn't help that every place she visited, she wondered if Gavin had been there and what he thought of it.

Ugh.

"God that sounds so amazing," Tenika gushed as she stopped at the resort. "I can't wait until Hamish and I go on our own European holiday."

"Honeymoon?" Nikki asked as they stepped out.

Tenika nodded as they went inside. "Four weeks around Europe, then we'll go back to Scotland for five months."

Litia bustled forward, interrupting their conversation. "Nikki, it's so nice to see you again! Welcome back to Maritimo Island!"

Nikki accepted her embrace, loving that she was remembered.

"Did she say yes?" Litia asked Tenika who nodded, and Litia beamed. "Oh good. We'll take you to the markets tomorrow to find the perfect dress. For now, let's get you checked in and settled."

Nikki stepped up to the desk just as Hamish exited the little office holding a clipboard with a pen under the clip. She caught sight of Eroni behind him. He spotted her at the same time and waved. She waved back as Hamish glanced over and grinned.

"Good to see you again, Nikki," Hamish said. "Gavin will be arrivin' tomorrow evening."

She froze and Hamish stopped mid-stride, his face paling as Tenika tutted quietly.

"Oh, sorry," he said, his smile sheepish.

Nikki swallowed and forced a smile. "No, it's fine." Her voice was hoarse, and she cleared her throat.

Hamish lifted his hand in a wave, then rushed away, his red cheeks matching his hair.

"You alright?" Tenika asked beside her.

Nikki nodded although her insides trembled. Now that she knew he *would* be there, it did nothing for her state of mind. She thought she was ready to face him, but she wasn't. Not at all. It still hurt so much that he couldn't return her feelings. But it was time to pull up her big girl panties and deal with it like a grown woman. The *new* Nikki.

"I'm good," she said, even though her voice trembled.

Tenika didn't look convinced but nodded. "Alright, well I'm going to check on Brenda." She grabbed a slip of paper, wrote something on it, then held it out. "When you're ready, come on by so you can meet her and Douglas, then I'll take you to meet Skye and Angus too."

Nikki took the slip of paper with a 'thanks', which had a bungalow number on it, and Tenika disappeared.

After checking in, Nikki made her way to the room inside the resort, which she'd share with Sophie. In the room's quiet, she took everything in. It was sleek and modern, decorated in island themes and colours of blue, green and brown. The balcony doors were open, revealing an idyllic view of rainforest and ocean.

She turned to the bed and dropped her luggage to the floor. That's when she saw it—the Fijian dress Tenika had lent her when she was last here. There was a note on top of it.

Nikki, I want you to have this. You looked so beautiful in it. Wear it tomorrow night for the hen's party before the big day.
   Nika xx

Grinning, Nikki picked up the dress and hung it in the closet. After unpacking her bags, she splayed out on the bed with a sigh. Jetlag was setting in, but she wouldn't sleep until after dark. A tip Monty had given her that had worked when she first travelled to England. As she stared up at the ceiling, the wooden ceiling fan twirling slowly, her head spun with how fast everything was happening.

Bridesmaid. Gavin arriving tomorrow. Two *massive* things she was unprepared for. The bridesmaid gig she could handle with help. Gavin... well, even after three months away, no one could help her there. Stomach in knots, she held onto the only hope she had. That she'd be too busy and wouldn't see him until after the wedding.

When her eyes began to droop, she forced herself up. A quick shower revitalised her and she changed into fresh clothes. Before heading out, she sent messages to her parents, Katie, and Monty.

The heaviness that had hovered over them for so long had lifted. Their family was happy and no one walked on eggshells anymore. She missed everyone a lot though and couldn't wait to see her parents when she returned home. Moving out of home would be hard, but it was long overdue.

Keycard in her pocket, Nikki drew in a steadying breath, then released it left her room. She took the elevator to the ground floor, then wandered past the pool area and beyond to the bungalows lining the L-shaped jetty. When she passed the one she and Gavin had shared, her heart pounded a little faster. Tears stung her eyes and even though she'd coped these last three months without him, she missed him so damn much.

All she wanted now was their inevitable meeting to be over so she could move on and start the next phase of her life.

The next day and a half were a blur of activity—meeting the rest of the wedding party, helping Tenika with last-minute wedding plans, and finding the perfect dress. Thankfully, Tenika's only stipulation was that the dress colour matched Skye's, otherwise Nikki had free rein to choose the style. It meant she could find something that suited her curves, which she did, and she looked and felt stunning in it.

She'd been so apprehensive about being a bridesmaid, but she needn't have been worried. Everyone was so welcoming and warm. Even Brenda, the poor sickly one, had been so supportive while staying close to the bathroom.

Sophie arrived mid-afternoon and at Tenika's insistence, was not only invited to attend the wedding but also swept up into the last-minute wedding mayhem. They finished off wedding favours, had the rehearsal, and ended the night with Tenika's hen's party.

By the time the rehearsal ended just before dinner, Nikki had a hard time standing upright. Even after an early night last night, exhaustion clung to her limbs. The jetlag didn't shift as quick as it did when she first arrived in London. Her only hope was that she'd be functional tomorrow and that makeup could hide the bags under her eyes.

Nikki couldn't be more relieved when Skye announced the hen's party would be held on the terrace of the resort's restaurant. Close to her room if she needed to depart early. Drinks, both alcoholic and non, and food were served frequently with music blaring, and even some games.

There were a lot of laughs and Nikki started off having a great time, but by her second cider, her heart grew heavy. Each second that drew her closer to the wedding, she was reminded of what she wanted. Sitting between Skye who raved about her young twin daughters back in Scotland, and Tenika who rattled on about her wedding and honeymoon, Nikki's mood soured.

How the hell was she supposed to live her entire life with this heartbreak?

Nikki cast her gaze over Brenda, who sat next to Sophie. Brenda still looked washed out and tired, but her cheeks had gained some colour. She sipped ginger tea and nibbled on a light platter of food that she managed to keep down.

Nikki then turned to Sophie, who looked over at her at the same time and her brow furrowed. She mouthed, "Are you okay?" and Nikki nodded on autopilot even though she knew Sophie wouldn't believe her.

The last thing Nikki wanted was to bring the night down, so when it reached eight p.m., she used her jetlag as an excuse and said she wanted to get an early night. After wishing everyone a good night, she disappeared.

Nikki stepped off the terrace into the bustling restaurant and navigated around the edges to the main door. When she stepped into the entry leading to the reception area, she came to a sudden halt.

There he was. Gavin.

He stood at the reception desk, side-on to her, completely at ease, chatting to the young man who checked him in. A bag over one shoulder, wearing shorts, thongs on his feet and a casual button-up shirt. He appeared more tanned than she remembered. His hair was longer too. It suited him.

Unable to move, she drank him in from head to toe. When she got to his calves, her eyes zeroed on in a new tattoo on the side of his left calf. She'd memorised nearly every tattoo he had, and he did *not* have that one. Her heart thudded as she remembered wondering if he'd get a new one after their time together. Did he?

Don't go there.

She swallowed and tore her gaze away, back to his side profile and her heart stuttered. Damn he looked *so* good. Relaxed. Carefree, even. His smiles came easier. He held his shoulders without so much tension. Las Vegas had clearly done him good.

Someone ran into her, budging her forward slightly, and she jerked back to attention. The young Fijian employee bustled off with an apology and Nikki took the moment to pull herself together. She wasn't ready for this interaction, *especially* tonight when she was so damn tired and fragile. Maybe tomorrow, after the wedding.

Until then, she had to avoid him at all costs.

He hadn't seen her yet, so she took in her surrounds and mapped out the best way to get past without him noticing, since there was no other way to get back to her room.

When she realised the best way was to simply walk right past, she sighed in resignation and prepared to do just that. This was ridiculous. She was a grown woman! This didn't have to be difficult. All she had to do was walk past and pretend not to see him. Simple. He still hadn't even seen her so quite likely this would be a piece of—

He turned to his left and looked right at her.

Having taken one step, she froze again as his eyes landed on her, eyebrows raising in surprise. Then he took her in, from head to toe. The way his eyes widened confirmed he recognised the dress, and this did nothing for her racing heart or the heat creeping up her neck.

For a few seconds they stared at each other. Nikki's brain screamed at her to move. Smile, act calm, just *move*. Then, because she was emotional and overtired, at least that was what she told herself, she did the worst possible thing.

She power-walked right past without even acknowledging him and disappeared into the depths of the resort.

So much for acting like a civilised adult.

Chapter 35

Gavin hadn't expected Nikki to bolt.

He'd waited for this moment for months. Had imagined every possible scenario, but never once did he consider she wouldn't want to see him. It stung like hell, but he wouldn't give up hope. Not yet.

But, *damn*, she looked good. More than good. Stunning. *Sexy.* Wearing the same dress Tenika had lent her on the night of the bonfire. He hadn't forgotten.

The young man behind the counter called his name and Gavin turned, shaking his head. He accepted his key with thanks and made his way to his room. He'd have to check in with Sophie later. She should be here already.

First, settle in, shower, change, then find Hamish who'd emailed him the details of their stag party and told Gavin to join once he'd arrived.

Under the hot needles of the shower, Gavin reflected on the last three months and how much happened in that time.

Las Vegas had always been a neon-lit playground for him. A place where nothing mattered, where he could lose himself in distraction like he was so used to doing. But it hadn't done what he thought it would do. The lights didn't dazzle. The noise didn't drown out the memories. No matter how much he gambled and chatted up women, it was all half-hearted. He didn't even bed a single one. He couldn't. They weren't *her*.

Three weeks he'd lasted. Bored in Vegas? It sounded ludicrous, but he'd realised it wasn't his dream anymore. One night when he'd almost drunk himself silly on a whole bottle of whisky, he'd phoned Sophie and they talked long into the night. A few times in the past she had suggested he should see a therapist, but he'd always shut her down. Convinced himself he could it do by himself. But that night he'd realised she was right. This was bigger than he could handle.

He missed Nikki so much. He wanted her... a future. The whole kit and kaboodle. He wanted to *love* her, but he had to learn how. And so, he finally did what Sophie suggested.

He changed his travel plans and travelled to Scotland. A place he'd visited in the past and connected with the same way he had with Maritimo Island. It was a place he could think, feel and heal. While there, he met Hamish's brothers, Douglas and Angus, and even helped them at the distillery some days when he wasn't hiking or exploring.

It was in Scotland he found a therapist online who specialised in grief and trauma. They chatted in weekly video chats, sometimes up to three times a week if Gavin really struggled. He learnt a lot. That he'd suffered from abandonment trauma and emotional detachment leading to fear of intimacy.

The first time he'd heard those words, he was sure he was a lost cause. How could anyone be so broken and live a normal life? Until the therapist revealed his own loss—his parents killed in front of him when he was a child. Rather than spiralling, he'd put his trauma into learning how to help others like him.

That was when Gavin knew he'd hit the jackpot, and since then, he worked hard to deal with his issues. The biggest takeaways for him were that trauma didn't disappear just because he pretended it didn't exist. That loving someone wasn't about being perfect. That fear wasn't weakness. Letting it rule him was.

It had been a gruelling few weeks. After that night on the ship when he'd broken down, the grief of his parents' death had hit him hard. Then picking at the same wound with the therapist had left him vulnerable and devastatingly sad. It'd taken a while, but he'd begun to find peace. He wasn't fully there, and he wasn't fixed—probably never would be—but he was strong enough to know what he wanted now.

Trauma never disappeared, a person had to learn how to live with it. Gavin was still learning, but he had the confidence to stop running and start living a life with meaning. He was even thinking about studying psychology too. The idea of helping others who'd suffered trauma the same way the therapist had appealed to him. He'd look into it once he was settled back in Australia.

One thing was certain though. Gavin wanted Nikki in his life. Forever. If she'd have him. Her runaway act hadn't given him much confidence. It confirmed there were no guarantees this would go the way he'd hoped, which was terrifying as hell, but he wasn't ruling it out just yet.

First, he had to prove he'd changed and that he was serious about her. About *them* as a couple. If not today, then tomorrow.

G avin had hoped he'd have another chance at seeing Nikki before the wedding until Hamish told him she was in the wedding because of a last-minute change of plans. Now he had to impatiently wait to speak to her.

By the afternoon, Gavin fidgeted in his seat between Sophie and Brenda. He'd met Brenda a couple of times when he was in Scotland.

The sun beat down on them, warm but not hot, and Gavin's stomach twisted tight as he waited for the wedding to start. Hamish stood at the front looking nervous, his brothers standing beside him.

"Will you sit still?" Sophie hissed from beside him, scolding him the way she would her boys.

"Sorry," Gavin muttered. He tried, he really did, but his right leg started bouncing instead.

Sophie's hand came down hard on it and she glared at him. "I swear, if you don't stop."

He managed a weak smile of apology and forced himself not to move. It took great effort and serious concentration. No easy feat when he was so damn impatient and nervous.

When the music started, he focused his attention on the wedding, which helped a bit.

Skye came down the aisle first. Nikki followed a few metres behind, and—good lord—she was *stunning*. His breath caught and suddenly he couldn't move *at all*.

Her hair had been curled and hung over one shoulder. A yellow hibiscus flower was tucked behind one ear, matching her flowing yellow dress that accentuated her natural curves he loved so much. Her skin glowed in the afternoon sun, and she had a soft smile on her face. His lungs screamed for air, and as he drew in a large breath, he watched her draw closer.

So beautiful. So confident. So damn *close*, yet completely unreachable.

It wasn't until she reached his row that she glanced over, flicking her gaze up to meet his. Held for a single beat before glancing away again. No smile. No hesitation. No recognition. Just calm indifference.

Then she moved past him and stopped at the front next to Skye. Gavin's shoulders slumped and he couldn't figure out what it all meant. Sure, she couldn't react right at that moment, but he'd expected to see something... *anything* in her eyes.

The indifference cut deep, and he feared the worst. That he'd royally screwed up and didn't have a chance in hell now.

"Stand up," Sophie whispered beside him, and he blinked a couple of times before realising the bridal march was playing and everyone else had got to their feet.

He scrambled to his feet, his legs heavy as he watched Tenika come down the aisle smiling so brightly it even made the sun shine brighter somehow. When she stopped in front of Hamish, he took her hands. They faced each other, smiling like a couple truly in love.

Something cracked open in Gavin's chest. This could be him and Nikki, and he suddenly wanted it so much it hurt.

He sat through the ceremony staring at Nikki as Tenika and Hamish promised to be together through thick and thin. Maybe it wasn't too late? He just had to be brave and hold on to hope.

When the wedding ended and the happy couple kissed while the crowd cheered and applauded, Gavin only had eyes for Nikki. Ready to pounce the moment she was free. Just enough time to tell her he needed to talk.

But then the crowd surged forward to congratulate Tenika and Hamish and Nikki became obscured. Gavin cursed under his breath and pushed through the masses. After giving Tenika a congratulatory hug and Hamish a handshake, Gavin searched for Nikki, keeping his eyes peeled for honey-brown hair and a bright yellow dress.

He found her a few minutes later, further down the beach chatting and laughing with Skye. This was his moment! He advanced forward but the rest of the wedding party moved past him and huddled together. A photographer joined them seconds later, shouting orders as he set up the camera on a tripod.

Nikki glanced up once and their gazes met. He lifted his hand in a wave, and he got the tiniest smile in response. His heart thudded at the small gesture that spoke volumes, giving him the slightest bit of hope.

"Don't give up yet," Sophie said when Gavin rejoined her and Brenda a moment later. "Maybe try again at the reception later."

Gavin nodded and sat, his knee bouncing again. The reception was still a few hours away.

Brenda rose. "I might take this time to have a nap."

"Let me come with you," Sophie said, then she turned to Gavin and added, "I'll see you later, okay?"

He nodded and watched as the two women made their way down the beach, away from the wedding party.

❧ ❦

By the time Gavin made it to the reception two hours later, his impatience had returned. Whenever Gavin had a free moment, he looked for every possible opportunity to take Nikki aside, but he was thwarted every time. He understood it was a busy day, weddings were hectic, but he was losing hope. It was like watching a tide pull her further away.

After dinner but before the cake was cut, the bride and groom had their wedding dance. The next song was another slow number, and all couples were encouraged to join the happy couple on the floor.

"Go get her," Sophie whispered in his ear.

He looked at her, brow furrowed, and she gestured with her chin towards the bar. He glanced over and saw Nikki leaning against a stool, champagne flute in her hand. Angus and Skye had stepped onto the dancefloor, and Douglas came over to see if Brenda was up for a dance, which she was, but just one, she'd said.

Finally, Gavin had his opportunity.

He downed the last of his champagne, then stood and strode over, his eyes never leaving Nikki. He wasn't letting her get away this time. A lot had to be said. Even if he couldn't say it all now, he wanted to set a time and he had a perfect place in mind. As he drew closer, she finished her champagne and placed her glass on the bar. She turned as though to walk away, and he picked up his pace.

Her back to him, he took two large strides and reached for her hand. She spun around, a look of surprise on her face, but when she spotted him, that surprise turned into something he couldn't quite pinpoint. He didn't have time to even consider it. Right now there was just *one* thing he needed to do.

Take a leap of faith.

Still holding onto her hand, he moved in close enough so she could hear him. He leaned in and whispered, "I love you," then closed the gap and pressed his lips to hers, wrapping his arms around her.

He heard a soft whimper, then her arms wrapped around his waist, gripping his shirt as she reciprocated. Gavin could've died right there and gone to heaven. Surely she wouldn't kiss him back if she didn't want to be with him?

Out of all the kisses they'd shared, this one held nothing back. He promised without words all the things she'd ever desired, and her reciprocation told him she understood that.

When they pulled away, panting, Nikki held his gaze, eyes shining, a smile on her lips. He rested his forehead on hers, her warm breath fanning his face. Neither of them spoke for a moment, and Gavin was vaguely aware of the reception going on around them, music playing, people talking, but his heavy breathing and pounding heart drowned out most of it.

"I've wanted to talk to you all day," Gavin said with a low chuckle. "Please tell me you'll have a free moment soon."

She nodded and pulled back. "After the reception. Let's meet at the resort entrance."

"Wear something you can hike in."

Nikki's brow creased but the music stopped and the emcee announced over the microphone, "It's time to cut the cake! Can the bride and groom come forward please?"

"I've got to go," Nikki said. "Can you at least tell me *where* we're hiking to late at night?"

"I thought we could do a spot of stargazing, if you're up for it."

A slow smile stretched across her face. "That sounds perfect. I'll be ready."

She disappeared and, with a smile plastered on his face, Gavin returned to his table, nerves subsiding and hope building within him.

Whatever happened from now on, he was so ready for it. The life Nikki wanted, he wanted too. He didn't care where they ended up, so long as they were together.

Chapter 36

It had taken every ounce of willpower for Nikki to hold it together all day. Then Gavin swept in, declared his love and kissed her with so much passion and *love* it made her head spin. She was still buzzing. Her lips still tingled. The words she never thought she'd hear him say had been spoken with such honesty.

Her own love had only grown stronger, and this time she held onto hope without having to worry it was going to be dashed.

The reception began to wind down, but the dancefloor still pulsed with music and dancers, the balmy nighttime breeze drifting through the marquee. Nikki watched Tenika and Hamish mingle with the guests, saying goodbye before they left for the night.

When Tenika spotted Nikki, she whispered something to Hamish, then came over, still beaming. She was the epitome of a glowing bride and Nikki could only hope she would one day look half as beautiful.

"I've been meaning to catch up with you," Tenika said breathlessly, stopping in front of Nikki. Her cheeks were flushed, and her eyes shone with happiness. "I have a favour to ask before I forget. Hamish and I leave early tomorrow morning for Suva so we can start our honeymoon, so I may not see you before then."

"Everything okay?"

"Yes, but I told you we'd be away for six months, right?"

Nikki nodded.

"Right, so the thing is, we've booked out the whole resort for a celebrity wedding. It's massive, Nikki. Nate Kilpatrick."

Nikki's eyes widened. "That big thriller author?" She wasn't a big reader, but she'd read some of Nate Kilpatrick's books and they'd hooked her.

Tenika nodded. "The one and only. He's an *insanely* private person, so this wedding is not only high profile but top secret. I'll be back in time for the wedding, but I'll be gone for most of the prep and Eroni's already panicking. He needs someone to help manage all the logistics. Someone calm. Detail-oriented. *Creative*."

"You want *me*?"

"I *need* you," Tenika all but begged. "I know you've got your web design business, and the last thing I want is to take you away from that. And don't think I didn't see that kiss between you and Gavin, so clearly there's *that*, but—"

"I'll do it," Nikki said without a second's hesitation. She wasn't sure why, she and Gavin still hadn't talked, but something told her this was the right thing to do.

"It's only temporary," Tenika continued as though not hearing her. "I just need you to make sure everything runs smooth and that nothing goes up in flames while I'm not here. If you can't do it, I do understand. There's no—"

"Tenika," Nikki said with a laugh. "I said I'd do it."

Tenika stopped and stared. Blinked once. "Oh. Really? Like that?"

"Like that. Now, you and Hamish need to go and enjoy your wedding night and your honeymoon. I'll talk to Eroni and Litia tomorrow."

"Thank you so much," Tenika gushed and came in for a tight hug. "You are an absolute godsend. I'll touch base from time to time."

Nikki pulled away. "No, you won't because you'll be enjoying wedded bliss with Hamish. By the time you get back, everything will be sorted, and the wedding will be on track. Don't worry about a thing."

Hamish came over at that point and wrapped his arm around Tenika's waist, kissing her on the cheek. "Come on, Mrs McNeill. It's my duty to take you to bed."

"Ooh I like the sound of that," Tenika said, her cheeks turning pink. "Nikki's agreed to help out at the resort."

Hamish gave Nikki a nod and smile. "Thanks, Nikki."

"Enjoy your honeymoon!" she called to their retreating backs.

Alone now, she stood thinking it all over.

Stay. Start again. *With* Gavin? Could this really work?

Wait... had she been too impulsive? Shouldn't she have talked to Gavin first? What if he had other plans?

Before her thoughts spiralled and she lost her nerve, she saw him walk away from the reception. She drew in a calming breath and took that as her cue to follow. There was only one way to find out.

⁂

Half an hour later, the full moon lit up the path as Nikki and Gavin commenced their hike to the peak. It was so fitting after the last time they stargazed. Where nothing was certain back then, now everything was.

Nearly.

They still carried torches with them for the thicker parts of the path where the moon was hidden behind thick foliage. Halfway up, Nikki realised with surprise that she did this hike much easier than last time. During her travels, she'd done a lot more walking and it'd paid off. She hadn't lost weight, but she was fitter and more comfortable in her own skin.

Old negative thoughts would probably always plague her, but she combatted them better. She could see her qualities and trusted that Gavin loved what he saw. That was enough for her.

Before they got to the top, Nikki had to ask, "Did you get a new tattoo?"

Gavin smiled at her. "Yes, why?"

"I saw it. Last night. On the side of your calf."

"Were you checking me out?" He smirked.

"Of course. I hadn't seen you for three months. Can I see it?"

He chuckled. "Yes, but let's get to the top first."

They reached the top ten minutes later and stepped into the clearing. Nikki stood with her hands on her hips, catching her breath as she stared up at the blanket of stars above her. The moon shimmered on the ocean, the islands in the distance were cast as silhouettes. To her left was the gravesite she noticed when she first came stargazing up here. Tenika had told her Hamish's father hand been buried here after an accident many years ago. It was all so tragic.

"I've missed you," Gavin said, interrupting her thoughts.

Her heart skipped and she tore her eyes away from the view and turned to him. "I missed you too."

"I hated Las Vegas," he continued with a quirk to his lips.

He reached out for her hand, and she let him take it. It was warm, solid, familiar.

"I'm sorry," he said, softer this time. "For everything. For not giving us a chance. For running away. Again." He smiled ruefully. "You changed me, Nikki. For the best. You helped me believe in love. Made me want to love and be loved, but it was terrifying. I didn't know what to do with that. Didn't think I was capable of loving anyone. Not even myself."

Her heart went out to him, but she still said nothing. Waited for him to continue.

He glanced up at the sky. While staring at the stars, he added, "I didn't realise how much my parents' death had a hold over me. That it had shaped my life so much." He turned back to her. "They died in a freak car accident. Did Sophie ever tell you that?"

She bit her lip and shook her head. Sophie had mentioned an accident but had never elaborated.

"The other driver had a heart attack at the wheel." His hand squeezed hers and she saw the glimmer of tears in his eyes in the moonlight. "I'd forgotten the details until recently. Pushed it out of my mind because it was too traumatic to talk about. I was so angry at them, but the anger was misguided. It was no one's fault, and I couldn't handle that. I needed to blame someone, so I blamed them for deserting me... and Sophie."

He tugged on her hand, and they moved over to a smooth patch of ground to sit.

"I'm so sorry, Gavin," Nikki said when he didn't speak for a long moment.

"You have nothing to be sorry for. I'm the one who hurt you, and—"

"No." She reached for his hand again and held it between both of hers. "I mean I'm sorry for all that happened to you. I can't begin to imagine what it must have been like to grow up without parents. I could never blame you for anything."

"But I hurt you."

"You didn't do it intentionally."

His gaze held hers. "How can you be so sure?"

"Because I know the real you, Gavin. The one who was on this island with me for four days, who revealed more of himself than he realised. You just had to be ready to be that man."

He leaned in and rested his forehead against hers. "I am now," he whispered. "I've been seeing a therapist for a couple of months and intend to keep seeing him. He's helped a lot. I know without a shred of doubt that I want you in my life Nikki. If you'll still have me."

Her heart stuttered. "Did you mean it when you said you love me?"

He shuffled back and moved his left leg so she could see the tattoo. It was difficult to see the detail in the moonlight, so Gavin shone the torch on it. It was a wave that curled up towards a star-studded sky with a crescent moon.

"I think this one's my favourite," Nikki whispered.

"So, yes," Gavin said with a wide smile. "I meant it. I love you so much, Nikki. I'm still figuring things out. I'm far from perfect, but I'm not running anymore, and I want a proper life. A messy, ordinary, terrifying life with you in it."

His leant in and brushed his thumb across her cheek, catching a tear she didn't realise had fallen.

"I love you too," she whispered, then surged forward and wrapped her arms around his neck, burying her face in his shoulder.

His arms wrapped around her, and she melded into him, relishing this moment and loving the feel of being back in his arms again. Right where she belonged.

She pulled back and blurted, "There's just one thing."

His brow creased. "Should I be worried?"

"Tenika asked me if I'd be able to stay here, on the island, while she and Hamish are away for six months. There's a big celebrity wedding coming up and Eroni needs some help. I-I said yes." She held her breath in anticipation, waiting for his reaction.

He breathed out and laughed. "Is that all? I wasn't sure what you were going to come out with then."

Her shoulders relaxed. "I wasn't sure how you'd react."

"I love this place. I'm more than happy to stay for as long as we need to. I'm sure I can pick up some odd jobs here and there." He paused, then added, "I've actually been thinking I'd like to study psychology. I'd really love to help people who've been through a similar thing to me."

Nikki's heart swelled with love for this man in front of her, who'd come so far. "Gavin, I think that's amazing."

"You do?"

"You'd be amazing at it. If you wanted to, you could even study remotely while we're here."

"Perhaps I'll study part time and pick up a job too." He looked at her expectantly and she nodded.

They laid back on the ground, holding hands, staring at the bright stars. For a long moment, neither of them spoke. Apart from the ocean below, a gentle breeze rustling the foliage, or nocturnal animals, it was blissfully quiet.

"By the way," Gavin said, "I owe you some money."

She shifted onto her side so she could see him. "Why?"

He moved his head. "Tenika told me you paid the invoice for when we were last here."

"So?"

"So, I think it's only fair I pay half. I got us stranded."

She laid back down with a smile. "Thank you, but I don't expect you to repay me. But if you insist, then maybe you can take me away one weekend."

He took her hand again, linking their fingers. "Deal."

Silence settled over them as they gazed at the stars once more.

"You looked beautiful today," Gavin whispered after a long silence.

Nikki smiled, her cheeks turning warm. "Thank you."

He moved beside her then, leaning on his arm and stared down at her. "What? No argument or denial?"

She chuckled lightly. "No, not anymore."

He grinned. "Good, because you're absolutely perfect just the way you are."

"There's nothing you'd change about me?" she asked.

He pretended to think then said, "Perhaps one thing."

Her eyes widened in surprise. "What?"

"Exactly that."

"What?"

"The worry that you're not good enough. You've come so far, Nik, and I'm so proud of you but I know those thoughts don't just go away." He smiled. "But if I could change one thing, it would be to have you see what *I* see. A beautiful woman with a personality overflowing with love. You're not one of those women who obsess over what they eat, what they wear, or how they look. You're *you* and that's who I fell in love with."

She didn't know if the self-doubt would ever go away, but being in Gavin's company lessened it. She hoped one day she *could* embrace the person Gavin saw. It was what she strived for, and with his help, maybe she would. As they settled back to stargaze some more, Nikki shuffled in closer so their shoulders touched. She took his hand, entwining their fingers. "Thank you," Nikki whispered after a little while.

"For what?" Gavin asked, squeezing her fingers.

"You kept your word."

"I did?"

"Mmhmm. The last time we were here, you told me that if you ever got your head sorted that it's me you'd want to commit to." She smiled, her heart fluttering at the memory. "And you did."

Also in This Series

Ocean's Embrace is the first standalone book in this series and is available in eBook and paperback.

When Tenika visits Maritimo Island for a destination school reunion, she hopes to finally find peace with her painful past. Meanwhile, Hamish arrives on the island following the death of his mother to follow a journey she went on over thirty years ago. Sparks fly when their paths collide in paradise and their connection soon deepens into something real. As they uncover long-buried truths and lean on each other through grief and growth, Tenika and Hamish must decide if they're brave enough to let love rewrite their stories.

Navigate to the URL below to purchase this book.

https://books2read.com/OceansEmbrace

Ocean's Echoes, the third standalone book in the series will be released in 2026. Sign up to my newsletter to be the first to learn all about it!

Other Books by Lisa Stanbridge

Series

The **Longing for Home** series follows the story of Jane and Jacques between Paris and Australia as their relationship evolves.

Lonely in Paris – Book 1

Jane has accepted a job in Paris, but she speaks very little French. With no friends to enjoy the city of love with, she's awfully lonely. Then she meets Jacques DuPont. From a rich family, he's living the dream. Just not his own. Trapped in a life chosen by his family, he's always been alone. Until he meets Jane. The two couldn't be more opposite, yet they will fall hard. With an expiring visa, a jealous colleague, and manipulative family, their loyalties will be tested.

<u>Troubled in Paradise – Book 2</u>

Things are coming together for Jane and Jacques, but the news of his father's illness has Jacques troubled. When his mother and siblings beg him to return to Paris, he reluctantly agrees. Jane is loving her new life, has a new job lined up, and an old friendship has been renewed. While Jacques is in Paris, she receives some devastating news. They need each other more than ever but the pressures of distance, manipulative family and friends, and life-changing events will put their relationship to the test.

<u>Finding Our Home – Book 3</u>

They've weathered the storms of manipulative family members and the ups and downs of their evolving relationship, and their dreams of a forever home is within reach. When Jacques' brother drops a bombshell, the foundation of their dream trembles. The surprise arrival of Jane's parents is perfectly timed and Jane is elated, but her joy is short lived when she learns of a devastating lie. Jane and Jacques must overcome the unexpected twists that will force them to reconsider what home really means.

Navigate to the URL below to purchase this book.

https://lisastanbridge.wixsite.com/lisastanbridgeauthor/series

Standalone books

Abandoned Hearts is my debut novel. A heartfelt story about two broken individuals who must learn to trust again.

Finally free from her abusive ex, Claire Stone accepts a job as a live-in nurse in the small beach-side town of Busselton, Western Australia. A new life is exactly what she needs. Move away, move on, forget. If only things were that simple. Even the intriguing but abrasive son of her new patient can't shield her from relentless memories. Michael Karalis is watching his mother die while battling his ex-wife for custody of his five year old son. He's bitter, broken, and distrustful, but Claire becomes a light in his world, despite his reservations. Two broken souls need to learn to trust again and open their hearts or they'll never find the love they both need.

Navigate to the URL below to purchase this book.

https://books2read.com/AbandonedHearts

Thank you for reading **Oceans Apart**. I hope you enjoyed it.

This is the second book in the Maritimo Island series, which I'm super excited about. Each book will feature the stunning fictional island, but each story can be read as a standalone. Some of the characters will return, but in a minor role, as you would have seen in this one. This will continue in the next two books.

This has been a work in progress for many years. I've always loved the story, but it never felt ready for publication. Creating Maritimo Island really worked because of how Nikki and Gavin meet. However, they were not always going to get stranded. Initially it was mostly set on the ship, but I found it needed more. Throwing in a spontaneous island adventure where they end up stranded was exactly what it needed.

So why the cruise setting and why do Nikki and Gavin get stranded? It wasn't just escapism and the whole forced proximity / one bed trope, which were certainly huge factors. But there were other factors too.

The first one was because of the movie *Titanic*. I watched it at the cinema and bawled my eyes out as the ship started sinking. I couldn't stop crying (literally sobbing), and I embarrassed my older sister (sorry Tracey). In my defence, I was only 15 years old and hormonal. But digress. Since then, I always wanted to write my own cruise ship story (without the disaster, of course).

The other factor was because of the British TV series *Keeping Up Appearances*, one of my favourite comedies. One of the episodes had Richard and Hyacinth going on a cruise and they miss the ship on their departure day. It's a whole hilarious escapade to finally get on the ship. While they never really got stranded, it fed the inspiration to have Nikki and Gavin get stranded and grow their romance.

So while it took me a while to perfect the story, I made it in the end!

Next in the series will be **Ocean's Echoes**, which is set for release in late 2026. This is another one I wrote quite a while ago, but needs a big rewrite to not only tie in the Maritimo Island location, but fix up a flawed story. I wrote it when I was still a budding author and I love the characters, which is why I'm giving it another chance. I'm really excited to share it with you in a much better form. While you wait for this, keep an eye out for a couple of novellas coming out in anthologies early 2026. To be the first to find out when they'll be released, and to follow my progress on **Ocean's Echoes**, pop over to my website and sign up to my newsletter.

Thank you, kind reader, for being with me on this journey. And thank you to everyone who's been involved in this entire process. You know who you are and I appreciate you all.

About the author

International award-winning Australian author Lisa Stanbridge has been writing ever since she could string sentences together. As a child, it started off with princesses in castles being rescued by Prince Charming. As a teenager she moved on to angsty teens struggling through life with raging hormones. Now, as a semi-mature adult, she writes sweet contemporary romances and romantic comedies about real people going through real struggles who want their HEA.

She has been shortlisted in many contests, and even won some! Her biggest award is for her debut novel, **Abandoned Hearts**, which won 'Best First Book' in the Koru Award of Excellence, run by Romance Writers of New Zealand.

When she's not writing, Lisa works full time as a Software Tester. She reads anything she can sink her teeth into, and loves binging on

TV shows, especially the British ones. Lisa loves lazy days at the beach reading or writing, but rarely swimming, and loves spending time with her husband and her friends.

Say hello to Lisa

Visit her website and subscribe to her newsletter. It will keep you up to date with:

- New releases

- Preorder links

- New cover reveals and excerpts

And lots more!

https://lisastanbridge.wixsite.com/lisastanbridgeauthor

Leave a review

Did you enjoy this book? The best favour you can do for an author is to leave a review. If you'd like to leave one, go to your place of purchase, or search for the book on Goodreads, Amazon, or BookBub and leave a review. Thank you.

Nikki Eckhart is searching for clarity and space to breathe. Ye
criticism from her older sister have slowly chipped away
confidence. A family cruise to celebrate her parents' thirtieth w
anniversary might be more than just a holiday. It could be her ch
figure out why her sister treats her so terribly, and maybe she'll
the parts of herself she's lost.

Gavin Fletcher is a master of running away. Haunted by a tr
childhood, he's spent years drifting from one place to the nex
Commitment? Not in his vocabulary. He's only on the cruise to sup
recently divorced sister, a rare display of loyalty. Once the cruis
he's moving on. Again.

On day one of the cruise, Nikki and Gavin crash into each other.
What starts as a harmless fling turns into something deeper as the
spontaneous island adventures and late-night conversations un
stars. Somewhere along the way the lines are blurred, and real
begin to bloom.

Gavin helps Nikki regain her confidence. Nikki helps Gavin see
more to life than running. As their emotional defences start to cra
wants all in, but Gavin wants out. Opening his heart means riski
and there's never been anyone there to catch him. Unless Nikki cc

ISBN 978-0-64566

9 780645 667394